Bewitched, Bothered, and Bitten

by

C.C. Wood

Table of Contents

Chapter One

I TOSSED ANOTHER LOG in the fireplace, using a poker to stoke the embers. I watched as the flames engulfed the log, crackling loudly. The house creaked and settled as the frigid wind blew outside. A cold front had moved through that afternoon and the temperature dropped to just a few degrees above freezing. I loved it.

Winter was my favorite time of year. Well, winter in Texas was my favorite. Snow was rare and the temperature almost never dropped more than a few degrees below freezing. This was the first truly cold night of the season and I intended to enjoy it.

Replacing the poker, I went over to the couch and curled up beneath the afghan my mother had crocheted the year before she died. A pang of sadness washed over me. Three years later and my heart still ached for the loss of my mother. I missed her every single day. The poignancy was stronger here at the country home where she'd spent the last few months of her life. I'd been spending more and more time here as opposed to the loft apartment above my New Age store in Dallas.

Those memories weighed me down, pulling me toward that dark place I didn't want to go. I sighed and reached for the wineglass on the side table. In the years since my mother passed away, it never got any easier.

I swirled the deep red wine in the glass and took a sip, letting it warm me from the inside out. I stared into the fire, trying not to think of anything at all. My life hadn't exactly been peaceful the last few months and things wouldn't be getting better any time soon.

Two of my friends were now playing house with vampires and I had another vamp sniffing after me. Then there was The Faction, a group of rogue vampires, with their malevolent plans, whatever they may be. If that wasn't enough stress for a girl, there was upheaval in my coven. I wasn't sure what worried me more.

Once again, I thought of my mother and wished she were here to give me advice. She was one of the smartest women I'd ever known. She could see into the heart of people with very little trouble and I would have been able to count on her opinions, her guidance. There were reasons she was next in line as High Priestess of our coven and it wasn't just because she had been the most powerful practitioner.

One of the logs in the fire broke apart with a crack, pulling me free of my thoughts. I drank more wine, hoping it would calm the tumult in my mind. There were too many things happening in my life right now and I felt close to breaking.

A whisper of sound echoed in my head. I felt as though something were shifting on the edge of my peripheral vision, yet I couldn't quite see it. It was then that I knew he was here.

I closed my eyes, resting my head on the back of the sofa. Why couldn't he leave me alone? Did I really want him to? Something unidentifiable shot through me at the thought.

Tossing the afghan to the side, I stood and drained my wine-glass, setting it on the coffee table with a little too much force. I shoved my feet into my fuzzy booties and went to the front door. The slap of cold wind made me suck in my breath and I wrapped my arms around my body.

My eyes scanned the tree line in front of the house, searching for any signs of an intruder. Tonight was the new moon, so the landscape was dark. I tried not to think about the symbolism of the new moon. It was supposed to be a time of beginnings, fresh starts. I ignored the trepidation that crawled along my skin, attributing it to the icy air that swirled around me.

"Why are you out here without a coat?"

I jumped and whirled toward the sound of his voice. His long shadow rose from the porch swing, his outline barely visible in the dark. Before I could respond, he shrugged out of his coat and draped it over my shoulders. Still hot from his body, the fabric smelled of him, spicy with a hint of vanilla. It reminded me of the mulled wine my mother would make for winter solstice and Yule.

I let myself enjoy the sensation of being surrounded by him for a split second. Then, I demanded, "Why are you here at all?"

Finn took another step forward and his purple eyes flared, glowing faintly in the shadows, a sign that he was either hungry, turned on, angry, or trying to use his powers. I was unsure which. "You know why."

The wind lifted the ends of his thick brown hair, tangling it around his shoulders. I stared up at him, anger and desire warring in my belly.

"Are we going to have this discussion again? Really?" I asked, my voice going up an octave.

I could see the flash of his smile, even in the deep shadows of the porch. His fangs had extended slightly and I was suddenly very aware of the throb of my pulse in my neck.

"Kerry." His voice drifted around me, so deep and rich I could feel it like fingers stroking down my spine.

Somehow, he was even closer than before, yet we weren't touching. Even in the frigid night, I could feel the heat pouring off his body as though he were burning from within. I couldn't take much more of this. He was haunting me. I saw him in my dreams and he seemed to arrive at my weakest moments, as though he knew when I might be pushed past my reserve and give in to the palpable chemistry between us.

For months, he'd pursued me. The first time he came to me in a dream, I thought it was my sex-starved imagination desperate for some relief, though we rarely did more than talk and kiss. Even our conversations felt intimate and erotic.

Until, one day, he slipped and mentioned something he shouldn't have known. Something I had never said aloud, except in a dream. I'd been angry, but mostly I was hurt. His tactics were underhanded and invasive. I tried to keep him out of my dreams after that, but I couldn't resist for long.

When I saw him in my sleep, I didn't have to worry about what the coven would think or what our High Priestess would say. I didn't have to consider the rule prohibiting me from consorting with a vampire. I could just….be. Once I was aware that I was truly talking to him in those dreams, I weighed my words a little more carefully, but, still, I told him more than I probably should. I talked about my past, my mother, and how much easier my life had become since I didn't have to hide my true self from my closest friends.

Finn told me things about himself. He talked a great deal about his life as a human and his wild adventures as both mortal and vampire. I'm sure there were things he didn't share with me, just as I kept certain tidbits of my history a secret. Still, I found myself liking him and feeling drawn to him, in spite of the fact that witches had been forbidden from engaging in relationships with vampires for centuries.

Over the last few months, it had become a constant game of tug o' war. He would do and say things in my dreams that made me feel close to him and want to know him better, then I would see him in reality and realize that I was building foolish fantasies of things that could never be.

"Why are you doing this, Finn? Why won't you leave me alone?" I whispered, desperately wanting to take a step back but my feet refused to move.

His hand lifted and brushed my hair back from my face where the wind had blown it. "You've been alone too long already and you don't have to be."

"That's not fair, Finn. I shouldn't have told you that. I shouldn't be talking to you, even in my dreams." My pulse kicked up another notch and I managed to back away slightly. Not that it helped. Finn's eyes flared brighter and he followed my movements. Shit, I'd forgotten Rule #1 when dealing with a vampire. Never run. "Stop."

Finn leaned down, his face a few scant inches from my own. "You don't want me to. All these months of pulling me in and pushing me away. Even I can see that you are fighting your own instincts."

I scoffed. "Yes, actually, I do want you to stop."

Once again I saw the gleam of bright white teeth, his fangs now completely extended. "Then you should let go of me."

I glanced down and saw that I had one hand flattened against his chest and the other fisted in his shirt. Now that I was seeing it, I felt it as well. The heat of his body beneath my palm, taut muscle, and the quick, steady thump of his heart. I tried to jerk my hand away, but Finn's fingers wrapped around my wrist. He pressed my palm closer. My fingers brushed the bare skin of his chest above the v-neck of his sweater.

My mouth suddenly felt dry. "Finn."

A low sound emerged from his throat. "When you say my name like that, I want to see what I have to do to get you to say it again."

It was official. I was no longer cold. In fact, I was so hot, I almost didn't need his coat. The heat that washed over me gathered low in my pelvis and throbbed with every beat of my heart. Before I could stop myself, I took two steps back, instinctively trying to put space between us even though he still held my wrist.

In a flash, my back was pressed against the front door and Finn's long, hard body was plastered to mine. I gasped when I felt his mouth touch my neck, his lips branding the skin over my carotid. My head fell back and my legs became useless, my will to resist this crazy attraction taking a major hit at the sensation of his mouth on my skin. I sagged into Finn's embrace. This was the first time he'd put his mouth on me. In the last couple of months, we'd danced around one another, Finn attempting to seduce me while I desperately yet unsuccessfully tried to remain unmoved. I wanted him. I didn't want to want him, but I did, probably more than was healthy.

Now that I'd spent so much time with him, I could see beyond the fog of lust that clouded my mind every time he was near, to the man he was beneath the surface. Finn was more than the fanged beast we were taught to fear as children. He was honorable, affectionate, and compassionate. He had flaws, arrogance for one, like anyone else, but, at his core, he was the best man I'd ever met. This knowledge made resistance even more difficult.

"Finn." His name was practically a soundless puff of air as it escaped my lips, but he heard it.

"You taste better than I imagined." I felt the vibration of his voice against my throat and shivered.

His hands parted the coat he'd draped around me, sliding under the thermal shirt I wore. While folklore said that vampires were the undead and unusually cold to the touch, it couldn't be further from the truth. Vamps ran hotter than humans, especially after feeding. His hands were so hot that I expected my skin to sizzle. Tendrils of icy air threaded between us and the juxtaposition of his fiery touch and the cold wind threatened to overwhelm me.

Finn's mouth moved up my throat as his hand slid up my body. I moaned softly as his lips touched my ear. "You're shaking, Kerry. Let me warm you."

My nipples tightened when the tips of his fingers brushed the underside of my breast. Then his palm cupped me, his thumb brushing over my nipple. It only took that simple touch to make me wet. His other hand smoothed down my spine and beneath the waistband of my pajama pants.

When his hand encountered bare skin, Finn hesitated and lifted his head, his beautiful eyes glowing like two amethyst stones. "Goddess help me, you're not wearing a stitch beneath these clothes are you."

He didn't let me respond. Instead he lowered his head and kissed me. He wasn't tentative or gentle as he had been earlier. Finn kissed me deeply, his mouth opening over mine, his tongue thrusting between my lips. He tasted the way he smelled, like mulled wine, spicy and a little sweet.

Finn groaned into my mouth and I realized I'd buried both of my hands in his hair, wrapping the silky strands around my fingers. His thumb and forefinger tugged at my nipple, the small pain arrowing through my body straight to my clit.

I could barely catch my breath. Sensation after sensation washed over me, making me forget why this was a huge mistake.

Finn released my mouth, his cheek sliding against mine. I whimpered when he used his lips and the tip of his tongue along the side of my throat, up to my ear.

"Are you wet for me?" he asked, his voice rough.

As his hand moved from my ass, around my hip, Finn sucked lightly at the skin right above my collarbone. Just as his fingers grazed my clit, he nipped me sharply with his teeth. The fog blanketing my mind vanished and I realized that I was moments away from being blooded and fucked by the very creature considered an enemy by my coven. I was already on shaky ground with them as it was, I couldn't afford to push my luck.

"Stop." My voice was shaky and weak even to my own ears as I grabbed Finn's forearm.

He heard me, the movement of his fingers between my thighs halting, though he didn't withdraw his hand. "Are you sure, Kerry?" My eyes almost rolled back into my head when he drew a light circle against my clit. "You're so swollen, I can feel your pulse here. I know it hurts. I can make the pain go away." He pinched my nipple lightly as he mirrored the motion with my clit.

I almost came as both pain and pleasure spread through my body. Somehow, I managed to speak. "Stop, Finn." I forced myself to meet his eyes, squinting against the intense light his irises emitted.

The movement of his hands ceased and he lowered his head. I heard him sigh and mutter something about stubborn witches, but the rest of the words were lost as a sudden gust of wind blew between us. He released my breast, smoothing my shirt down once he was done. My hips jerked when he inched his other hand from between my thighs. I fought to ignore the ache between my legs. I watched wordlessly as he lifted his fingers to his mouth and they disappeared inside.

He removed his hand from his lips, humming in the back of his throat. "You taste of honey and wine. I could spend hours savoring such a delicious treat."

I could see and feel it after he spoke. His face between my thighs, the swipe of his tongue over my clit. Unable to speak, I fumbled with the doorknob behind me, stumbling backward into the house and slamming the door shut between us. I leaned my forehead against the rough wood of the front door, panting while my body burned with need.

My harsh breathing stopped completely when I heard him speak, muffled by the door and the howling wind outside, yet still clear.

"I'll be back for my coat, Kerry. And another taste of honey."

Then he was gone.

Chapter Two

AFTER FINN LEFT, I couldn't sleep. My body hummed with a sexual tension that couldn't be relieved and my mind whirled with all the reasons I shouldn't get more involved with him. As long as I only saw him in my sleep, I could continue to pretend that this dangerous attraction wasn't real. If we slept together, I could no longer luxuriate in denial and there would be consequences.

I had to do something to clear my mind and relieve the tension coiled in my lower body. I tried, dear Goddess, I tried. The orgasm did nothing to relieve the ache within me. After tossing and turning for a couple of hours, I prepared a cup of my mother's special tea. She always dried herbs from her garden and brewed them as a tea to help with insomnia. I continued the ritual when I couldn't sleep, the scent and delicate, almost floral flavors bringing back memories of her.

It was after midnight before I drifted off. When he came to me, I knew it was only a dream. At least, that's what I told myself. In reality, I didn't care. I was still so aroused from our earlier encounter on the porch that I couldn't bring myself to give a damn if this was a shared dream or a fantasy whipped up by my fevered, horny brain. Over the past few months, he'd held me and kissed me in our shared dreams, but that was all.

When I rolled over, I found Finn lying next to me in bed, the blankets pulled up to his bare chest. His tanned skin and dark brown hair glowed in the firelight.

We didn't speak. Somehow it wasn't necessary. Finn stretched out over me, his mouth and hands voracious. I touched him in all the ways I imagined, running my hands over the skin of his back, down to his ass. Then I did what I wanted to do earlier on the porch, I brought my hand around to the front of his body and cupped his cock. Finn groaned, his hips thrusting against my touch. I slid my palm against the hot, smooth skin of his erection and wanted to use my mouth instead.

I wrapped a leg around his hip and used my body to turn us. When Finn realized what I wanted, he rolled over onto his back and I knelt over him. I wrapped my fingers around his cock, stroking him from root to tip slowly and firmly. Keeping my eyes on his, I leaned down and used my tongue to trace the same path as my hand. His hands twined into my hair, lifting the long curly strands out of the way so he could see what I was doing.

I took him into my mouth, tightening my lips around him and sucking strongly. I let my mouth slide down his length, using my tongue on the underside. I fell into a rhythm, sucking and stroking, and gloried in the harsh sound that seemed to be torn from Finn's throat.

"Kerry, I'm going to come," he groaned.

I intensified my movements, wanting to feel and taste his orgasm. His abdomen went rigid just before his release filled my mouth. I swallowed it down, humming in the back of my throat at the taste of spice and salt.

When his body relaxed beneath me, I gave the tip of his cock one last teasing lick before I slowly released him.

Suddenly, he lunged and flipped us so that I was lying beneath him. "That was incredible," he rumbled. "But now it's my turn."

I watched as he moved down my body until his shoulders rested between my legs and anticipation flooded my body. Finn ran a fingertip over my clit and down to my entrance, sliding inside and causing me to gasp. Bringing him pleasure and making him come had aroused me so much that I knew I was wet.

My IQ shrank to the single digits at the first pass of his tongue. My toes curled and my back arched as he clamped his lips around my clit and sucked. He added another finger to the first and thrust them inside of me smoothly, pressing up and rubbing a spot inside me that made all my internal muscles spasm. As he suckled my clit, he flicked it with his tongue firmly, and I felt the climax unfurling rapidly inside my pelvis.

If it hadn't been a dream, I would have been embarrassed at how quickly he brought me to orgasm. I cried out as wave after wave of intense pleasure crashed through me.

I looked down my body at him and his amethyst eyes burned brightly. He gave my clit one more teasing lick and tremors rippled from my center. Finn smiled, revealing that his fangs were fully extended. Then he sank them into my inner thigh and I screamed as his bite showed me the true meaning of ecstasy.

Gasping, I sat up in bed, my thighs still trembling and the echo of my climax resonating throughout my body. I looked down, realized I was still dressed in my pajamas and alone. Though it seemed incredibly real, it truly was just a dream.

Flopping back on the pillows, I threw my arm over my eyes to block out the harsh morning light and the aftershocks of a mind-bending orgasm. It was official. Sexual frustration was going to drive me insane. I could be the first documented case.

My cell phone rang and I abandoned my plans to submit myself to scientific study.

"Woman, why aren't you at home? I've been calling your landline for an hour."

I had to laugh. Leave it to Ricki to get right to the point. "I am at home. Just not my home in the city."

"Oh." She paused. "So, does that mean you're not coming to Donna and Conner's engagement party tonight?" She sounded a little off.

"No, I'll be there. Are you okay?"

"Yeah, yeah. I'm fine."

I started counting down from five, knowing she wouldn't be able to keep it in long. *Five, four, three….*

"It's just….well, have you met Conner's friend, Calder?"

I had. As the beta of MacIntire clan, Calder wasn't exactly my best buddy, but I did know the handsome wolf. "Yes, I've met Calder a few times." Ricki was silent for so long, that I thought she'd hung up. "Ricki?"

She sighed deeply. "Well…shit, I slept with him at Donna's Halloween party a couple of weeks ago."

"What?" My voice was louder than I intended. I cleared my throat before I continued, trying to keep my tone neutral. "Seriously?"

"Yes. And, Kerry, it was the best sex of my life."

"Okaaay. Then what's the problem?"

Ricki groaned. "Donna warned me it would happen, but I didn't listen. She told me that werewolves hook up with two, three, sometimes even four different people at these parties. I thought she was exaggerating. Well, after we, ya know, he had a *problem* and had to leave. He asked me to stay in his room and wait for him. When I woke up, he wasn't back, so I got up to see if he was still even around. I, uh, I saw him with another woman."

Outraged on Ricki's behalf, my voice was harsh when I asked, "You found him screwing another woman?"

"Well, they weren't doing anything when I saw them, but she was in her underwear and he was shirtless and there were these huge scratches on his back."

With a human male and female, I would agree that the evidence was damning, but werewolves were nothing like humans. It wasn't unusual for them to walk around naked in front of each other and even snuggle with no sexual intent. It also wasn't unheard of for wolves to change forms to fight out an issue of dominance, then change back and go have a beer, buck naked. Unfortunately, Ricki didn't have the same understanding of werewolf culture that I did. Though she knew that supernaturals existed, she hadn't spent a great deal of time around them, probably because of how overprotective Donna, Ivie, and I were.

"What did he say when you talked to him?" I asked. Surely, Calder would have explained what happened. Werewolves were not big on lying. Actually, they were disconcertingly blunt and aggressive about what they wanted.

"I didn't. I just got the hell out of there. I felt dirty just by association. I mean, you know how my dad was and my ex. No way am I getting involved with a man who can't keep his dick in his pants, especially if he screws two or three women in one night!"

I loved Ricki dearly, but she did tend to leap before she looked, which was probably why Donna warned her about shifters in the first place. "Okay, I can understand why you were upset, sweetie, but werewolves aren't like humans. What we consider inappropriate is completely normal for them. They walk around naked in front of each other and it's no big deal and it's also not sexual."

"Kerry!"

"Ricki, I am your friend and I love you. Do you want me to tell you the truth or what I think you want to hear?"

She sighed, obviously put out with me. "Okay, okay. You're right. Maybe I should have talked to him. It's just that I thought we had this amazing connection and it….well, it hurt that he could screw me six ways to Sunday, then go chasing after another piece of ass as though it meant nothing."

"Honey, you don't know if that's what happened. And, if it is, would you rather know or torture yourself with whatever scenarios you can concoct in that brain of yours?"

I could practically hear Ricki thinking before she conceded with a frustrated sigh, "Yes."

"I'm always right," I answered, laughing when she snorted. "Okay, I have stuff to do before I drive back to Dallas, so I need to get up and get moving. I'll see you tonight."

We said our goodbyes and I lay in bed, staring up at the ceiling. I hadn't thought about this last night, but Finn would probably be at the party. After the insanity on my porch and the exquisitely pleasurable dream I'd had, I wasn't sure I could manage to stand in the same room with him, much less look him in the eye and talk. Finn wasn't just a vampire, he was an extremely powerful practitioner of magic. I wasn't certain, but I believed he may have been a Druid before he was turned. He'd never outright stated it during our nocturnal conversations, but certain things that he said and did hinted at his origins. If that was the case, it would be child's play for him to see into my thoughts and exploit my weakness for him to his advantage.

Feeling tension returning to my body, I threw off the blankets and shivered when the cold air hit me. I didn't hesitate, though. I rolled out of bed and headed straight for the fireplace downstairs. Once I had a fire burning, I would shower before putting together an amulet for the party tonight. Something that would strengthen my mental barriers. I would need every defense I could muster to keep Finn out of my head and likely my panties as well.

✧   ✧   ✧

AT SEVEN THAT evening, I pulled up in front of Conner's palatial home, feeling the shimmer of nerves in my belly. I was always on edge around other supernaturals. Witches and vampires had a long, bitter history of mutual loathing and shifters considered us little better than humans. Despite the fact that both species were susceptible to a witch's magic, neither was willing to acknowledge the elemental strength of witchcraft. Probably due to the fact that most witches sought to prevent harm and to heal. All practitioners knew that magic carried a price. Evil begets evil and black witches usually died an early, excruciating death, which is why they were rare among our kind. I had only witnessed it once when I was still a child and the taint of that followed me throughout my life.

I yanked myself out of my thoughts. This was not the time to allow painful memories to overwhelm me. I needed to have all my mental and magical defenses in place. While I trusted Donna with my life and had slowly allowed myself to relax around her vampire fiancé, Conner, suspicion of the fanged had been too deeply ingrained in me since childhood, and, tonight, I would be sur-rounded by bloodsuckers.

Still, I had to become accustomed to interacting with other supernatural beings. Conner and several other younger Council members were making an effort to establish a civil relationship with witches and shifters. It had been centuries since peace existed between the species. Distrust was still rampant among the coven and the MacIntire pack when it came to vampires, but things were improving.

I flinched when I saw a flash of black next to the passenger side window. My suddenly coiled muscles relaxed when I realized it was just the valet that had been hired for the evening. Shaking my head at my skittishness, I opened my door and climbed out of the car, accepting the ticket stub from the young vampire. Before I had a chance to give him a tip, he jumped in my car and zoomed off.

I climbed the steps to the front door, still feeling off balance. Before I pushed it open, I closed my eyes, took a deep breath, and released it slowly, focusing on exhaling all the tension in my body. Feeling slightly less stressed, I lifted my eyelids to find the front door open and Conner's friend, Lex, standing in front of me with a smirk on his handsome face.

Alexander Dimitriades was another vampire I was gradually beginning to trust. He had fallen hard and fast for my friend, Ivie, so I saw him often. He did nothing to hide how much he doted on her and that alone softened my attitude toward him. Unfortunately, he read me like an open book and, like any typical male, decided to use my weakness against me and tease me relentlessly every chance he got. If I'd had siblings, I imagined an older brother would behave a great deal like Lex did toward me.

"Communing with fairies, witch?" he asked, dark eyes sparkling with humor.

"Actually, I was summoning a demon and here you are," I quipped.

Lex laughed and grabbed my hand, pulling me into the house and a tight hug. His affectionate behavior surprised me. Though he strove to be friendly to all of Ivie's friends, he rarely touched us except for a handshake or a peck on the cheek.

Awkwardly, I patted him on the back. "Down, boy. Don't make me zap you."

He released me with another chuckle, looking more relaxed and happy than I'd ever seen him.

I frowned at him. "Okay, this is just weird. Aren't you supposed to be all dark and broody and sparkle in the sunlight?" When he merely grinned and shook his head, I sighed. "Fine. Tell me why you're so happy."

His smile widened until I was afraid his face would split in two. "Ivie finally agreed to a Claiming ceremony."

I went still at the announcement. "Really?"

Lex nodded.

"How did you manage that?" When his grin became absolutely wicked, I shook my head. "Never mind. I think I know."

He laughed and threw an arm around my shoulders. "All's fair in love and war, little witch. You'd do well to remember that."

Scowling up at his face, I allowed him to lead me toward the ballroom. "What's that supposed to mean?"

His dark brown eyes were amused, but also gentle. "War and love are quite similar, Kerry. Both are full of battles and, sometimes, you have to fight dirty to win." Lex looked up as we entered the ballroom, still smirking slightly.

Before I could ask him what in the hell he was talking about, an arm wrapped around my waist, pulling me away from Lex. I stiffened, knowing exactly who had just grabbed me. The smell of vanilla and spice assaulted me and I felt a hot, muscled body against my side.

I glanced up at Finn, fighting to keep my face neutral. "Why are you touching me?" I asked evenly.

He merely hugged me closer, leaning over to whisper in my ear. "You liked it when I touched you last night."

Lex cupped my elbow, trying to tug me away. "Finn, leave the little witch alone."

Immediately, I decided that I would never give Lex shit again, since he was trying to save me from this awkward situation. Anxiety filled me when Finn growled low in his throat and tightened his grip on my waist.

I elbowed Finn in the ribs sharply. "Knock it off!"

Suddenly, I was crowded between Lex and Finn, in danger of being smashed by two hard chests. Over my head, Finn hissed, "Stop touching her."

Abruptly, I'd had enough. Taking a deep breath, I pressed one hand to each of their chests and gave each of them a nice little shock.

They leapt away from me, Lex rubbing his pectoral and Finn his sternum.

Finn grimaced. "What was that for?"

"Just a reminder that you should keep your hands to yourself," I stated. I hoped my voice didn't sound as shaky as I felt. My fingers tingled painfully where the charge had escaped.

"What about me?" Lex complained.

"That was just a bonus," I answered.

With a little wave, I turned and headed toward the bar. It would be rude to get a drink before finding Donna to say hello, but I really needed one. I was sure she would understand.

Chapter Three

AN HOUR LATER, I was feeling much more mellow. When I'd gone to the bar earlier, I'd ordered a shot of tequila and a glass of red wine. The bartender hadn't even blinked, just smiled politely and gone about filling my strange request.

After I tossed back the shot, I took my wine, sliding a ten dollar tip across the bar and earning a genuine smile from the stone-faced bartender. Then I went looking for Donna. I saw her across the ballroom, looking radiant in a dress that was both blue and gray. The color looked fantastic on her. I made my way across the room, nodding politely to people as I passed.

Donna's eyes lit up when she saw me. "Kerry!" She hugged me tightly. When she stepped away, she looked down at my dress. "You look great!"

The bad mood brought on by Finn's earlier antics disappeared. "Thanks. You look beautiful."

Donna smoothed her hand down the material of her gown. "Really? Conner picked this out."

I had to laugh. She loathed shopping and avoided it at all costs. Conner usually had to blackmail or trick her into it. Many times, he would just buy her clothes and have them hung in her closet. She hadn't liked it at first until she realized that, by allowing him to purchase her clothes and have them delivered, she could avoid shopping altogether. Now, I think she also enjoyed wearing things that she knew Conner would like. Donna jokingly called him her style fairy.

"He has excellent taste in clothing and women," I answered, lifting my glass in a mock toast to her.

"Thank you, Kerry."

The sound of Conner's voice and that sexy Scottish brogue startled me. He kissed my cheek as he stepped past me to pull Donna against his side. I smiled a little at the picture they created. They fit.

Donna rolled her eyes. "Kerry, don't let him hear you saying things like that. His ego is big enough as it is. Too many compliments and he'll become an unbearably arrogant jackass." She squeaked when he playfully bit at her neck in retaliation.

Conner lifted his head, raising a single brow. It was a sexy look. "For every compliment your friends give me, you usually have at least one complaint. I think I'm safe from the delusion that I'm perfect."

I shifted my weight, intending to excuse myself.

"Kerry." Conner's face was suddenly serious. "Have you spoken to Belinda today?"

I shook my head. As the High Priestess of the coven, Belinda rarely had time to call me for a simple chat.

He frowned. "She's here this evening and said it was important that she talk to you."

A small kernel of unease settled at the base of my spine. "Okay. I'll be sure to find her."

Donna looked a little concerned, but Conner didn't say more. They were distracted by another vampire, so I gave Donna a discreet wave and moved away.

I looked around as I made my way through the throngs of vampires and werewolves. There were a few witches from the coven here, but most chose to politely decline their invitation to the party. I knew that Belinda would have a hard road ahead of her if she wanted to convince other coven members that witches should form alliances with vampires and shifters and I didn't envy her the job.

I was pleasantly surprised at how many vampires acknowledged my presence and spoke as I passed. After centuries of distrust and bad blood, it seemed a new generation of the fanged were willing to put all that aside.

"Kerry!"

My head turned when someone called my name. Shannon and Ricki were standing a few feet away. I changed direction and headed their way.

Shannon hugged me. "You look gorgeous."

I smoothed down the skirt of my dark blue dress. "Thanks. You both look fantastic."

Shannon wore black, which wasn't unusual, and Ricki wore red. I had to suppress a smile because Ricki must not have realized that wearing red while attending a vampire function alone was akin to wearing a halter top and miniskirt to a bar. It was guaranteed to capture attention and maybe even inspire a few crappy pick up lines. Then again, the shifters and vamps were pretty suave, so the pick up lines might be decent.

Ricki leaned closer, whispering, "He's here."

Confused, I asked, "Who?"

"Calder!" she hissed. "He's here and…" She trailed off and stiffened as someone walked behind her.

I glanced up and realized it was Calder. He smiled and winked at me. I also noticed that he trailed his hand across the bare skin of Ricki's back. Then he disappeared into the crowd.

"Holy shit, what the hell am I gonna do?" Ricki asked me, her eyes huge. "Every time I turn around, *he's right there!*"

"Are you afraid he's going to hurt you?" I asked.

"No," she muttered. She fiddled with the halter neckline of her dress and I saw a small scar where her neck met her shoulder. It was obviously a bite.

My body tensed when I saw it. I leaned forward and pulled the strap of her dress a couple of inches to the side. She'd been marked. Yet, Calder was still keeping his distance and Ricki seemed to want nothing to do with him.

"Kerry, what are you doing?" Ricki sounded annoyed but also a little anxious.

I released the strap of her dress and stepped back slightly. "Who bit you?" I had a strong suspicion and, if I was right, it would explain a lot about Calder's behavior.

Her face flushed. "Calder."

"What's going on, Kerry?" Shannon asked, her eyes sharp.

I met Ricki's eyes. "You need to talk to Calder, and you need to do it soon."

"You're starting to freak me out," Ricki whispered.

I grabbed her hand, squeezing it lightly. "Don't be afraid, sweetie. I promise, it's not bad. Remember what you and I were talking about this morning? How male shifters and human guys are very different from each other?"

She nodded.

I didn't want to tell her everything, because Calder should really be having this conversation with her, but, I knew Ricki. She would avoid him as long as possible until she had no choice but to talk to him. I took a deep breath, not sure I was doing the right thing. "Well, when a shifter bites their partner deeply enough to scar, it's sort of....marking their territory."

"*What?*" Ricki's voice was loud enough to have people around us turning to stare.

Realizing that I should have chosen my words more carefully, I grabbed Ricki's other hand. "Wait, I'm sorry. It came out wrong. I just mean that a bite like that one, well, it's a statement of intent. And it's usually an indication that they are serious about that relationship."

"*WHAT?*"

Shit. I should have kept my damn mouth shut and just told Calder to talk to her. Ricki knew next to nothing about werewolves and she had no idea what she was getting into. However, she was a strong, smart woman and I knew she would have her freak out then calmly consider the situation.

Ricki noticed that we were under scrutiny and lowered her voice, but it vibrated and I knew she was fighting not to scream. "So, you're telling me that Calder did the werewolf equivalent of pissing on me to keep other men away and didn't bother to mention it?"

"No, no. It's not like that. Marking someone is instinctive for shifters. Especially during sex. They usually only mark one partner in their lifetime, though it's not unheard of for a wolf to mark two, sometimes three partners, since they have longer life spans." I didn't mention that this marking instinct was part of their mating ritual and was only repeated if their mate was killed. No need to freak her out more than she already was.

Ricki's face was pale. "So, biting me was his way of saying he was serious about me?" Shannon grabbed her arm as she swayed. Ricki blinked. "Then why would he have sex with another woman after he left me the night of the Halloween party?"

I took a deep breath. Things were about to get a hell of a lot trickier. "He wouldn't."

"Shit," Shannon whispered. I knew Ricki had given her a run-down of what had happened as well, so she probably thought Calder had screwed other women that night too.

"Kerry." Belinda's low voice came from behind me.

Perfect timing, as usual. I glanced over my shoulder. "Hey, Belinda."

"I need to talk to you."

"Can you give me just a minute and then we can find a quiet place for a conversation?"

Belinda nodded and stepped away slightly to give us a little privacy.

I turned back to Ricki in time to see her drain her wineglass. Her eyes were suspiciously bright when she looked at me.

"Thanks for telling me all this, Kerry. I'm going to the powder room and then I'm going to get drunk. I'll see you later." She hugged me and kissed my cheek before she walked away.

Shannon and I exchanged looks.

With a sigh, I asked, "Will you go with her? I think she'll be fine, but I don't want her to do anything she'll regret later." While Shannon was just as new to supernatural culture, she'd acclimated astonishingly fast. I knew she could comfort Ricki and probably scare off any lecherous vamps.

"Too late," Shannon joked.

Unfortunately, she was right. Ricki was going to have to face the consequences of her night with Calder and, being uninformed of shifter customs, she would probably have difficulty dealing with them.

"I'll find you later, okay?"

"Okay." Shannon smiled. "I'm sure we'll be somewhere near the bar, so we should be easy to spot."

We both chuckled before she turned to follow Ricki.

I looked around until I found Belinda and walked over to her. "Hey."

Her eyebrows rose at my familiar greeting. Though she was only a decade or so older than me, Belinda had a decidedly old-fashioned attitude towards etiquette. Still, she didn't say a word about it, which surprised me. At the very least, I usually received a gentle reprimand.

"Why don't we go outside for a bit?" she asked. "I could use some fresh air and there are things we need to discuss."

"Sure."

Yet again, she didn't comment on my casual attitude toward her. Interesting. Usually, I did this to needle her, but it seemed to be useless tonight.

We walked through the house and out the back door. Since the evening was cool, there was no one out there except the two of us.

"So why did you need to talk to me?" I preferred to get straight to the point. Belinda rarely spoke to me, except at coven gatherings, so I didn't feel the need to dance around the subject. I respected her, but I hated all the social niceties that she seemed to expect.

Once again, Belinda said nothing about my borderline rude behavior. Instead, she crossed her arms over her chest and studied me closely.

Accustomed to this, I was silent as I waited for her to answer my question. The High Priestess often looked at me as though she thought I must be from another planet. However, she was one of the few witches in the coven who treated me as a friend. Despite my sometimes bad attitude, she never shunned me or made me feel lesser because of who my father had been and what he had done. In fact, she'd known me since I was a child and often spent time at our house with my mother and me, studying, practicing spells, and asking question after question. The elders, well, they hated my guts and probably pestered Belinda weekly to kick me out of the coven.

"Tomorrow afternoon, I'll be meeting with the vampire Council and the alpha of the MacIntire pack in order to hold a sort of diplomatic summit. It's time for the different supernatural races to learn to coexist, because if we can't accomplish this, then I fear we will all perish."

I wanted to believe that Belinda was being melodramatic, but she was one of the most gifted Seers of the coven. Her instincts were always spot on.

"Okay. Do you need me to handle some coven business while you're busy there? I'm happy to do it."

Belinda shook her head. "No, I want you to come with me."

I almost choked. "Pardon me?" For once, I was polite.

The High Priestess' eyes shimmered with amusement. "It's time for me to begin training my successor."

I didn't speak, unsure where she was going with this conversation.

"It's time for me to begin training *you*, Kerry."

That was the last thing I expected her to say.

Chapter Four

THE NEXT MORNING, I stood in front of my closet with both hands on my hips, clad only in my underwear. What exactly did one wear to a meeting of the leaders of the supernatural species? I pulled out my charcoal pantsuit, but put it back almost immediately. As a plus size girl, the boxy jacket and pants made me look like a gray blob. I continued to dig through my closet, cursing Belinda under my breath. I couldn't believe that she sprang all this on me the day before the meeting.

I pulled out a pair of black slacks and a knitted tunic with a cowl neck. It was dressy without being staid and, after a glance at my clock, I realized it would have to do. I pulled on the pants and sweater and stared at my shoe collection. Black pumps would be the obvious choice, but it was also the boring one.

Instead, I picked up a pair of pumps with a peep toe and a striking pattern of black, white, red, and yellow. They were uneven, random slashes of color, but I adored them. I predicted that Belinda would give these shoes a thinly veiled look of distaste, but I wasn't going to change who I was because she suddenly decided I'd make a good successor. In fact, she and I would be having a conversation about that as soon as I saw her. I wasn't at all sure I wanted the job of High Priestess. Ever. Not to mention the fact that the elders would likely conspire to have me removed if I accepted, perhaps even plan to do worse.

I hurried into the bathroom and swiped on some light make-up, just enough to make my cheeks glow and bring out my eyes. My curly brown hair refused to be tamed, so I rubbed a little product in it to fight frizz and hoped for the best.

Five minutes later, I was sliding gold hoop earrings in my ears and walking out the door with my purse. Though the meeting wouldn't take place until later in the day, Belinda asked me to pick her up at ten. Probably because she knew I intended to interrogate her.

I drove the thirty minutes to Belinda's home. She wasn't very far away, but in Dallas traffic, even a short trip usually took a half hour. It always surprised me that she lived near Southern Method-ist University. Then again, while she definitely wasn't a Methodist, she was prim and proper and always slightly disapproving. So, maybe she fit right in.

I pulled into her driveway and walked up to her front door. She was quick to open the door when I knocked and I was surprised that she looked genuinely pleased to see me.

"Good morning, Kerry. Please come in."

"Good morning, Belinda."

She ushered me inside. "I'll brew us some tea."

I hadn't been to her home in a long time and I was surprised by the bold colors and cozy feel. It certainly didn't coincide with my perception of the High Priestess or my memories of her from the past. Honestly, I expected several shades of white and cream, blended with black and grey with a distinctly modern edge. Something a little cold.

Instead, she had cushy micro suede couches in navy, scattered with throw pillows in shades of teal, magenta, and lighter shades of blue. Her kitchen was beautiful, full of clutter and herbs on the counter near a huge window that looked into her back yard.

"Your home is beautiful," I told her.

She smiled serenely as she put the kettle on a lit burner. "You seem surprised. Did you expect me to live in a cave or a dungeon?"

I had to smile in return. "No, it's not that. Though I did expect a little bit of modern minimalism."

Belinda brought the teacups to the table and paused. "You think I'm cold?" I thought I saw a glimmer of hurt in her eyes.

"Reserved and refined," I answered.

"Very diplomatic response. Not exactly what I expected from you either."

I laughed. "Good point. Tact is not one of my strengths. Still, I don't think you're cold, Belinda. I do think you have to keep yourself removed in some way due to your position in the coven."

The kettle began to whistle and she poured the water into the warmed teapot and lowered the large tea ball into it. She brought the tea pot over and sat down, putting the pot on the table. Each motion was graceful and efficient.

Belinda folded her hands on the table in front of her, her eyes intent. "And that is why I chose you."

"I'm sorry?"

She smiled a little. "I understand you, Kerry. I knew you would have a lot of questions, which is why I asked you to come here before we meet with the Council. I also know you were wondering why I chose you as my successor." She paused to pour the tea. "And what you said a few moments ago is why. You have a great deal more wisdom than even I realized. Your personality may differ dramatically from mine, but, at your core, you have what it takes to lead the coven. In many ways, you are exactly like your mother."

My chest hurt at her assertion that I resembled my mother. I liked hearing it, but that didn't mean it didn't make my heart ache. If my mother were here, she would be the High Priestess.

Belinda's eyes grew distant, as though she were looking through the walls, out to something only she could see. "We need to begin your training immediately. Though you probably know everything you need to about coven politics, there is information only the High Priestess and her successor are privy to. We'll begin today."

Since my throat was tight, my only answer was a nod. We sipped our tea in silence for a few minutes. All I could think about was how proud my mother would be that I had been named successor and that I wasn't certain I wanted to take on that responsibility. I was all too aware of the scrutiny Belinda had faced when she succeeded my mother. Just thirty-six at the time, many of the elders of the coven considered her to be too young. Now, four years later, she proved herself to be an excellent High Priestess.

"Since we have time, why don't we have lunch before the meeting? You need to get up to speed on what's happening and what will be discussed this afternoon."

I blew out a sigh. "Yeah. That'd be a good idea."

✦   ✦   ✦

TWO HOURS LATER, we were on our way to Lex's home. The Council, the pack, and Belinda had decided to gather away from the Coven House, the large house that held our library, for security purposes. After my lunch with Belinda, I was nervous about the situation I was walking into. I had no idea how bad things had gotten.

Apparently, the Faction was no longer recruiting only vampires. Their reach was now extending into the shifter community. There were also rumors that Cornelius had acquired a powerful warlock to his ranks. That was unsettling. Black witches and warlocks practiced the darkest of magic; death magic. The law of magic states that what a witch casts, she receives in return.

Warlocks and evil witches used spells to circumvent this law, casting their negative energy onto others. It was a never-ending cycle and it brought suffering to innocent people.

Every instinct I had screamed that this would be war. A war that could out the supernatural community to humans. If that happened, well, I'm sure the government would keep us in very comfortable testing facilities that supplied the finest sedation available. There was more than survival at stake. The outcome of this fight could change the future of supernatural beings forever.

My mood was somber as I pulled up in front of Lex's home. It seemed the size of a vampire's home was directly proportional to their age. The older they got, the bigger the house. It must be nice to have centuries to build up your bank account.

Belinda was silent during the drive from the restaurant. After I turned off the car, she faced me. "Kerry, I want you to watch and listen during this meeting." When I started to scowl, she shook her head. "Don't take my words the wrong way. I'm not telling you to keep your mouth shut. I need you to watch the others closely. If you notice strange behavior or you think one of them is lying, I want you to use this."

She handed me a truth amulet. They were hard to come by as the level of skill and power required to make them was rare among witches. This one was set in a bracelet in order to camouflage its purpose.

A truth charm was simple but only worked on one person if you were standing directly in front of them. An amulet could work in a much larger area and be used on multiple people. A witch would have to focus on the person speaking to see if they were being truthful. Each amulet was different based on the witch that created it. Some would have green for honesty and red for deception, others blue and yellow. My mother had been powerful enough to create them and, when I demonstrated that I would have the power as well, she taught me. I preferred to use white for honesty and black for deception. Rarely in life were things that clear cut, but it seemed poetic.

A truth was a truth and a lie was a lie. That was all the amulet could tell us. It couldn't account for the intent behind the untruth, malice or protection. A wise witch wouldn't rely solely on an amulet or charm, but also on her own instincts. That was something my mother drilled into me while teaching me about my craft.

"The amulet will remain purple for truth and orange for lie."

Belinda's words brought my focus back to the task at hand. "Are you suspicious of any one in particular?" I asked.

She shook her head. "I think they are all trustworthy, but I want to be sure I don't believe that because I want to. I've wanted to establish a relationship with both the shifters and the vampires for a while. However, in situations such as this, I have to be sure I'm not placing the coven in danger."

"I understand."

"Ready?" she asked.

We got out of the car and walked toward the front door. Brian, one of the younger MacIntire pack members, stood on the steps, looking surprisingly stern.

He nodded to us. "Ms. Smythe, Ms. Gayle."

Just the night before, I'd chatted with Brian during the engagement party. He seemed like a young, flirtatious shifter, but there was no trace of the wolf I'd met last night. His face still looked young, but his eyes were hard, guarded. He appeared formidable and cold.

The smile on my face faded as he opened the door and stepped to the side to let us pass. I glanced over my shoulder at him, suddenly wary. Brian winked, his eyes once again warm as they had been the night before.

Still feeling unsettled, I returned my focus to the task ahead of me. Belinda seemed to know where we were going, walking through the foyer to the hall that led directly to the back of the house. She knocked on a door to the left.

It opened almost immediately by none other than Finn.

Chapter Five

I F HE WAS surprised to see me, Finn didn't show it. He
gestured for us to enter. I realized that we must be in Lex's
study, only it was bigger than any study I'd ever seen before.
Three of the four walls had built in bookshelves, all filled with
books. A polished cherry table was a few feet from the door,
surrounded by twelve chairs, most of which were occupied, and a
fire burned in the fireplace on the far end of the room. There was
an ornate desk that matched the table set at an angle in the left
corner.

Conner rose from the head of the table. "Ms. Smythe." He
looked surprised by my presence, unlike Finn. "Kerry, what are
you doing here?"

Before I could answer, Belinda spoke, "Kerry is my successor."

The room fell silent, all eyes turned to us. I wanted to fidget
under the scrutiny, but forced myself to remain still. Showing
weakness or discomfort in a room full of vampires and shifters
would be a very bad idea.

Conner smiled at me. "Congratulations, Kerry."

"Thanks."

"Please, have a seat. As soon as Lachlan arrives, we'll be ready
to begin." Conner remained standing as Belinda sat at the table.

I leaned in to speak in her ear. "I'll sit on the sofa so there will be room for Lachlan and his group." I also wanted to be far enough away that I could use the truth amulet discreetly.

Her only answer was a nod.

I walked around the table to the sofa, settling in the corner and crossing my legs. I glanced at the vampires seated around the table and my eyes met Finn's. The expression on his face was disconcerting. He studied me intently, as though he were trying to figure out what I was thinking. Unconsciously, I ran a finger over my necklace. Another amulet was set in the pendant and it prevented others from reading my thoughts through natural talent or spell. In Finn's case, his vampire powers of mind-reading and persuasion were rendered useless. His gaze rested on my neck and I lowered my hand. Shit. Now he knew why he couldn't read my thoughts.

Finn's smile was decidedly smug when our eyes met again. I rolled my eyes and went back to ignoring him, which is exactly what I had done last night after Belinda and I returned to Donna and Conner's engagement party. Instead of annoying him, my refusal to acknowledge his existence seemed to amuse him greatly.

Conner, Finn, and Lex were all Council members. After Donna's kidnapping and near death, Conner had killed one of the original Council members, Vanessa Santino, for her part in the plan. The power-hungry bitch had been replaced with Gabriel Crow. Before he was turned he'd been a Cheyenne shaman. Gabriel wasn't as tall as Finn, but his demeanor made him seem larger. His dark eyes seemed as hard and cold as black ice. While his face was too harsh and his bones too sharp and prominent to be handsome, he was a striking man. His black hair was cut short and hugged his skull.

The final member of the vampire Council was a female who had been turned in her forties. I did not recognize her, but knew

Conner would make introductions shortly. I assumed he was waiting for Lachlan and Calder to arrive.

There were supposed to be seven members on the Council, but, with the upheaval and distrust among the community, I assumed that they were leery of bringing in two more members until it was over.

There was another knock on the door but Calder opened it before Lex could move to answer it. He and Lachlan entered the study, their expressions neutral.

Lach greeted Lex with a nod and a simple, "Lex."

He and Calder greeted Conner and Finn as well and I felt a whisper of awareness run down my spine as Lachlan's gaze shifted to Belinda. There was something in his eyes that I didn't recognize, yet it didn't seem malicious. I didn't think he and the High Priestess had met before, but maybe I was wrong.

With everyone present, Conner did as I expected. He introduced Gabriel and the female vampire named Johanna. Once polite greetings were exchanged, everyone took a seat.

Casually, I pretended to toy with my bracelet, making sure that the amulet was turned toward me and not visible by the others. I regulated my breathing and heart rate as my nerves jangled. Typically, I loathed subterfuge, but I also understood that this was necessary. If I allowed my anxiety to get the best of me, everyone in the room would know something was going on. Vampires and werewolves could literally smell fear and hear the heartbeat of a person nearby. Those were the traits of a predator.

As the meeting began, I watched everyone, including Conner, Lex, and Finn, for signs of deception. Though I didn't think any of them were lying, I used the amulet to evaluate their truthfulness periodically.

I also listened to what they discussed. Undoubtedly, Belinda would want to know my thoughts on the suggested changes. I knew Conner, Lex, and Finn were eager to establish good relations with the witches and wolves, and it seemed Lachlan and Calder were open to that as well. Gabriel and Johanna were difficult to read. While they didn't seem completely opposed, I could see they were hesitant.

Finally, the meeting began to wind down. During the last half hour, I'd desperately needed to pee. After catching Belinda's eye, I slipped out of the room and down the hall in search of the bathroom.

A few minutes later, I finished washing my hands, checked my make-up in the mirror, and left the little powder room. My mind was still back in the study, thinking about everything I'd heard. It seemed that the vampires and werewolves were serious about establishing a relationship between one another and the coven. Perhaps there was hope.

Lex's home was a maze of halls and rooms and, as I wandered through them, I quickly became lost. Irritated, I stopped and tried to get my bearings. Turning on my heel, I headed back the way I came. When I rounded a corner, I hit a boulder. A warm boulder that smelled like vanilla and spice. Son of a bitch.

All the air left my lungs and I stumbled over my feet. Strong hands closed over my arms, keeping me from falling flat on my ass. While my dignity was shredded, at least my tailbone was saved.

"Careful." Finn was standing too close, his thumbs caressing my biceps.

"Sorry." I knew my voice was insincere, but I was shaken. Throughout the meeting, every time I looked up, Finn had been watching me. He had done the same last night when Belinda and I returned to the party.

Though he always watched me, this was different. Before, I felt appreciated....wanted. This felt more like a threat, as though he were waiting for the perfect moment to strike.

"You've been avoiding me." Finn's voice was mild when he spoke, but there was an underlying tension to his words and in his muscles.

I shrugged. "You haven't given me much choice."

His eyes brightened, beginning to glow, and his grip on my arms tightened. "Why are you so stubborn? You want me, I can feel it, so why are you resisting?"

I tried to pull away, but Finn only followed me. "You know why," I whispered. I gasped when my back hit the wall. This infernal vampire was constantly backing me against an immoveable object.

"That argument won't carry any weight for much longer and you know it. Any day now, the coven will have a truce with the vampires and wolves. Old hostilities will no longer stand in the way."

I smirked, ignoring the press of his body against mine as he crowded closer. "You think it's that simple? The elders of the coven are not so easily swayed. Just because there is a truce between us, doesn't mean that all the tensions between the supernatural communities will be resolved."

Finn moved even closer, his torso plastered against my chest. He lifted a hand, his fingers gliding along my cheekbone. His thumb brushed my lower lip, tugging it down and pressing into my mouth and between my teeth. I could taste his skin, salt and spice. It took every ounce of willpower I possessed not to suck his thumb deeper into my mouth. While reason told me it was a horrible idea to extend a blatantly sexual invitation, my hormones were all on board with it.

"I think you are reaching for any excuse to keep your distance."

When the man was right, he was right. "I don't need excuses, Finn. I don't want to be close to you." It almost hurt to let that lie fall from my lips.

The fire in Finn's eyes flashed, almost painfully bright. "Your mouth says one thing, Kerry, but your body says something else." He lowered his head, his stubbled jaw brushing my neck. I shuddered, though I tried to keep still. His lips tickled my neck slightly as he spoke again. "I can still taste you, you know, and hear your moans when you come."

I felt as though every cell in my body stilled right before it exploded. "What did you just say?" A hot wave of anger washed over my skin. I put my hands to his shoulders and shoved. "I can't believe you snuck into my dreams and...and...." I couldn't even bring myself to say it. A little voice whispered in the back of my mind that I had no right to be angry because, on some level, I had known it wasn't just a dream.

Finn was completely unmoved after my push. "I didn't sneak. You invited me."

Though I was more angry with myself than Finn, my frustration got the best of me and I let it flow to my hands and out my fingers. I felt the bolt of heat and electric spark leave me, shooting through his body. He stiffened.

"Oh Goddess, Finn, I'm sorry." No matter how it happened, what we shared two nights ago had been consensual. I had no right to be mad at him.

He smiled. "Prove it."

"What?"

"Prove how sorry you are," he answered, his smile growing wider and revealing that his fangs were fully extended.

"And how do you expect me to do that?" I asked. When he opened his mouth, I narrowed my eyes. "Think very carefully about what you're about to say. I could probably set your entire body on fire with very little effort."

He chuckled. "How about a little kiss to make it better?"

"Stop pushing me, Finn."

His hands framed my jaw, thumbs tipping my chin up. "I think it was you pushing me a few moments ago."

I rolled my eyes.

"C'mon, Kerry. Surely, if you're that unmoved by me, you could kiss me with no problem."

I scoffed. "What? Are we twelve? Next you're gonna double dog dare me."

Finn's thumbs met under the center of my chin. He leaned forward enough that our lips nearly touched. I could literally feel the heat of his mouth on mine.

"I double dog dare you," he whispered right before he kissed me.

Damn, but the man could kiss. Any resistance I might have dissolved beneath his lips. Finn's hands moved from my face, down my back to grip my ass so he could lift me off my feet.

Shocked, I turned my head, panting so heavily I could barely speak. "Finn, put me down. I'm heavy."

He dragged the tips of his fangs along my collarbone, causing goose bumps to break out on my arms. "No, you're not. Wrap your legs around me." Finn moved his hips so the hard ridge of his cock rubbed over my clit.

I moaned and lifted my legs, circling his waist with my thighs and locking my ankles together behind him. He rolled his pelvis, grinding the length of his erection against me over and over again. It was almost ridiculous how quickly he brought me to the edge of orgasm with a kiss and a few thrusts of his hips. I hadn't been this horny since dry humping was a regular occurrence in the backseat of my first boyfriend's car.

Dear Goddess, what in the fuck was I doing? Despite what Finn might think, the coven elders would never accept a High Priestess with a vampire lover. They were convinced vampires either wanted to control or turn witches. Then there was the fact that he pushed his way into my dreams constantly, undermining my will to keep my distance. It was manipulative.

Despite the fact that I was one breath away from an orgasm so strong it would incinerate my underpants, I tore my mouth away from Finn's, dropped my legs, and pushed at his shoulders. I could practically feel his frustration as he released me, but he still let me go.

"There's your kiss. I need to return to the meeting." I was glad my voice wasn't shaking as much as my thighs.

I vaguely heard his low, growling laugh as I hurried down the hall. I still had no clue where I was going, just that I needed to put some space between myself and the sexiest man on the planet, fangs or not.

After a few wrong turns and backtracking, I managed to make my way back to the study. Finn was already there, looking completely unruffled. There was no sign that he had been seconds away from bringing me to orgasm five minutes ago. I wanted to zap him for that alone, especially since I was pretty sure I had no lipstick left and my hair looked as though it had gone a few rounds with a weed whacker.

Conner and Lex exchanged looks after I entered, both of the handsome bastards were smiling smugly. Belinda gave me a questioning glance but I gave a slight shake of my head.

"I'm glad you're back," she said. "We were discussing what safety precautions the coven and the pack should take until the Faction is dismantled. Conner and Lachlan suggested that you and I stay with shifters or vampires until a safe house can be arranged."

Scowling, I asked, "Why would we need a safe house, Belinda? The coven has been protecting itself for centuries without the help of vampires or wolves."

However, it was Conner that answered my question. "You know we have information that suggests the Faction already has a warlock among their ranks and they are in search of stronger witches. You and Belinda are the strongest in the northern hemisphere."

"Why would they want us? They can't compel us."

Lex's face was harsh when he chimed in. "No, but they can torture you into submission."

I felt a stab of fear near my heart. "Belinda and I are perfectly capable of taking care of ourselves," I argued. I turned to the High Priestess. "Right?" Her face told me all I needed to know. "Seriously? You want to stay with Conner or Lex until they find a place to hide us? If the Faction has a warlock, what's the use of hiding? They'll find us eventually."

Belinda sighed. "Kerry, we have strength in numbers. What intelligence we have of the Faction suggests they are still a relatively small group. They won't risk coming for us if they think the collateral damage would be too high. The vampires have their own security details and the pack lives together just outside the city. It will be safer for both of us. You and I both know that the knowledge we hold would be coveted by the Faction. Only the High Priestess and her successor have access to certain information." She left out the fact that we were also two of the most powerful witches in North America and that alone made us valuable.

I bit my lip against further argument, tasting blood when my teeth sank too deeply into the flesh behind my bottom lip. Fucking hell, she was right.

Confident my arguments were done for now, Conner spoke up. "Lachlan has offered Belinda the pack's protection."

I nodded. "Okay, so am I staying with you and Donna or Lex and Ivie?"

"No, you're staying with me."

I looked over at Finn, saw his triumphant expression, and lost my ability to control my tongue. "No fucking way."

Chapter Six

I COULDN'T STOP the self-satisfied smile that spread across my face as I pulled down the long driveway of my mother's country home. After the meeting ended, Lachlan had taken Belinda to her home so she could pack a few of her things. Finn insisted on following me to my loft in order to "protect" me. More likely, he wanted to make sure I didn't give him the slip.

I had anyway.

I managed to lose him in the crazy traffic that was part of everyday life in Dallas. I didn't bother to go by my apartment because I knew that was the first place he would check. Instead, I pointed my car east and headed out of the city. On my long drive, I called Saundra Abrams, the assistant manager at my store and asked her if she could reschedule the clerks for the next few days because I would be unavailable. Though war was brewing, I needed to be able to pay my bills. She was worried and curious, but I managed to evade most of her questions and calm her fears somewhat.

I knew my little house in the country would be the next place Finn would look, but I intended to have a few surprises waiting for him. I was sick and tired of the way he used my attraction to him against me. Somehow, over the last three days, I realized I could no longer deny that I wanted him. He'd managed to sneak past my shields. That was why I was so easily angered by his attitude and melted beneath his touch.

However, that didn't mean I wasn't going to make him work for it. I had a feeling that women came easily for Finn, in every sense of the word. Maybe it was selfishness or pride, but I wanted to be different from his past lovers. I wanted him to truly see me.

My mother once said, "People appreciate the things they have to work for. If it comes too easily, then it can be just as easy to let it go." I knew, in this instance, that her advice was spot on.

I climbed out of my car, groaning when I realized that the cooler weather that moved through a few nights ago had been followed by warmer air. The temperature had to be in the mid-sixties. A bank of dark grey clouds was building in the west, probably the leading edge of another cold front. It wouldn't be long until those clouds built into a storm.

I grabbed my purse, locked my car, and hurried into the house. If I wanted to set up my little *surprises* for Finn, I needed to get it done before the rain began. Since he seemed to enjoy sneaking up on me, I intended to make it impossible for him to do so.

Before she died, my mother amassed quite a collection of spell books and magical texts. Several of them held detailed instructions for setting protection wards and casting perimeter spells. I intended to welcome him with fireworks and fanfare.

I went directly to the small library just off the living room and began choosing my spells and wards. I laughed to myself as I set three perimeter spells and several wards on the house. None of them would damage Finn, though quite a few of the protection wards might give him a little shock.

Within a half hour, I finished casting and made myself a cup of tea. I expected Finn to arrive in the next hour or so. Once he realized I wasn't going to show at the loft, he would likely come straight here.

He started this little game, but I would damn sure be the one to finish it and on my terms.

The house began to cool down as the sun set, so I started a fire in the living room fireplace. About an hour after I arrived, I heard the first rumbling of thunder and knew the storm building in the west was closing in.

As the clouds moved over head, the sun disappeared behind the horizon, leaving behind an oppressive darkness. I could hear the wind picking up as flashes of lightning burst outside the window.

Rain began to fall, heavy and fast, and the lightning became more frequent, as did the thunder. The wind blowing across the chimney sounded like a banshee's wail. Something wasn't right. I felt…unsettled. A chill crept across my neck, lifting the hair at my nape.

Over the cacophony, a resounding boom echoed inside the house and within my head. The first perimeter spell I'd cast had been breached. However, the entity heading toward my home wasn't Finn. And they definitely weren't alone.

Red and orange light filled the house as the second of my spells was broken. I snuck to the window and took a peek toward the driveway. The fireworks display my spell created was still exploding against the black clouds, brighter than even the lightning arcing across the sky. While I couldn't see my enemy, I could feel them.

The invaders were rapidly approaching my third and final perimeter spell. When I cast it earlier, I'd only wanted it to give off a mild electrical shock when breached. Since I was completely certain that Finn was not among the beings coming toward me, I closed my eyes, released my breath, and recited the words of the spell, changing them slightly.

Mere moments before the perimeter was crossed, I completed the spell and felt the snap of a circle completed. Indescribable power hummed beneath my skin. It was rare for me to call on so much of my magic. Aside from Belinda, no one in the coven knew exactly how strong I was. According to the tests my mother and Belinda had administered to me over the years, I was the most powerful witch practicing in North America, perhaps even the Western hemisphere.

It seemed, however, someone outside the coven was aware of my abilities, there was no other explanation as to why they would be here. Knowing it would take my enemies a while to break through the strong electric current generated by my new spell, I focused on the wards I'd placed on the house.

I closed my eyes, forced myself to breathe slowly and deeply, and centered my thoughts on reinforcing the wards. My body jerked when my final perimeter spell fell under the assault, the power I'd released into it flowing back into my body. Still, I didn't allow the almost painful sensation distract me.

Now that they were closer, I could feel five individual energies. I studied each in my mind's eye. Four were vampire and the fifth... a warlock. An immensely powerful warlock. I could feel the weight of his magic as he tested each of the wards on my house. A frisson of fear knifed through my chest. I understood it was likely that he was as strong as I.

Knowing what was coming, I began to call up a protection spell more difficult than any I'd ever attempted before. While most protection spells were defensive, this was not. Most witches would never be able to achieve it because it required a vast amount of skill and power. The incantation was meant to deliver a debilitating strike to one's enemies and destroy as many as possible in one blow. I never would have considered the spell if I were facing humans or other witches because it would almost certainly result in their death.

Vampires and warlocks, however, might be seriously injured but their wounds probably wouldn't prove fatal.

There was a rather large problem, though. In order to cast this spell, I had to drop the protection wards surrounding the house. I would be a sitting duck if it failed.

I felt the first slam of the warlock's attack and knew there was no time for doubt. While spoken spells were the strongest, I couldn't risk the vampires hearing me cast. Even with the tempest raging outside, two of the vampires were close enough to hear me if I used my voice.

Instead I crouched down to the floor, flattening both palms against the hardwood and lowering my head. In preparation for the incantation, I began to gather myself. The storm overhead filled the air with electricity and I could use that to boost the force of my attack.

In order to unleash a strike that would end this, I would have to let loose every bit of power I could muster. Usually, when casting, I needed only a small amount of magic, so, after years of training, I automatically controlled the flow. My mother often likened it to a dam. The amount of water released was based on the need. In this case, I would have to lower all the floodgates of my mental barriers.

The air in the living room became heavy as I called up my magic. I could almost feel it pressing into my skin like a physical touch. Then the static electricity created by the storm was drawn to my body, dancing over my skin, leaving the hair on my head standing on end.

In my mind, I began to recite the spell, never allowing my concentration to waver. If I let even a small amount of power slip before I struck, the warlock would know what was coming and have time to warn his companions.

Magic pulsed in my extremities. I felt as though a wild animal was trying to claw its way out of my body. I allowed the power to crescendo within me as I repeated the incantation three times in my head.

As I will it, so mote it be.

With those final words, I surged to my feet, my arms flying forward. The wards I'd placed on the house crashed down and a split second later, the ferocity I unleashed with my spell exploded with enough force that the entire structure shook.

A brilliant white light filled the room, so bright it was as if I were standing in the midday sun. I suddenly realized there was no way I could control the wave of destruction I released. Even to a vampire, this would be a fatal spell. It was too late to stop the chain reaction I'd begun. Instead, I rode the crest, my entire body sparking with electricity and magic.

Vaguely, I heard screams and felt the leading edge of the spell hit the four vampires surrounding my house. Then, they were devoured by pure, elemental magic, not even a trace of their bones left behind. The warlock vanished a moment before he would have been consumed.

From the epicenter of the spell, I searched the outside edges of my property and felt no one lurking. Satisfied that I was now alone, I lifted my arms above my head, calling for the power to return to me. Though I'd released it in a rush, it would take time for the surge to come full circle.

Slowly, the magic retracted, dispersing into the earth, the air, and my own body. While many books portrayed challenging spells such as these as draining, in reality, they were energizing. Residual magic swirled in the air and within my body, fizzing like champagne in my veins.

As I stood in the center of my living room, arms hanging limply at my sides and chest heaving, my front door flew open. Before I could think, my right hand lifted and a bolt of energy shot from my palm.

Wide-eyed I watched as the streak of light struck Finn's chest and a blinding shower of sparks erupted. Blinking rapidly to clear the black dots that filled my vision, I gaped when I realized that Finn was not only still standing, he was completely unharmed.

"Goddammit, Kerry! What the fuck were you thinking?"

Rubbing my palms together to relieve the intense tingling in my right hand, I apologized. "I'm sorry, Finn. I have never done that before. I didn't even know I *could* do that." I hadn't even thought of a spell, merely called up the magic and used it as I willed.

He slammed the door shut forcefully, causing the frame to creak ominously. "That's not what I'm fucking talking about and you know it!" he roared. "You KNEW that you were in danger and you willfully ignored the warnings. You could have been kidnapped, or worse, killed."

Still riding on the sharp edge of magic, which was more intense than a high by any drug, my eyes narrowed and very air around me sizzled with little sparks of electricity.

"I don't see anyone else standing here but you and me, Finn. I've told you before and I'm telling you again, I can and will take care of myself."

In a blink Finn was in my face, his large hand circling my neck. While he wasn't squeezing, his touch was threatening.

"I could crush your windpipe before you could even utter the first word of a spell," he hissed. "And there is nothing you could do to stop me."

Anger, wild and out of control, erupted inside me. Quickly, I lifted my right hand and tapped my finger in the center of Finn's chest. As I had moments ago, I didn't even think of the words needed to cast, merely used the magic as I wanted.

To an observer, the move would seem almost playful, but Finn groaned in pain, releasing my neck and collapsing to the floor, whatever prevented him from being hurt moments ago no longer seemed to protect him.

Leaning down to stare straight into his glowing lavender eyes, I whispered, "And I could have made your heart explode with that simple touch. Don't play this game with me, Finn. You wouldn't like the outcome."

An expression of grudging respect flickered across his features. "You are stronger than I thought," he muttered. "But you are an idiot if you think you can take on a warlock and his vampire apprentices alone."

Steel filling my spine, I straightened. "I just did and I could do it again."

Finn rose to his feet. "And how do you think you could do that?" he asked.

"You practice magic, yes?" Something wild and reckless filled me. Deep in my mind a voice whispered that I should stop, pull back, that I was dancing too close to the edge of the cliff that led straight down into the pit of black magic that had swallowed a man I once loved. The words of reason were interrupted by a devilish voice that insisted I needed to prove myself.

A glimmer of understanding filled his eyes. "Yes."

"Do you consider yourself to be powerful?" I asked.

Goddess help me, I had to be a nutcase, challenging a thousand year old vampire to a duel. He'd had a millennium to perfect his craft. He could probably kick my ass with his pinkie. Still, that devilish little voice inside me demanded that I garner his respect. Anything less would be an insult.

The glow in his purple eyes flared brightly and his voice dropped as he answered, "Yes."

"Then why don't you take me on and see who's still standing in the end?"

Chapter Seven

"**T**HIS IS A ridiculous idea," Finn complained.

As we squared off in my front yard, rain soaking us to our skin, I realized he did have a valid point. I'd regretted my suggestion as soon as I'd begun to calm, but my pride wouldn't let me back down. My mother and even Belinda had always said my pride and fierce independent streak would be my downfall. At least the storm had calmed somewhat, the lightning and thunder had stopped, so we likely wouldn't be electrocuted.

"Probably," I answered, "but you need to understand what I'm capable of. I can protect myself quite adequately, as I'm sure you noticed tonight."

Finn scowled at me. "You can't watch your back 24/7, Kerry. Whether you like it or not, you're vulnerable and you need help."

"Enough. Let's do this." The longer I listened to his logical arguments, the sillier I felt. Still, I couldn't let this go. Somewhere, deep within me, I *needed* him to respect me and to understand exactly how strong I was, even though I knew I was acting like a child.

"Kerry…."

Rather than continue the argument, I zapped him. Okay, so there was a more technical name for it, but, for lack of a better description, I threw a ball of static electricity at him. After that, there were no more words.

Finn managed to deflect my attack, barely, and he countered. We continued hurling spells at each other, gaining speed as the battle progressed. Though he was a vampire and wouldn't die from a more powerful attack, I didn't use anything stronger than I would when sparring with another witch. I wanted to prove my point, not injure him.

At first, I was surprised at how evenly matched we were. I thought he would be stronger than me. As we continued, he seemed to be losing focus. Finn cursed when he didn't deflect all of my last energy ball. I knew from experience that, while it wouldn't seriously damage him, the electric sensation was very unpleasant.

"Fuck this," he shouted, coming toward me. His speed was preternatural, bringing him right in front of me in a blink of an eye.

I backpedaled, lifting my hands to cast, but he moved too quickly. As I retreated, my foot slipped in a patch of mud and I went down. My breath left my lungs when I landed hard on my back.

I was still struggling to take in air when Finn's face appeared over me.

Eyes angry, he snapped, "Goddess, Kerry. Are you okay?"

Feeling foolish, I shoved at his shoulders. "I'm fine," I croaked then laughed. "You can get off me now." The sharp blade of anger was dulling beneath the ridiculousness of the situation.

Finn wrapped his fingers around my wrists, pinning my hands above my head. "No, not until you listen to reason."

"Seriously? I'm calm now. You can let me up."

"Are you going to come with me to a safe place tonight?" he asked.

I frowned at him, refusing to answer because I knew he wouldn't like what I had to say.

"By the god and goddess, you are the most stubborn, independent, proud woman I have ever been cursed to know."

I struggled beneath him, my irritation returning. Panting, I retorted, "Then leave." I didn't mean the words, but that same reckless and immature urge that had driven me to challenge him goaded me on.

"I don't want to."

Then he kissed me.

I could almost taste his anger as his mouth opened over mine, his tongue tangling with my own. He released my wrists, but laced our fingers together, holding my hands still. The heat of his body burned through my wet clothes, making me aware of how cold the night had become. Suddenly aware of the drop in temperature, I shivered violently.

Within seconds, Finn stood, lifted me into his arms, and carried me into the house. I could still feel the frustration emanating from him in waves. I responded by unleashing my own ire. Our mouths clashed as he lowered me to the rug in front of the fire.

Finn tugged at my shirt, trying to pull it over my head. When the wet material clung stubbornly to my body, he yanked and I heard the fabric rip. My pants quickly followed. He didn't even try to fight the hooks at the waist or the small zipper, tearing the material instead. I kicked off my shoes and lifted my hips as Finn wrestled me out of my slacks.

I couldn't think. I was angry, yet painfully aroused. I'd never experienced anything like it before. As Finn literally shredded my satin bra and panties, my hands twisted in the hem of his sweater and I yanked it over his head. My fingers fumbled with the button on his jeans, practically ripping them open. When my cold hand encountered his hot cock, he grunted, his hips jerking. I wrapped my fingers around the head of his erection and ran my thumb over the tip.

I yelped as Finn sucked my nipple between his lips. The warmth of his mouth almost hurt as it surrounded my icy flesh. My back arched when his hand slid up my inner thigh to my center. I lifted my hips as he thrust two fingers inside my body.

When his thumb pressed my clit and rotated, I clutched his biceps. "Finn."

He smiled slightly, revealing his fangs, then removed his hand.

"No! Don't stop." My anger forgotten, all I could think about was the pleasure of his touch. When he laughed, I reared up and sank my teeth into his chest as he shoved his jeans down his legs.

I felt the hot, hard length of his erection glide over my clit before he angled his hips and thrust inside me with one smooth motion. I cried out, wrapping my arms around his torso and digging my nails into his lower back. His hands pushed my knees higher, leaving me open and helpless to his powerful thrusts. The muscles in my lower abdomen tightened in preparation for a blinding climax.

Our coupling was fast and ferocious. I scratched and bit, straining against him, alternating between pleading and threatening. When my movements became too wild, Finn lowered his upper body, caging me between the floor and his chest, his arms providing a cushion for my shoulders and his hands cupped the back of my head.

"You feel more incredible than I imagined," he murmured in my ear. "Tight and hot."

I turned my head and sank my teeth into the curve where his neck and shoulder met, sucking hard enough to leave a mark.

Finn growled, his fingers tightening in my hair hard enough to hurt, but I liked it. His hips slammed into mine hard and fast, hitting my clit on each stroke.

My pulse thudded harder as he used his grip on my hair to turn my head, completely revealing my neck to him. I knew what was coming and, damn, I wanted it badly. Unlike my human friends, I knew exactly what to expect from a vampire's bite and I knew I would enjoy it.

When his fangs sank into my throat, an orgasm exploded within me, almost blinding in its intensity. With each pull of his mouth, another wave of pleasure would crash over me. Vaguely, I felt Finn stiffen as he came, then the world went dark.

✧   ✧   ✧

I WAS WARM and dry when I awoke. I smelled wood burning, vanilla and spice. Inhaling the comforting scents, I stretched languidly. So that was what angry sex felt like. I definitely should have tried it before now. When my eyes opened, I saw that I was lying in my bed, a small fire burning in the fireplace. It was the only light source in the room.

I shifted, wincing as sore muscles made themselves known. Our coupling had been wild and rough, and my body was letting me know it didn't approve of my enthusiastic activities.

Turning over, I was greeted by the same sight I saw in my dreams a few nights ago. Finn was stretched out on my bed, chest bare, and the blankets pulled up to his hips. His arms were bent, his hands locked together behind his head. His eyes followed my movements, an inscrutable expression on his face.

I tucked my hands beneath my chin, smiling a little. "Hey."

Finn didn't smile in return. I tensed, suddenly unsure of myself. He rarely hid his thoughts or emotions when we were together, in reality or in dreams. I hadn't realized before how much I relied on his openness to read his mood and thoughts.

Unconsciously, I gripped the top of the sheet covering me and clutched it to my chest. "What?" My voice sounded hesitant and meek, and I hated it.

"You realize this changes everything, don't you?" he asked, his expression still closed.

"What do you mean?"

Finn turned toward me, rolling over onto his side, his elbow cocked and head resting on his hand. "What do you think I mean?"

"Well, it could mean several things. Off the top of my head, it could mean that you think us having sex means we're in a relationship. Or that I'm going to flagrantly ignore coven edict and flaunt our hypothetical relationship in front of other witches. Or…"

In a flash, I was on my back, Finn looming over me. He was definitely back to being angry. "Shut up, Kerry."

I raised both eyebrows. "Did you really just tell me to shut up? Because that's just not nice." Even his grumpy behavior couldn't kill my good mood.

He growled and muttered under his breath, something about stubborn, prideful witches.

"What was that?" I asked, mostly teasing him.

Finn closed his eyes and took a deep breath. When he opened them, his purple eyes were aglow. "You're playing a dangerous game. We shared something rare and you know it. You understand exactly what I mean." He lowered his head until his lips touched the side of my neck. "To you, my bite is more than merely pleasurable, it is ecstasy. We're meant for each other. You belong to me."

I swallowed hard. I knew exactly what he was talking about. Vampires would often marry and have other long-lasting relationships, but, in their extended existence, it was rare for them to find a true soul mate. These mates could sustain each other. They often were unable to drink from anyone else, even when necessary. Finn was telling me that I was his mate and it scared the shit out of me.

"I can't belong to you, Finn," I whispered. "Even if I wanted to, it's impossible."

"You can," he stated. "You will."

I shook my head. "No, I won't. Even if the coven wouldn't condemn me, I still won't do it, Finn. If you turn me…." I trailed off. The process of turning a witch could have unforeseen consequences. Most of them were not good.

He sighed. "Please tell me you do not believe that bullshit that the coven distributes. You realize that most of it is fabricated to frighten young, open-minded witches away from vampires, right?"

I frowned up at him. "There are documented cases, many of them, in which witches either died in the transition, lost their powers, in some instances, even their minds."

Finn scoffed. "No, there aren't. Five hundred years ago, when the Council banned the forced turning of witches, there have only been a handful that have volunteered. Most are warlocks or practice black magic. There are two that left their covens because they mated with a vampire."

"That can't be," I argued. "Why would the coven lie?"

He smiled but it didn't reach his eyes. "Power, Kerry. It's always about power. What other things have they told you about witches that are turned?"

I thought for a moment and mentioned the second reason I was reluctant to consider mating with Finn. "Our powers are weakened when we become vampires."

He laughed. This time it did reach his eyes. "And you believed that?"

My frown turned into a fierce scowl. "Of course. It's a widely known fact among covens."

His amethyst eyes shimmered, hypnotic as they bored into mine. "Then why would vampires even want to turn witches? If your talents are diminished so greatly by transition, why bother doing it at all?" He had a point. Before I could mull it over, Finn continued. "I was a great deal weaker than you when they came for me. Within the first year of my change, I gained almost double the power. While my growth slowed considerably after that, it did continue. I'm at least ten times stronger than I was as a mortal."

I gaped up at him. "You were weaker than you are now?"

He nodded. "Yes. That's why they chose me, you see. My magic was too weak to fight them off, but just powerful enough to be of use. And I did prove myself to be very useful, even though I didn't want to be."

"But, surely you could keep them from compelling you to do what they wanted. All witches have at least some ability to withstand vampire powers."

"There are other ways to coerce a newly changed vampire into doing as he is bid," Finn whispered.

My eyes widened. I wasn't sure I really wanted to know, but I asked anyway. "Like what?"

He stroked my temple, letting his fingers slide down into my hair. As he played with a curl, he didn't look at me so much as through me. "They starved me. After the first six months, I lost count of how long I went without blood, food, or water. Then, they broke me."

Unable to stop myself, I lifted a hand and placed my palm against his cheek. This was the first time he'd spoken of the time when he'd changed. Once again, Finn's eyes focused on my face. "How?"

His expression became grim. "They waited until I was so desperate for blood, food, any sort of sustenance, that I couldn't control myself. Then they brought in a sixteen year old girl and locked her in the cell with me." He closed his eyes and I could literally feel the echoes of his pain. "I…I killed her as she cried and begged for mercy. I couldn't stop myself from gorging on her blood until she was dead and I was sated." When his lids lifted, Finn looked haunted. "It's been nearly a thousand years and I still haven't forgotten a single detail of that day. I can still smell the flowers she had braided in her hair."

I should have thought him a monster, but I couldn't. I could see the guilt and the sorrow his actions caused him. "What did you do after?" I asked softly, stroking his cheekbone with my thumb.

He blinked. "I told them that I would do whatever they wanted, as long as they never brought me an innocent human again. For years, I never fought back, never tried to escape, merely did as commanded and fed off the blood of criminals and prostitutes. They ridiculed me for my unwillingness to kill when I fed, but they never pushed me on it until fifty years later. I bided my time, but I waited until it was almost too late."

"Too late?"

Finn looked haunted. "As time passed, I became more and more like them. I was losing what was left of my soul. There were things I swore I'd never do that I did because I couldn't bring myself to care any longer. Then one night, they found a pregnant woman and they kept talking about the power in the blood of a woman with child. I suddenly realized I had a choice; I could join in their plans and become a monster, or I could stop them. I didn't have to be what they expected me to become."

I felt his words wind around my heart like a ribbon. Finn and I were alike in more ways than one. The people around us expected us to be monsters, to choose the darkness because of what we were and who we were, but we didn't. Surprisingly, I wanted to tell him about my father, the things he had done, and how being the daughter of a warlock had almost ruined me. Instead, I swallowed the words, stroked his face, and asked, "What happened to the woman?"

He shook his head. "She died in childbirth a few weeks later, her son not long after."

"I'm sorry." I could see that talking of the past was hurting him, but I had to know one last thing. "What happened to the vampires that turned you?"

The light in Finn's eyes flared so brightly I squinted and the ice cold triumph on his face sent a shiver of fear down my spine. "I destroyed them. I destroyed them so thoroughly that only ashes remained."

Chapter Eight

AFTER OUR CHILLING bedtime conversation, neither of us was in the mood to continue talking. Finn reclined on the pillows and watched me as I slipped on underwear, shorts, and a t-shirt. Once I'd washed the remnants of make-up and mud from my face and brushed my teeth, I returned to the bed.

Surprising Finn and myself, I pressed myself into his side, resting my head on his shoulder and curling my leg around one of his. He hesitated only a moment before bringing both arms around me and holding me closer.

At first, my body relaxed into his and I felt myself drifting toward sleep, both giving and taking comfort in his closeness. When my eyes began to close, a moment from the fight earlier flashed in my mind. Just after I released my power and it swallowed the vampires surrounding my home, a shard of dark pleasure pierced my soul. I had taken life and enjoyed it.

Despite vampire lore, they weren't the undead, merely changed. It was similar to lycanthropy. It could be inherited or shared through blood. However, their change was facilitated by magic rather than a virus. The magic ran in their veins, mingled with their blood.

Tonight, I had killed a living being, the worst of the crimes a witch could commit. Our purpose was to help, to heal. It was one of the first edicts we were taught as children.

Shudders began to wrack my body, shaking me down to my bones. Though the fire burned bright and hot, I was ice cold. A fine sheen of sweat broke out on my skin. Dear Goddess, what was happening to me?

Finn tightened his arms around me. "Just breathe, Kerry. Focus on the sound of my voice."

"W-w-what's happening?" I gasped.

He was silent for a moment. "If I had to make an educated guess, I'd say that you're having a panic attack or an adrenaline crash."

"But I was perfectly fine before." I stuttered over every other word in the sentence, making it nearly impossible to understand.

Another strong tremor twisted my body, tightening my muscles to the point that they ached. My teeth clacked together violently.

Finn shifted us so that I lay panting, sweating, and shaking beneath him. Unfortunately, it was the least sexy thing I'd ever experienced.

"Look at me, Kerry," he said, his eyes boring into mine. "Listen only to me. Stay here in this moment."

I blinked rapidly. My vision was becoming hazy and my head spun sickeningly.

"Kerry!" Finn snapped. "Breathe!" I sucked in a deep, shaky breath, the dizziness receding. As I exhaled, he said, "Good girl. Again."

I kept inhaling and exhaling until the shaking in my limbs calmed and my heart rate slowed to its normal pace. When I knew I would be able to speak, I croaked, "For future reference, if you call me *good girl* again, I'm going to bite the shit out of you."

Finn's eyes lit with humor. "Little witch, did you forget that biting is foreplay for vampires?"

I sighed, too tired to give him shit as I normally would. "Whatever. You know what I mean."

He smiled slightly, smoothing my hair back from my face with his hands. "Yes, I do." He studied my face for a few seconds. "Do you feel more like yourself?" he asked.

I nodded. "Yeah, I'm okay now."

Finn placed his lips against my forehead in a soft kiss. "Good. Let's get some rest. We both need it."

He rolled to the side, reaching out and turning off the lamp beside the bed. Then he pulled me into his side, the same position we'd been in earlier before my panic attack or adrenaline crash, whatever it was.

Though I didn't think I'd be able to sleep after such a traumatic night, I cuddled with Finn, letting his body and his warmth seep into my soul. We lay there silently in the dying light of the fire. Surprisingly, after a long while, my eyes grew heavy and I sank into sleep.

✦   ✦   ✦

THE SCREAMS WOKE me.

I sat straight up in bed, my head twisting, searching for the source of the bone chilling wails. It wasn't until Finn's face filled my vision, his hands cupping my jaw, that I realized the shrieks were coming from my throat.

I choked on the scream, cutting it off, refusing to let it loose again. Instead, I whimpered. I hated the pitiful sounds escaping from my mouth, but I couldn't seem to stop.

Finn released my face and wrapped his arms around me, dragging me into his lap. I pressed my forehead into his neck, trying to gain control over myself. He rocked me, rubbing my back gently. I felt wetness trickle down my face and knew I was crying.

"It's a dream, Kerry. Just a dream."

I took a deep breath that caught in my throat and I hiccupped. I tried to calm down enough to remember what the dream had been about, but it was no use. All that remained in my memory was a black void.

After a long while, I finally relaxed against his body.

Still stroking my back, Finn asked, "Do you remember what the dream was about?"

I shook my head.

"Do you want some water?"

Again I shook my head and burrowed closer.

Finn maneuvered us so that we were back beneath the blankets and my back was to his front. Then he surrounded me. There was no other word for it. His long arms wrapped around me, one under my body, the other coming over my ribcage. Then he moved so close that I was plastered to him from the crown of my head to my feet.

We didn't speak anymore, which was a relief. I didn't want to talk. I didn't want to think. The slow tempo of his breath helped me sink deeper into relaxation. I dozed, never completely awake or asleep, until dawn. I could tell by the looseness of his body that Finn was sleeping soundly. Unable to stand lying in bed any longer, I decided to get up and let him rest.

Moving slowly, I slid out of bed, shivering at the chill in the air. Both fires must have gone out last night and I hadn't thought to turn on the furnace. I snagged a pair of thick flannel pants and socks from a basket of clean laundry and crept out of the room. I was surprised that Finn didn't wake up.

I moved downstairs on silent feet, avoiding the steps that squeaked. Once in the living room, I switched my shorts for the pajama pants and pulled on the thick, fluffy socks. Already feeling somewhat warmer, I went to the large fireplace and poked at the ashes. The fire was completely dead.

I tried to be quiet as I scooped out the ashes and started a new fire. Within a few minutes, it was crackling steadily, the flames growing bigger and brighter. After I was satisfied that it wouldn't go out, I rose from my crouch next to the hearth and headed into the kitchen. I was in desperate need of caffeine. The stress and lack of sleep from last night were taking their toll.

As I prepped the old fashioned percolator, I heard the sounds of Finn moving around upstairs. I lit one of the gas burners on the stove and set the percolator on it. While I waited for the coffee to finish, I set a pan on the stove to fry bacon but didn't turn on the burner yet. I required coffee before I would have the ability to concentrate on cooking.

Though I wasn't very hungry, I needed to eat and Finn was a big guy. Even if he didn't need blood this morning, he had to have food for fuel. Funneling the amount of magic I'd used last night took a toll on me. I might not be a skinny girl, but that sort of casting depleted my entire body and mind.

The coffee was just beginning to perk when Finn came down the stairs, wearing only a pair of mud-stained jeans. He had my cell phone in his hand.

Pausing by the counter, Finn tilted his head and ran his eyes over me. "How are you feeling this morning?" he asked.

"Tired and sore." I was tired from lack of sleep and sore from our joint activities after our showdown in my yard last night.

For the first time, Finn didn't smirk when I made a reference to sex. Instead, he glanced over at the stove and was visibly surprised when he saw the enameled percolator there. "Is that…"

I smiled a little and nodded. "Yeah. My mom always said brewed coffee didn't taste as good as perked. I still make my coffee that way when I come here. It…reminds me of her and makes me feel closer to her."

He nodded, his expression serious. "Belinda called." Whatever he saw in my face made his jaw tighten. "I didn't answer. She left you a voicemail message." He held my phone out to me.

Surprised he hadn't listened to the message, I took it from him and murmured, "Thanks."

Finn didn't respond, merely turned on his heel and headed back upstairs. I watched the muscles play in his back as he ascended as I fought the urge to go after him and apologize for whatever I'd done to upset him. Frowning, I shook my head when I realized the direction my thoughts had taken. Since when did I worry about hurting a vampire's feelings? I preferred to be direct. I often tried to be tactful, but I never sacrificed my honesty, even with my friends. No wonder I only had a few.

With a sigh, I selected my voicemail app and listened to Belinda's message.

"Kerry, Finn called Lachlan last night and told us what happened. I need to speak to you as soon as possible, preferably in person. There's something…." She paused. "There's something you need to know before things go any further."

The message ended. I noticed the coffee was ready, went to the stove and turned off the burner. Then I called Belinda.

After one ring, she picked up. "Kerry. How are you feeling this morning?"

"I'm fine." My voice caught and I cleared my throat and repeated, "I'm fine."

"You're sure?" she asked.

My voice was stronger when I answered. "Yeah, I'm okay."

Though she probably knew better than to believe me, the High Priestess didn't push me for the truth. Instead, she said something that shocked me. "I had a vision but I don't think we should discuss it over the phone. Are you still at your mother's house in Farmersville?"

"Yes. Are you sure you can't tell me now? Won't it be dangerous to come out here?" I asked, my heart beating faster.

"It will be easier if I talk to you in person. Lachlan and Calder will bring me in a couple of hours and we can discuss it then."

"Okay."

"I'll see you soon, Kerry." Belinda paused. "Be sure and tell Finn we're coming, okay? I don't want to surprise him."

I doubted that would happen, but I knew she was right to remind me. I was so used to being alone, I often forgot my manners. "I will."

"Good-bye."

I disconnected the call without responding, curious as to what Belinda had foreseen.

"Is everything okay?"

At Finn's question, I gasped and whirled around, clutching my chest. "Dammit, you nearly gave me a heart attack! Can you make at least a little noise to let me know when you're around?"

He smirked. "I'll try."

Grumbling under my breath, I grabbed the mug of coffee I'd poured and handed it to him. "Belinda, Lachlan, and Calder are coming by in a couple of hours. She had a vision and she wants to discuss it with me."

"That sounds ominous," he muttered.

Without saying anything else, Finn went to the fridge and began to rummage around inside. A few moments later, he emerged with bacon, a carton of eggs, and butter in his hands. I watched as he placed them all on the counter and reached into a cabinet for a bowl.

"I'll make breakfast while you take a shower," he stated, without turning to look at me.

I didn't argue. Finn might be right that I was stubborn, but I wasn't stupid. If I could have a meal that I didn't have to cook myself, I'd take it. Though I would probably bite my tongue off before I admitted it, it was nice to be taken care of from time to time.

Chapter Nine

AFTER I TOOK my shower and discovered that I had dried mud in places I could barely reach, I dressed in a pair of jeans and a incredibly soft navy sweater that brought out my blue eyes. I didn't bother with shoes, just a pair of fluffy, warm socks.

I could no longer ignore the smell of frying bacon and decided to skip primping. I twisted my hair into a bun before I headed downstairs, my empty coffee cup in hand. I paused when I entered the kitchen because Finn was still shirtless and barefoot, standing in front of my stove with his back to me.

For the first time since we'd met, I let myself really look at him and openly appreciate what I saw. His dark brown hair was tousled, just brushing his shoulders, and his lightly tanned skin felt as smooth as it looked. Though he wasn't as bulky as Conner and Lex, his shoulders were broad and the taut muscles of his back flexed with each movement of his arms. The jeans he wore rode low on his hips and, while they weren't tight, they molded perfectly to the curve of his ass and left my mouth watering. I wanted to sink my teeth into the firm muscle. Which was strange, because I'd never thought about doing something like that before.

"Are you going to stand there and stare at my ass all day or come eat this breakfast I'm slaving over?"

I jumped at Finn's voice and felt my face heat up. I moved to the side of the stove and picked up the percolator to refill my cup.

Desperate to change the subject, I said, "Frying bacon shirtless is a little risky, don't you think?"

One corner of Finn's mouth lifted and he looked sideways at me. "How so?"

"Hot grease and bare nipples are not two things I'd want to put together."

He chuckled as he began to shift the bacon from the frying pan to a plate covered with a paper towel. "You're worth the pain," he answered wryly.

I rolled my eyes toward the ceiling. "Save the corny lines and finish my eggs. I'm starving."

Finn's hand shot out and gave my ass a light smack as I added sugar and creamer to my coffee, but he didn't reply.

A few minutes later, he brought two plates to the table, each filled with eggs, several strips of bacon, and toast. My eyebrows rose as I looked at all the food in front of me, then my stomach rumbled, reminding me that I could indeed eat it all.

After channeling so much power, my body needed to be fed and I would probably need a nap later in the day as well. All magic carried a price and the more you used, the more you paid. Residual magic gave you an energy high that would last a few hours before you crashed hard. I paused at the thought. Last night, I'd cast the most powerful spell I'd ever attempted, then, later, I began to shake and sweat. I realized that the two could be related and decided to ask Belinda if she knew anything.

I took a bite of eggs and was pleasantly surprised at the texture and flavor. They were just right. The bacon was crispy and well done, exactly the way I preferred it.

"Wow, this is delicious, Finn," I murmured, taking another bite of egg.

"Thanks." His eyes twinkled with good humor. "Although this is one of the five things I can cook well."

After I finished another bite, I asked, "What are the other four?"

"Spaghetti and meatballs, grilled steak and baked potato, just about any kind soup, and fish and chips."

"That all sounds pretty good."

He shrugged. "It is until you've been eating it for a decade. Before he met Donna, I ate at Conner's a lot because he's the best cook I know."

I chuckled. He had a good point. Having tasted Conner's food, I had to agree. He could probably make cardboard taste good.

We finished our breakfast in companionable silence. I started to wash dishes, but Finn insisted on helping me, so he dried them.

I couldn't help thinking about the strangeness of this situation. Just twelve hours ago, I'd been in mortal danger, and now I was standing in my kitchen doing mundane chores with a vampire. The concept of vampires was so exotic that the idea of one of them keeping house seemed foreign. Yet, here we were, washing dishes together like an old married couple. Well, maybe not married, since most of the married men I knew couldn't put their dirty dishes in the dishwasher, much less help with actual hand washing and drying.

After we finished cleaning up the kitchen, Finn said he had some calls to make and I poured myself another cup of coffee and headed into the study. Years ago, before she died, my mother had the house expanded to include a spacious library that connected to a solarium. In the solarium, my mother had grown herbs and medicinal plants needed to cast spells, create potions, and make charms. I continued this practice, but also included cooking herbs and a few orchid plants. There was even a small cast iron wood stove in the corner of the library.

It was by far my favorite room in the house.

I walked around the room, trailing my fingers along the spines of the books on the shelves. I wasn't looking for anything in particular, but, as my finger tips slid across the back of one book, I felt a tremor go up my arm. I paused and pulled the text from the shelf.

There were no markings or writings on the binding, so I opened the book. When I realized what I was holding, my stomach plummeted to the floor.

It was a translation of an ancient Latin text that had been banned by the coven. The elders claimed that, while it wasn't true black magic, it was a gateway to the dark arts. My mother obviously hadn't agreed. It surprised me that she kept it on her shelf so openly. Even more shocking was that I hadn't noticed it before. While I hadn't catalogued her library after her death, I had spent many hours in the study during the last few years.

I took the book to the table and sat. As I turned the pages, a feeling of recognition sparked through me though I'd never read them before. Midway through my scan of the text, I found a folded paper tucked inside.

My heart stopped when I saw my name in my mother's handwriting. With shaking hands, I unfolded the sheet and began to read.

Beloved Daughter,

If you are reading this letter, then you have found the Book of Shadows. There is speculation that this is one of the first in history.

It also means that you are in need of the information it contains.

The spell I cast on this book keeps it hidden until it is needed by my blood. When its contents are required, it will appear on a shelf in the library when you are near. You will also feel it call to you, as though you've been looking for something but you're not sure what.

Don't ignore that call. It may mean the difference between victory or defeat, life or death.

I hope, Kerry, that you never need the spells and prophecy in this book. However, if you do, please use them wisely. Don't be fooled into believing that some of the spells aren't verging on dark magic.

In some ways, the coven elders are correct about this text. Should it fall into the wrong hands, it would be extremely dangerous.

I love you, my sweet girl.

~Mom~

"Dear Goddess," I whispered. My emotions were in turmoil and impossible to separate or recognize.

I ran my hands over the binding. The book seemed to vibrate beneath my palms, urging me to explore what lay between the covers. Moving slowly, I lifted my hands. Goose bumps broke out on my arms and energy seemed to be gathering around me, centering on the text that sat on the table.

I jumped to my feet, knocking over my chair, as the front cover flew open and the pages turned on their own, moving so quickly they were only a blur. When they began to slow, I backed away and watched in shock, until one last page flipped and the book lay flat and still. The power that had gathered around me began to fade.

Wary, I took a hesitant step forward. Nothing happened. There was no surge of power or movement from the Book of Shadows.

I bent and righted my chair, yelping when Finn barreled around the corner, a fierce snarl on his face. When he saw that I was alone, his expression cleared, but his body remained tense.

"What happened?" Unable to speak, I merely pointed at the book on the table. "The book?" he asked.

I nodded.

He approached the table and looked down at the pages. Frowning slightly, he lifted his gaze to me. "I'm not sure, but I think it's a prophecy."

I moved to stand next to him and, careful not to touch the tome, I read what was written on the page.

> *One will live*
> *Two will die*
> *Three will return the Fourth to life*
> *Together the Five will right the past,*
> *Create the future and hold it fast*
> *All hold keys to power untold*
> *And will find their Fate as evil grows bold*
> *Five may live*
> *Five may die*
> *Five may love*
> *Five may fall*
> *Should this come to pass*
> *Then ten will save Creation*
> *Or lose that which they have found at last*

"Oh shit," I breathed.

"Do you know what it is?" Finn asked.

"Yes. You were right, it is a prophecy." My voice cracked, so I cleared my throat. "It's something that no one has seen in centuries and most witches in the coven consider it pure myth."

"What does it mean?"

"It means, that unless we figure out how to stop the Faction, we're fucked," I answered.

Chapter Ten

HALF AN HOUR later, Belinda, Lachlan, and Calder arrived. I immediately grabbed Belinda's hand and practically dragged her to the study.

"Well, hello to you too, Kerry." She looked around the library and out into the solarium, smiling. "I always loved this room. I used to come here as a teenager and sit and read for hours."

"No time for reminiscing. We have a major problem." I knew I sounded melodramatic, but I was still on edge after what had happened with the Book of Shadows.

Belinda sighed. "I should say so, since you and I have to go into hiding just to avoid being kidnapped or killed."

Gesturing to the book, which was still open on the table, I explained, "No, really, we have a *huge* problem. This whole situation, the Faction, it's been prophesied. There's more at stake than just the vampire council, wolf pack, and our coven. This could change the entire course of supernatural history, and not in a good way."

Frowning, she went over to the table and began reading. When she finished, her face paled. "It's the prophecy of the Five," she whispered.

According to legend, the prophecy of the Five was the supernatural version of the Apocalypse. We could all live or die. Our fate was in our own hands.

"I know."

"But who are the Five? You and I and three others? Or five people we don't know?" she asked.

My body tensed. I hated the idea that I was about to suggest because it meant my friends were in danger. "I think that my friends and I are the Five."

"But ancient lore…"

I nodded. "I know what the books say, but I think they're wrong. I don't think the Five are only witches."

Belinda stood and walked into the solarium. I followed, knowing she would have something to say.

"Tell me why you think that your friends are involved," she murmured.

Before I began, I took a deep breath. "First of all, there are five of us." When Belinda sighed, I hurried on because I knew she thought my idea was ridiculous. "Two will die….Donna technically died before Conner turned her. She almost didn't make it. I think she's the first. One will live. I think that each of the numbers means two different things. It's not just how many will live or die, but each number represents a person. Donna is One. Ivie is Two." I paused, my voice dropping. "I think I'm Three."

"Do you have any other reason to believe that you and your friends are the Five? That's a very flimsy foundation for your theory." She sounded skeptical and I couldn't blame her.

"Think about it, Belinda. Twenty years ago, hell, even ten, what would happen to a human who learned of the supernatural community? They were eliminated, either through memory wiping or death. No one could know. Yet, for some reason, the Council makes an exception for Ivie, Ricki, and Shannon? That's not a coincidence. That's destiny. They were meant to be involved and, whether the Council, coven, or pack is willing to admit it or not, the fate of our species lies in their hands as much as ours."

The High Priestess didn't speak for a long time. She stared out the glass wall of the solarium, deep in thought. Finally, she asked, "Who is Four?"

The book intimated that the fourth would die before being brought back, the second of the two deaths. As much as I hated to even consider it, I said, "I think it's Ricki. She and, uh, Calder, they…." I swallowed hard because I hated the idea of something bad happening to someone I cared so deeply about. "He marked her."

"I see."

Belinda began to walk around the sunroom, studying the herbs and other plants I had growing there. I tried not to fidget, but her silence was making me nervous, so I had to stop myself from shifting from foot to foot several times.

Finally, she stated, "We need to get them all here and then to safe houses. Though I doubt the Faction is aware of the prophecy, we can't trust anyone not to share what they learned. If this is coming to pass, then you're right. The peril isn't just to the Dallas underground, it's to supernaturals around the world." She seemed distracted as she ran a hand over her hair, smoothing invisible stray hairs back into her bun.

"I'll make the calls."

Belinda nodded her assent, but she seemed lost in her own thoughts as I turned to leave the room.

"Kerry."

I stopped and looked back at her. Her face was pale and composed, but something in her eyes seemed wild.

"Promise me that you will do everything in your power to get the coven to agree to the truce between the Council and the pack."

Confused, I answered, "Of course I will."

"I need to hear the words."

The sliver of worry in my gut expanded. "I promise I will do everything in my power to see the supernatural community united."

Her shoulders slumped, as though my declaration relieved her.

"What's going on, Belinda?"

She didn't answer, merely turned her back on me, an effective dismissal.

Unsettled, I left the room, my pace much slower than before. I had a feeling her demand was a precursor to something much, much worse. I would make a point to pull Lachlan to the side today and talk to him. A whisper of premonition fueled my paranoia. I sensed that he would need to keep an even closer watch than he thought on the High Priestess.

✧   ✧   ✧

TWO HOURS LATER, my house was filling up with vampires, werewolves, and humans. It was like some sort of twisted, paranormal menagerie. All we needed were a couple of ghosts, goblins, and some zombies.

Though the males were impatient, Belinda and I only wanted to explain things once, so we were waiting for Ricki and Shannon to show up. When Calder heard that Ricki was on her way, I thought he was going to crawl out of his skin. He hadn't stopped moving since.

Lex and Conner were watching him closely as he paced in the living room by the front window, looking out every thirty seconds or so. I had a feeling they wouldn't hesitate to intervene if Ricki was overwhelmed by Calder's intensity.

Calder stopped prowling, his gaze fixed on something outside the window. I heard a car door slam and assumed that Shannon and Ricki were here. A few minutes later, the front door opened, and a blast of cold air followed my friends into the house.

I took their coats and, as I was hanging them up, I noticed the expression of longing on Calder's face when he looked at Ricki. When he saw me looking at him, his face closed down and he shrugged before turning away.

A few moments later, after she hugged me, I saw a similar look on Ricki's face when she looked in the wolf's direction.

Despite the seriousness of our current situation, I wanted to smile. Whether she liked it or not, Ricki had finally found a man who would stick with her for the rest of her life.

Since there were too many people to fit in my library and solarium, we gathered in the living room. Conner sat on the couch with Donna on his lap. Lex and Ivie sat side by side next to them. Lachlan, Calder, and Finn stood near the fireplace, talking quietly. The other two members of the vampire Council, Gabriel and Johanna were seated in my cozy armchairs by the fire looking a bit uncomfortable. I'm sure that they were unused to being surrounded by witches, werewolves, and humans.

Shannon and Ricki were sitting on the floor in front of the fireplace. Ricki worked very hard to avoid looking at Calder and Shannon was eyeing Gabriel and Johanna curiously.

"Are you ready?" Belinda asked from behind me.

Glancing over my shoulder, I shrugged. "No, but I don't have a choice."

The corners of her mouth lifted in a semblance of a smile and she handed me the Book of Shadows. "Let's get this done. Lachlan and Calder appear as though they're ready to make their escape."

Together, we moved to the center of the room, commanding everyone's attention. I was glad when Belinda took the lead and spoke first.

"Thank you all for coming. As you know, there has been unrest among the vampires in this area and a rebellion against Council rule. It now appears that the mutiny has reached beyond the vampire population. Last night, members of the Faction also made an attempt on one of my coven. I believe it is only a matter of time before they turn their attentions to the MacIntire pack." She paused, letting her words sink in. "It's time that we stop playing politics and dancing around an alliance. There are too many lives in peril to waste more time. We need to work together in order to protect all of those we lead."

I saw a small smile of approval on Conner's face and Lex tilted his head in acknowledgment at her words. The tension that had wound within me began to relax slightly. I glanced at Gabriel and Johanna, since I didn't know them as well as I did the other vampires on the Council.

Gabriel seemed unaffected, his face composed and calm, but Johanna appeared to be on the verge of, for lack of a better term, losing her shit. Her hazel eyes glowed brightly with what I assumed was anger. She leaped to her feet, moving so quickly that her long brown hair seemed to float around her head.

Staring at Conner and Lex, she asked, "You will allow a witch to tell you what to do? She knows nothing and she is weak. You have allowed your love for humans," she sneered the word as though it were unclean, "to affect your judgment. Vampires are the strongest. We should be telling them what should be done, not listening to the sniveling of mere witches."

I knew that Belinda wouldn't speak up for herself. She was too diplomatic and I had never, in the years I had known her, seen her lose her temper. Me, however, well, I was fucking done.

I stepped forward, keeping my posture relaxed as I called on the magic around me as I had last night. I didn't want to use it, but Johanna seemed on the edge of doing something stupid, so I wasn't going to take any chances. "That is enough," I murmured, fighting to keep my voice calm.

I almost flinched at the snarl on her face when she whirled toward me. "Do not speak to me, *witch*." She turned her back on me and continued with her tirade. "You're living with a human, Lex. She's food, not a pet."

Ivie's face paled at Johanna's words. Since early in their relationship, she'd been dealing with feelings of inferiority and insecurity around his vampire colleagues.

That was when I lost my temper. A wave of power crashed over me, so strong I almost fell to my knees. Unable to stem the flow, I managed to control it enough to keep it from exploding in the room like a stick of metaphysical dynamite.

I focused the energy on Johanna. "I SAID, THAT IS ENOUGH!" My voice had taken on an unnatural depth and volume, heavy with the weight of my magic.

The vampiress fell to the floor, curling into a fetal position, as I stalked toward her. I knew the amount of power I was forcing into her was hurting her badly, but it seemed that Johanna hadn't encountered a powerful practitioner in all her centuries of life and I intended to teach her a lesson she wouldn't soon forget.

I crouched down beside her and, hissing, she tried to strike out at me. Somehow, even though she was moving so quickly most humans would only see a blur, her attack looked slow and clumsy in my eyes.

Lifting a hand, I commanded, "Stop." Her body froze, but her eyes burned into mine, promising pain and most certainly death if she escaped my grasp. My voice was still distorted as I spoke, though not as loud. "You are in my home and you have treated me and my guests with contempt." I leaned a little closer, staring deep into her eyes and feeling her mind trying to force its way past my mental barriers. Shaking my head, I admonished her, "I can feel what you're trying to do, Johanna, and it won't work. Now, what does vampire law say about insulting one's host?"

Her internal struggles stopped and I could feel the niggle of fear within her.

"Since I don't trust you to answer honestly," I stated, "let's ask another vampire."

To my surprise, Gabriel Crow spoke. "An affront of this magnitude would have the most dire of consequences, including exile or even death."

I glanced over at him, and something he saw in my face caused him to stiffen. I realized that the amount of magic I was channeling was lifting the ends of my hair as though I were sitting outside in a light breeze. To one who had never witnessed a witch in her full glory before, it could be an extremely unsettling sight.

"Your eyes," he whispered.

"What about them?"

He blinked several times, a look of awe on his face. "They're glowing. In fact, at this moment, you look almost like a vampire in the throes of bloodlust."

His comparison hit me in the gut hard enough to make me catch my breath. I could sense that he didn't mean it as an insult, but rather a strange sort of vampire compliment. I tucked those emotions away to deal with later. I reminded myself I didn't have to become the witch my father had been. Right now, I had a chained tiger in front of me and I needed to handle her first.

"All right, Johanna. It seems that I can choose your punishment. However, I might be inclined to be lenient if you apologize."

She spat out words in a language I didn't know. Maybe Polish or Ukrainian. I didn't think I wanted to know what she was saying anyway.

I clicked my tongue at her. "Now, Johanna, that's no way to treat the person who holds your life in her hands."

"You cannot kill me, witch. You are too weak and spineless."

Before I could respond, I felt Finn come up behind me. "You're wrong, Johanna. I saw her last night as she destroyed four vampires, three of them older than you, and she did it without uttering a single spell."

For the first time, the vampiress' eyes showed true fear. She stared up at Finn. "Please don't."

"Oh, but I must," he answered, his voice as calm and unruffled as though he were asking for another cup of coffee.

"What's going on?" I asked.

Finn didn't respond. He merely focused his vibrant purple eyes on Johanna. I watched as his pupils constricted to pinpricks, then expanded until only a corona of electric purple shone around the edges.

His voice held a strange echo when he spoke again. "Dear Johanna has been recruited by the Faction. Unfortunately, they haven't shared much information with her, only accepted what she offered them."

My heart stopped. How could I have forgotten? One power Finn had developed after he was turned was the ability to read and control other vampires. Though all vampires could play mind games with humans, it was extremely rare for them to possess the ability and strength to do so to one another.

"Is there anything else you can see?" Conner asked.

Finn shook his head. "Not right now. I will need more time with her. She's under some sort of spell to protect any secrets she knows. The warlock aligned with the Faction is powerful. It won't be easy to break through his spell and, even if I do, it may kill her."

Conner's face was harsh when he said, "That's a risk we'll just have to take." He removed his phone from his jacket pocket and made a call. To whomever was on the other end, he stated, "I need you. Johanna's been compromised and we need to have her taken in for interrogation." He paused. "No, you need to come now."

Again he listened to the person on the other end. "You won't be seen, now get your bloody arse over here."

I felt my eyebrows lift as Conner's accent thickened during his last words. It was actually very sexy.

Donna must have noticed my surprise because she muttered, "I know, right? Every time he's pissed off, I get turned on."

I swallowed a cackle at her wildly inappropriate and ill-timed comment. Unfortunately, Shannon snorted and the rest of my friends dissolved into howls of amusement. The vampires and werewolves around us did not look amused as all five of us laughed until we cried. Goddess, my friends were twisted bitches and I loved every one of them for it.

Chapter Eleven

A FTER OUR HYSTERICS over Donna's poorly timed humor, Finn had done something to Johanna to make her sleep. Then Belinda cast a spell to keep her from hearing us as we spoke. I'd never heard of it before and I would have to ask her where she found it as I'm sure it would come in handy in the future. Maybe it was overkill, but we weren't taking any chances with what we were about to share.

Once we were sure that Johanna would not be able to eavesdrop, we continued our meeting while we waited for Conner's man to arrive. It hadn't taken long to explain what I had found in the library that morning. Since Belinda and I weren't yet sure exactly what the prophecy meant, we couldn't answer the questions asked by the remaining Council members and Lachlan.

Donna, Ivie, and Ricki seemed excited at the idea that they had such an important role in the upcoming battle, but Shannon was the only one of them that seemed to comprehend the gravity of their position. As an administrator for a security firm, she understood what war looked like. Most of the employees at her company were military veterans or ex-government operatives. Her questions were intelligent and relevant. Even the vampires and werewolves looked at her with respect and approval by the end of the meeting.

After we were done, Lachlan pulled Calder to the side and they spoke quietly for a few minutes. The conversation looked tense.

Finally, Lachlan nodded and the rigid muscles of Calder's back relaxed.

As they continued their conversation, Belinda wandered over to me. "In all the hubbub, I forgot to tell you why I called. I had a vision of a vampire with black eyes and I'm almost certain he's the warlock that was here last night. He was in a dark room, lit only by a few candles, and you were sitting on the bed, talking to him. I could see you, but not hear you. I know it's not much help, but I hoped talking to you would help me see more."

I nodded. "I understand. Anything shake loose?"

"Shake loose?" she asked with a smile. Shaking her head, she answered, "No, nothing else. I've been a little distracted with your discovery. If I have another vision, I'll call you."

"Okay."

Before our conversation could go further, the MacIntire alpha left his beta standing in the corner alone and came over to where Belinda and I were standing.

"Bell, it's time to go," he growled impatiently.

Bell? Really?

To my surprise, the High Priestess of my coven smiled serenely and nodded. "No problem." I stared at her as she said to me, "I'll call you later, Kerry."

I watched as the alpha helped Belinda put on her coat before resting his hands on her shoulders and stroking the back of her neck with his thumb. When I realized that my High Priestess definitely had an intimate relationship with the MacIntire alpha, I gaped at them, dumbfounded. I watched as Lachlan placed a hand on Belinda's lower back and guided her out my front door. Shit, after all the insanity before our meeting, I'd forgotten to talk to him about keeping a closer eye on Belinda.

"I thought you knew that they were together," Finn murmured in my ear.

"No clue."

I walked away from him without another word. Despite our easy rapport that morning, I really didn't want to discuss my High Priestess' sex life. Or think about it in any way, shape, or form.

A half hour later, a tall, blonde vampire came through the front door. He did not look happy. In fact, he looked downright enraged. However, when Donna saw him, smiled, and waved, the anger left his face as he nodded at her.

I was sitting on the floor in front of the fireplace with all four of my friends, trying not to worry about everything that was happening.

"Whoa, who is that?" Ricki asked quietly. "He's hot."

We all jumped when a low, rumbling growl filled the room. Ricki shot Calder a dirty look before turning her back on him.

I couldn't stop my smile. The sexual tension between those two was palpable and I knew it wouldn't be long until Calder lost his patience with Ricki's 'hard to get' act.

"That's Asher," Donna answered, ignoring Calder's possessive behavior. "He's a friend of Conner's and he's part owner of Concord."

"The restaurant?" Shannon asked.

"Yeah."

We all watched him as he walked over to where Conner stood with Finn and Lex.

"Damn, that is a whole bunch of sexy," Ivie whispered.

In unison, all four vampires turned and looked at our group.

"Shit, do you think they heard me?" she asked Donna.

I chuckled when I saw Lex look right at Ivie and nod his head.

"Somebody's in trouble," Ricki trilled.

"Shut up."

We all started giggling at Ivie's petulant response. Conner, Finn, and Lex went back to their discussion, but I noticed that

Asher seemed to be distracted and still staring in our direction. I glanced over and realized that he and Shannon were studying each other as though sizing up an opponent. Something clicked inside me and I realized that the final woman in our group had found her match. Not that I would tell Shannon that. The woman carried a gun and she knew how to use it, even if it was pink and girlie. I wasn't about to get on her bad side.

"Shannon, will you quit eye-fucking Asher and pay attention?" Ricki quipped.

I bit my lip to hide my smile as Shannon's eyes cut to the side and she gave Ricki a look that would have made a grown man flinch. Ricki just flipped her off and kept talking.

We chatted and watched as Conner and Asher carried Johanna out of the house. Finn, Lex, and Gabriel followed. They returned a few minutes later, minus Gabriel and Asher. I assumed those two were handling Johanna's relocation to whatever make-shift dungeon they had set up.

Conner approached our group and hauled Donna to her feet. "Lass, we need to go so Kerry can get to the safe house."

I stifled a sigh at his endearment to my friend.

The rest of us stood as well. We exchanged hugs and kisses and I promised to call them as soon as I was settled in the safe house. Since Lex and Ivie had ridden with Conner and Donna, they left together. Shannon and Ricki were just putting on their coats when Calder approached them.

"If it's all right, I'd like to ride back to the city with you." Calder phrased it politely, but it was not a request.

Shannon shrugged. "No problem."

I watched as Ricki's eyes widened and, once again, had to bite my lip to hide a smile. It seemed Shannon was getting revenge for Ricki's eye-fucking comment earlier. Though I know she wanted to object, I watched as Ricki fought for her composure. They had driven out here in Shannon's car, which meant that Shannon had the final say.

Calder watched Ricki closely, obviously waiting for her to rise to the bait, but she merely snapped, "Fine." Then she stormed out of the front door, leaving Calder and Shannon to trail behind her.

A few moments later, Finn and I were alone in the house.

With a sigh, I headed toward the stairs. "Well, I guess I should pack a few things. Should I follow you to the safe house in my car?" I asked.

"No need. One of Conner's employees came out with Asher and drove it back to your loft."

I stopped, one foot hovering over a stair. "What?" I turned and stared down at him, unsure if I'd heard him correctly.

Crossing his arms over his chest, Finn replied, "Your car is at your loft. You'll ride back to Dallas with me."

I mirrored his position, feeling irritation building in my belly. "Don't you think that you should have, I don't know, *asked* my permission?" My voice was tight because I was struggling not to yell at him.

He shook his head. "No. You would have argued with me about it, then, after a nasty little spat, I still would have had Conner's man come out here and pick up your vehicle whether you liked it or not."

Oh, hell no. "Now, wait just a damned minute…" I began. Somewhere in the kitchen I heard my phone ring. Concerned it might be important, I darted down the stairs, but not before pointing a finger at Finn and saying, "Don't think this is over, buster."

He merely bared his teeth at me in a poor semblance of a smile. "It's over and done. Anything you have to say won't change that."

I almost zapped him as I passed by, but somehow managed to control the childish impulse. "We'll see about that," I muttered.

I found my phone on the counter next to the coffee pot and answered.

"Hello?"

"Kerry! Thank the Goddess." It was Sally Abrams, Saundra's sister. She sounded extremely upset. She began speaking, her words slurring and disjointed to the point that I couldn't understand what she was saying.

"Whoa, whoa. Slow down, Sally. I can't understand you."

Then one word in the jumble became very clear. "....DEAD!"

"What?" I whispered.

With a choked sob, Sally finally spoke clearly. "Saundra is dead!"

Chapter Twelve

I DON'T REMEMBER much of what happened after Sally's call, only that Finn removed the phone from my numb hand.

It seemed only seconds had passed when Finn squatted in front of me, worry in his eyes. I glanced around and wondered how I ended up sitting on the couch. I didn't remember walking over to it, much less collapsing on the cushions.

"Kerry, we need to leave."

I blinked at him, feeling as though I were underwater. I could hear and see, but it was garbled.

His hand cupped my knee. "Kerry."

"Okay."

Finn helped me stand, his arms taking most of my weight. He practically carried me out to the car, settling me in the passenger seat, and even buckling my seat belt for me. We didn't speak on the drive back, but Finn cradled my hand in his the entire time.

I finally woke from my stupor about fifteen minutes from the city. "I need to speak to Sally."

Finn stared at me, his expression empty of emotion. "No."

"I need to know what happened, Finn," I insisted. Saundra's body had been found at my store and, though I didn't yet know the specifics, I was almost certain that her death had something to do with me.

He turned his eyes back to the road, still so calm and collected that I wanted to kick him. "You will, but not right now. I need to get you somewhere safe. Then, I'll tell you what happened. When the time is right, I'll allow you to call Sally."

If I had hackles, they would have been standing on end at his words. "Allow?" I asked, my tone dangerous. If I was angry then I didn't have to feel this horrendous grief.

Finn growled. "Bloody fucking hell, Kerry! I want to keep you safe. Why are you fighting me every step of the way?" The steering wheel creaked as his grip tightened.

"Because a good friend of mine is dead and it's my fault!" I screamed. "It's my fault she's dead. It's my fault." My voice broke as the tears started to fall, all my anger falling away.

Finn pulled over and stopped the car. His arms came around me and he tucked my head into the crook of his neck. "Shhh. I've got you," he murmured. "I've got you."

I don't know how long it took before the storm of sobs, guilt, and regret passed, but my throat felt raw and my eyes burned. I pulled away from Finn, trying to dry my face with my hands. He held out a clean white handkerchief.

I took it from him and dabbed at my eyes. "Thanks."

"Look, I know you're upset, but we need to get to the safe house. Once we're there, I'll tell you what I know and you can talk to Sally tomorrow. You're vulnerable as long as we're out in the open."

Since it was obvious that he wasn't going to budge on the safe house and me speaking to Sally in person, I decided to pick my battles and let him have this one. "Okay."

Finn's eyes narrowed. "That was easier than I thought it would be."

I barely refrained from rolling my eyes. "What? I can be reasonable."

The expression on his face clearly showed his disbelief, but he didn't speak. He rebuckled my seatbelt, then his own, and maneuvered the car back onto the highway. I was surprised when he exited the expressway and headed into a subdivision. The neighborhood had cookie cutter houses and was solidly middle class. He drove to the end of the street and turned left. A sign declared it a dead end.

He turned into a vacant lot at the end of the cul de sac. "We're here."

I looked around at the large, empty lot in front of us. The grass was neatly manicured and there were good-sized trees along the perimeter in both the back and the front. "Um, are we camping? Because, I hate to point this out, but that's pretty fucking out in the open."

Finn chuckled softly. "Look with more than your eyes."

Frowning, I stared at the bare land. Then I noticed something shimmering in the air. I blinked several times and looked beyond what my physical body could see. Suddenly, it was no longer empty. While the other homes on the block had smaller lots, this one had almost triple the amount of property and a large two story house in the middle. It looked a great deal older than the rest of the neighborhood. Almost as though it had been sitting here for decades and the expansion of the surrounding area somehow left it untouched.

Finn followed the driveway around to the back of the house, pulled a garage door opener out of the console, and pressed the button. I gaped as the garage door lifted to reveal a four car garage. Three bays were empty, the other held a nondescript beige sedan. He pulled in next to the sedan and shut off the car.

"What is this place?" I asked.

"It's one of the safest buildings in the city. It's protected and hidden by some of the strongest magic in history and even a powerful warlock wouldn't be able to pinpoint your location if he attempted to scry for you. Still, I'll need to take your cell phone. While the protection prevents you from being located through magical means, I don't think it extends to the GPS locator in electronic devices."

I nodded and gave him my cell before we got out of the car. He insisted on carrying my bags for me and led me into the house. We walked through a mud-slash-laundry room, then entered a spacious kitchen. I realized that the house was much larger on the inside than it seemed from my view of it before entering.

"This is beautiful."

"Thank you," Finn replied.

"Who does it belong to?" I asked. "I'm not displacing someone from their home, am I?"

He chuckled, gesturing for me to follow him out of the kitchen, through a gorgeous foyer, and up the stairs. "No, you're not kicking anyone out of their house."

I trailed my hand on the banister as we climbed the stairs, admiring the warm tones and smooth finish of the wood. "So, who does it belong to?"

Finn didn't respond, merely walked down the second story hallway to a door at the far end. When we entered the room, I saw it was a suite. There was a small sitting room with a television, couch, and chaise and French doors that were open to reveal a large bedroom with an enormous sleigh bed in the center.

He carried my bags into the bedroom and set them on a bench against the wall. Suspicion curled in my belly as I watched him shrug out of his jacket. I approached him as he carried the garment to what appeared to be a walk-in closet and disappeared inside. Determined, I followed, then stopped short and gaped as I took in every fashionista's dream. There were rows upon rows of racks, shelves, and drawers. Only half the closet held clothing and all of it was for a man. I had a strong feeling I knew who's home I was in, but I wanted Finn to say it out loud.

"Who's house is this, Finn?" I demanded. "Tell me."

Calm and completely unruffled, he hung up his jacket. "It's mine."

Anger surged inside me. "I thought you said we were going to a safe house?" I snapped. "I'm sure that the Faction is aware of where you live, Finn. Please explain to me how that is safer than my cottage, especially since I will need my books, herbs, and other tools to research this prophecy, make amulets, and brew potions." He stepped toward me, his hand out, and I batted it away as I retreated.

Finn advanced quickly, his hands gripping my upper arms. My back hit the open closet door and I glared up at him. I opened my mouth to hurl insults at him, but Finn put his hand over my lips, effectively shutting me up.

"Mmmmhhhmmm bhhhmmmm." Though it came out completely unintelligible, I still tried to call him a motherfucking bastard.

"Now, now, Kerry. That's not nice." I jerked my head, trying to dislodge his hand, but he gripped me more firmly. "Let me finish what I was trying to tell you. I've owned this house for decades, but only moved in a few weeks ago. There is no way the Faction knows that this house is here. The Council doesn't even know of its existence."

I stopped struggling and just stared at him.

"Are you going to calm down?" he asked.

I nodded slowly. The hand he had over my mouth loosened slightly. I was tempted to bite him, but knew he would enjoy that too much, so I settled for stalking away.

"Dammit, Kerry. Why are you being so irrational?" he snapped.

I whirled on him. "Why didn't you tell me you were bringing me to *your* house?" I already knew that answer, but, once again, I was going to make him tell me because he was a close-mouthed bastard and I knew he hated it.

"You know why," he growled.

I crossed my arms over my chest. "Yes, I do, but you're going to say it out loud."

"Why?"

"Because I know you hate explaining yourself," I answered, nearly yelling.

Suddenly, the scowl on Finn's face disappeared and he smiled. "You are a piece of work," he muttered.

The tension and anger that had been holding me up leaked out of my body and my shoulders sagged with fatigue and sorrow. He was right, I was behaving irrationally and out of character. I might enjoy giving Finn a hard time, but he didn't deserve what I'd been dishing out. "Yes I am, but I shouldn't be left out of the loop, Finn, and you know that. I need to know the details."

"Why?"

I threw my hands up in the air. "I'm not going to just sit by while the Council and the pack fight this battle. The coven is in just as much danger as all of you and we need to know what's happening! I can help. The coven can help."

Finn studied me carefully. "Is this about the coven helping or something else?"

I sighed. He saw right through me. This wasn't just about the fact that he'd brought me to his personal home without telling me where we were going. "What happened to Saundra, Finn?"

His face went hard, all emotion wiped from his expression, but he didn't speak.

"I have to know." My voice was low. I didn't want to know, didn't want any more guilt on my conscience, but, as the next High

Priestess, I *had* to know. The coven would have questions and they would expect me to have the answers.

Finn ran a hand roughly through his hair. "Fine. Let's go downstairs. I have a feeling that we both will need a drink before this conversation is over."

✧ ✧ ✧

FIVE MINUTES LATER, we were in his study. I watched from my position on the sofa as he started a fire in the fireplace. Once logs were alight and crackling, he walked over to a set of decanters on a small bar in the corner. He poured an amber liquid into two snifters and brought them to the couch.

"It's cognac," he murmured as he handed the glass to me.

"Thanks." I sipped it tentatively because cognac had never been my favorite drink, but it was smooth and left a trail of warmth from my tongue to my stomach.

Finn sat down next to me, rolling his glass between his palms. "Are you sure you want to know the details?" he asked.

"Tell me, Finn."

He leaned back against the cushions and grabbed my legs where they were curled beneath me. As he straightened them and pulled them across his lap, he gently pushed my shoulder so that I reclined against the arm of the sofa. Once I was comfortably settled, he began.

"Yesterday afternoon, it appears as though members of the Faction entered your store. Rather than finding you there as they expected, they found Saundra instead. From what Conner's men could gather, they then went up to your apartment. When the warlock and his lackeys discovered you had packed a bag and were gone, they attempted to coerce your employee into giving them your location."

A chill permeated my body. They had likely missed me by less than an hour and instead hurt someone I should have protected.

"She was more than my employee," I whispered. "What did they do to her?"

He shook his head. "Kerry....no. I don't think...."

"TELL ME!"

"No," he stated, his face stony. "You don't need to know that. I will tell you that she fought hard and wounded at least two of them before they subdued her."

"Is that how they knew where my cottage was?" I asked quietly.

Finn nodded.

I took a large swallow of the cognac, gasping when the warmth turned into a fiery burn in my esophagus. "She wouldn't have told them easily. They....they would have had to hurt her badly before she would have given them that information," I rasped. I closed my eyes, imagining the horrors my friend would have endured in an effort to protect me.

"Stop, Kerry," Finn whispered, his hand cupping my face.

"She shouldn't have been there. I should have just closed the store, but I didn't think." I lifted my lids and stared at Finn, my eyes welling with tears. "You tried to tell me, but I didn't listen."

He pulled me into his lap. "No, don't blame yourself. I didn't explain how perilous your position truly is. I should have made you understand what was happening and I never should have let you out of my sight."

Finn might not hold me responsible for what happened to Saundra, but I knew in my heart of hearts, that the coven would not feel the same way. The High Priestess and her successor were held to the highest of standards and were expected to put the safety of the coven and its members above even their own. Just as the witches of our coven were expected to do in regards to their High Priestess. We were supposed to have each other's backs.

Finn plucked the snifter out of my limp hand, set it on the side table, and, for the second time that day, rocked me gently as I sobbed against his neck.

Chapter Thirteen

I T WAS NO surprise that I had nightmares again that night.

After my tears subsided, Finn made me eat some soup and take a hot bath before he tucked me into his bed. Though the room was warm, I lay shivering beneath the covers. Finally, Finn climbed into the bed behind me, his long body stretched out behind mine and his arms wrapped tightly around me. I despised feeling weak, but the last forty-eight hours had been overwhelming and I didn't have the energy to put on a brave face.

It was a long time before I fell asleep. That was when the dream began.

My eyes were covered, but I knew I was in my apartment because I smelled the vanilla and lavender candles I burned habitually. I could hear the low rumble of men's voices but couldn't make out what they were saying.

I was frightened. I tried to lift my hands to remove the blindfold, but they were tied down. I realized that I was flat on my back, my wrists and ankles securely fastened to my bed frame. My terror sharpened, slicing through my mind, removing my ability to think rationally.

Whimpering, I tried to twist my arms and legs in an effort to loosen my bonds. A spell. I should cast a spell. But when I attempted to speak the words, a gag prevented me. Tears of pure fear welled in my eyes, soaking into the fabric of the blindfold. Goddess help me.

"Ah, she is awake."

I froze at the sound of that lightly accented voice. The blindfold was suddenly jerked off my eyes and I squinted at the bright light. Blinking, I stared up into the beautiful face of a vampire. His hair and eyes were both black and his olive skin was tanned from hours in the sun. Coupled with his accent, his appearance suggested he was from South America.

"Hello, darling," he crooned.

His endearment contrasted vividly with the cold, soulless light in his eyes. I wasn't his darling. I sincerely doubted he cared about anyone, even himself.

"Now that you're awake, there are some things we should discuss." He sat down on the edge of the bed, his hip resting against the curve of my waist.

I looked down my body and realized that I wasn't myself. I was naked, but my body was not my own. Oh, Goddess, I was Saundra.

The vampire slapped my face lightly, but it was enough to make my ears ring. "Now, now, it's rude to ignore your guests." My eyes flew back to his. "Good, now that I have your attention, I have some questions for you and I expect you to answer them honestly. If you don't, I'll know and I'll have to punish you." His hands went to the gag. "If I remove this, you won't scream, will you? Because I would hate to have to punish you for that too."

I shook my head. As he pulled the cotton from my mouth, I licked my lips. I wanted to ask him who he was and what he wanted, but instinct told me that would be a horrible idea.

"Now, I know you are not Kerry Gayle. You do not possess enough power. But, I assume you do know where she is. Is that true?"

I shook my head, but did not speak.

Quick as lightning, his hand shot out and he pressed his palm to my stomach. He murmured words in a language I didn't understand and excruciating pain, the likes of which I'd never felt before, suffused my body. My back arched so hard that only my heels and my head were touching the bed. When I opened my mouth to scream, he clapped his other hand over it.

When the sensations faded, I collapsed back onto the mattress, panting.

"I told you that you would be punished for lying to me," he stated. There was no expression on his face. No disgust. No enjoyment. This entire process held no meaning for him. He didn't dislike it, nor did he relish in my pain. This was just business.

He must have noticed my epiphany in my face because he said, "I don't necessarily want to hurt you, Saundra Abrams, but it doesn't bother me to do it either. Your suffering has no effect on anyone but yourself."

Another vampire entered the room, one side of his face covered in scorch marks. He stared at me with rage and hatred in his brown eyes.

"Now, Anthony, he wants you to hurt. In fact, he's hoping you'll hold out against my questions because he has plans for retribution for what you've done to his face."

At the vampire's words, Anthony trailed his fingers down the burnt flesh of his cheek. Now that the last bit of fogginess was leaving my mind, I remembered the fight downstairs and how I had hurled the strongest spells I knew at these vampires, but they had little effect. Any hopes I had toward fighting my way out of the situation died. The vampire beside me was a warlock and he was one of the most powerful I'd ever encountered. He was also on the knife's edge of madness. That's why he was so cold. All that evil was destroying him from within.

I swallowed hard, steeling myself for what was to come. Though I was terrified and in pain, I had to resist as long as possible. It was my duty to protect other members of my coven. Though Belinda hadn't announced it to the rest of us yet, I knew she intended to make Kerry her successor for High Priestess. That made her even more valuable to us.

"Now, I'm going to ask you again. Where is Kerry?"

For the first time since I awoke, I spoke. "I won't tell you."

Once again, I was overwhelmed with unimaginable pain. This time I screamed.

When it ended, the unnamed vampire leaned over me, his black eyes gleaming. "This is the last time I will ask. If you don't answer, I will let Anthony have you for a while and then we'll see how accommodating you are. Where. Is. Kerry?"

"No." Though I knew it meant even more pain, I wouldn't give them the satisfaction. It was clear that I wasn't going to survive the night. Even if Kerry's life wasn't in danger, if I broke, they would kill me. The longer I could hold out, the greater the chance I would be rescued.

Black Eyes sighed. "Very well." He looked over his shoulder. "Anthony, she's yours for the next thirty minutes. Just be sure she can still speak when you're done with her."

I stared at Anthony in horror as he approached the bed, his hands dropping to his belt buckle.

"You're mine now, witch." His eyes moved over my nude body, an unholy light gleaming in them. "Now, should I cut you first or fuck you?"

Despite knowing it was futile, I opened my mouth to cast a spell, only to have Black Eyes shove the gag back into it.

"Bad girl, Saundra. Casting spells at Anthony would only anger him further. That's not a smart idea in your position."

Bound and gagged, I lay helpless on the bed as Anthony finished undoing his pants, his intention clear. Though I knew it was fruitless, I screamed against the gag over and over again, hoping someone, anyone would hear.

"KERRY!"

My eyes popped open and I jerked upright in bed. The room was pitch black. Hands closed over my arms, holding me still.

"No!" I cried, fighting his hold. I couldn't let it happen. I had to escape. I lashed out with my power.

"Dammit!"

The hands holding me down left my body and I sprang out of the bed. Suddenly, a lamp clicked on, revealing my surroundings. I stilled, looking around in confusion. This wasn't my apartment. I looked down at the bed and saw Finn sitting on the edge of the mattress, watching me as he rubbed his abdomen.

"Finn?"

He stood, walking slowly over to me, his hands in front of him, palm up. "It was just a dream, Kerry. You were having a bad dream."

Gasping for air, I shook my head vigorously. "No, it wasn't. It wasn't a dream. It was a vision. I saw her. I saw Saundra and I know what happened to her."

Finn moved into me, wrapping his arms around me as my legs collapsed.

"I saw it all," I whimpered. "Everything they did to her." Tears streamed down my face at the pain and terror I knew she suffered. "I'm glad I killed them. I know I shouldn't be, but I am. I only wish I had killed that fucking warlock too! The bastard deserves to die for what he did to her!"

Finn released my body and cupped my face. "He will. The Council and the pack will find him and they will kill him."

I shook my head. "No, you won't. He's too powerful. You'll need a witch to help you." I covered his hands with mine and stared into his eyes. "You'll need me."

Finn grimaced. "Kerry...."

I pulled away from his hands and paced around the room. "Stop it, Finn! You know I'm telling you the truth. Belinda might be able to pull it off. *Might.* And that's only if you can talk Lachlan into letting her out of his sight." I caught the surprised look on his face. "What? You know that it will take an act of the Goddess to separate them if he's attached to her, if he's marked her. And there's no guarantee she's strong enough. I know I am. I've tasted his power and he's tasted mine. The warlock won't be able to win against me and he knows it. He's as strong as me, but his complete lack of connection or emotion weakens him."

"Slow down, Kerry."

I whirled and marched over to Finn. "That fucker deserves to die slowly and painfully. He deserves to suffer a hundredfold more than Saundra. If I can't have that, then I'll settle for him dead. Period. I don't have to be the one to do it, but you will need me if it's to be done at all."

Finn's jaw locked down as though he were gritting his teeth. I knew he didn't want to agree with me, but he had no other choice. Everything I was saying was true.

"No."

"Yes," I hissed. "If you won't help me, then I will leave. I'll go to Lex. I know he'll have no compunction about using me as he deems fit."

Though I'd seen Finn angry before, I'd never seen him snap, which is exactly what he did.

His hands clasped my biceps and he lifted me onto my toes so that our faces were just a few inches apart. "NO!" he roared. "You are mine, Kerry, my mate, and I will not let you put yourself in harm's way!"

I shoved at his chest, hard, but he didn't move. "Fuck you, Finn! I never agreed to any of this. You can't just come into my life and take over and expect me to go along with it. You're a leader among your people, you know you have a responsibility to them. Guess what? I have a responsibility to my people, too! I'm supposed to lead them when Belinda steps down and there is no way they'll respect me if I don't do something about this entire situation."

He released me so abruptly that I stumbled back. "You are the most fucking stubborn woman I have ever met. I don't care if you do have a death wish, I will not allow you to sacrifice yourself." Finn moved around me, heading for the door. He stopped in the doorway. "I'll be back later. Do not leave this house. If you do, I swear, I will bring you back and lock you in this room. You may be more powerful than me, but I promise you, I can find a way to keep you contained."

With those parting words, he exited the bedroom, slamming the door behind him.

Enraged beyond words and filled with grief and frustration, I screamed, wishing I could destroy everything around me. I jumped when a book flew off one of the nightstands and slammed into the heavy wooden door. I was so worked up that I was losing control of my powers.

Closing my eyes, I sat on the floor, crossing my legs, and focused on my breathing. I had to calm down before I did something drastic, like reduce this house to a pile of rubble and ash.

As I forced myself to breathe slowly and deeply, I began to plan. Finn might not want my help, but the Council would need it. The black-eyed warlock was too strong, even for Finn's magic.

Though I would never tell Belinda, he was stronger than my High Priestess as well.

Despite what Finn thought, I didn't have a death wish. What he didn't seem to understand was that I would likely die at the hands of the Faction in the future if I didn't stand and fight now.

They would never admit it, but the vampires, werewolves, and the coven would lose against the Faction's warlock. Somehow, I had to persuade enough of them that I was necessary to their success. If I could convince Conner, Lex, and Gabriel of the truth, then Finn would have no choice but to accept my involvement. Especially if Belinda and the MacIntire pack stood behind me.

It was the only path to victory. And retribution.

Chapter Fourteen

SOMEHOW, I MANAGED to doze off and on until dawn, despite my stress and the fact that I had lit both the lamps in the room. Sometime very early in the morning, I realized I would have to put aside my grief over Saundra's death in order to do what must be done. There would be time for sadness after we were safe. I managed another hour or two of sleep before my eyes opened as the weak light of day leaked around the edges of the curtains.

I rolled over, pushing myself into a sitting position on the edge of the bed. My body ached, likely from fatigue and stress. I dragged myself into the bathroom and took a hot shower. Once I was done scalding myself, I dried my hair, moisturized, and brushed my teeth. I didn't bother with make-up. My curly hair was wild so I pulled it into a haphazard knot on the back of my head.

Since I doubted Finn would allow me to leave the house, I didn't bother to dress in street clothes, just a pair of soft fleece pajama bottoms, t-shirt, and warm socks. I took a deep breath and left the bedroom, feeling determined, yet slightly hesitant. Finn had been so angry with me last night. Furious, in fact. I didn't relish being on the receiving end of his ire. So much so, that I was tempted to tell him I would back off and let the vampires and werewolves do their thing. Now that I was thinking more clearly, I regretted my emotional outbursts. I had taken out my anger and pain on Finn and it shamed me.

Still, I hadn't been wrong when I told him that they would need me. I *knew* in my bones that we would lose if I didn't get involved. There was a reason why the prophecy said five and ten. My participation was necessary to our survival.

I padded down the stairs and into the kitchen, greeted by the smell of frying sausage and coffee. Once again, Finn was making breakfast, but, this time, he was wearing clothes. My eyes moved over him, taking in the navy Henley, the faded jeans that hugged his ass in all the right places, and the thick socks on his feet.

He glanced over his shoulder at me, his face impassive. "Good morning."

Though I still felt ambivalent, I'd be damned if I let him see it. Finn had centuries to learn how to spot vulnerabilities and exploit them. "Good morning," I murmured.

"Coffee mugs are in the cabinet right above the pot. Help yourself." His tone was cool and distant. Apparently, he was still very unhappy with me.

"Thanks."

I walked across the kitchen, pulled a mug out of the cabinet, and poured myself a cup of coffee. When I opened the fridge to get milk, I was surprised to find a container of pumpkin pie spice coffee creamer on the top shelf. I loved the stuff and always looked forward to fall because it would be available again. I also noticed that he'd stocked some of my other favorite foods.

Seeing evidence of his consideration weakened my resolve to remain cold toward him. I finished adding sugar and creamer to my coffee, putting everything neatly away afterwards.

After I took the first sip, I cleared my throat. "Finn, I just wanted-"

For the first time since I entered the kitchen, he turned and looked at me. My voice stopped working at the expression on his face. He wasn't angry. If I didn't think it was crazy, I would have thought he was ravaged by fear.

"Shut up, Kerry."

My teeth clicked together and the cracks in my resolve began to heal and harden. I swallowed hard, fighting my initial angry response. Screaming out the words *fuck you* wouldn't help our situation, and I'd likely regret it later. My temper was usually slow to boil over, but my nerves were raw.

He reached over and, in short, angry motions, turned off the stove before removing the pan from the burner. Then he placed the sausage on a plate and reached inside the oven and pulled out a huge plate of pancakes.

"Sit," he barked, jerking his chin toward the kitchen table.

Even though my feet wanted to carry me straight out the kitchen door, then the front door, I went to the table and sat down, placing my coffee mug next to the plate already there. I realized that he'd even taken the time to set the table. Why did he have to be such a contradiction?

Finn put the plates down with a clatter before he went to refill his coffee mug and grab the warm maple syrup out of a small pan of water. I crossed my arms over my chest and watched him as he prowled through the kitchen. The indigo color of his shirt made his eyes seem more blue than purple and the predatory motions of his body seemed completely out of place in the homey room.

Finally, he sat in the chair across from me, plunking the syrup down next to the pancakes. Then he used his fork to put two pancakes and two sausage links on my plate.

"Eat."

I leaned back in my chair, my arms still tightly wrapped around the front of my body. Our eyes met and I stared right back at him, even though it was likely a bad idea. Vampires were, in essence, extremely efficient predators. There were certain things you didn't do to a carnivorous animal and the first was stare them in the eye, especially if they were agitated. Secondly, you didn't run, which was the last thing on my mind.

At first he tensed, his body coiling as though he were preparing to pounce. Then he blinked, somehow controlling the instincts that wanted to take over.

Groaning, Finn scrubbed his hands over his face. I could hear the scratch of his stubble against his palms. "Okay, okay. What were you going to say?" he asked.

"It doesn't matter now," I answered tightly. And it didn't. No way in hell was I apologizing now. Maybe it was small and petty, but his attitude had killed any genuine regret I'd had about our fight last night. Did I hate that we argued? Absolutely. Did I want to continue that argument this morning when I got up? Yes and no. This wasn't something I merely wanted to do, just to be contrary. This was something I *had* to do.

"Kerry." He growled my name rather than speaking it.

"I was going to apologize for our argument last night," I snapped, "but I'm honestly not sorry anymore."

The black expression on his face began to clear and he stopped scowling at me. In fact, the corners of his mouth tilted up slightly as though he were fighting a smile. "Would it help if I told you I'm sorry we fought?" he asked.

I nodded. "Maybe a little." I sipped my coffee. It was time to bite the bullet. I didn't want to continue our argument, but we did need to finish the conversation. I wanted to at least try to bring him around before I went behind his back to the Council and the pack. I didn't enjoy the thought that I would have to do something so sneaky and under-handed. "Look, I don't want to fight with you and I understand why you are resisting this, Finn, but I think you know that I can't get away from this situation, even if I want to. I'm already involved and I'm supposed to be involved. I think the prophecy proves that."

He grunted. "I know."

Since I had already been formulating a response to any and all possible arguments he might have, it took me a moment to realize what he just said. "What?"

He arched an eyebrow at me. "I know that you can't be left out." His shoulders slouched and he rested his elbows on the table. "I realized it when I was re-reading the prophecy for the tenth time at 3 a.m. this morning. That doesn't mean I have to like it. Or even pretend to like it."

Relief rushed through me. He understood and though he wanted to stop me, he wouldn't. Finn reached across the table, placing his hand over mine.

"However, I don't want you to get too cocky. If you let your guard down, even for a moment, you know that they will kill you, right?" he asked.

I nodded. "I know." I did. Despite knowing that I was the more powerful of the two of us, that didn't mean he wouldn't be able to best me with sheer cunning and madness.

"Are we done with this conversation?" he asked. "It's ruining my appetite and probably yours and we both need fuel."

Again, I nodded and focused on buttering my pancakes and pouring syrup. We ate in companionable silence, the only sounds were the light scraping of our forks on the plates and the wind outside the windows.

When we finished, we washed the dishes together as we had done the day before. It seemed like a week had passed rather than twenty-four hours. So many things had happened and someone I cared for had been lost.

After the last dish was dry, I refilled my coffee mug and Finn's. "I hate to bring this up, but I will need to speak to Belinda today. I'd like to talk to Sally as well."

Watching me over the rim of his mug, Finn sipped his coffee. "I know I can arrange a conversation with Belinda, but Sally may not be available. She probably has arrangements to make."

He was right. I sighed. "I'd still at least like to call her and offer my condolences."

Finn's long fingers closed over my forearm. He slid his hand down my arm and laced our fingers together. I took the comfort he was offering. While I still resented his tendency to be high-handed, I appreciated his strength and his intuitive understanding of how my mind worked. Finn lifted my hand and kissed my knuckles.

I cleared my throat and took another sip of my coffee. "Well, I guess I'd better get started on research. I don't know anything about the prophecy of the Five. I always assumed it was just a myth told to the children of the coven and thought it was boring, so I didn't pay much attention. Now, I have to figure out what it means and what we should do."

Finn squeezed my hand. "You will. *We* will, together."

I rose up on my tiptoes and brushed my lips against his. "Thank you and I am sorry for the things I said to you last night," I whispered into his mouth. When I rocked back, he blinked down at me, a surprised look on his face.

"That's the first time you've kissed me without me having to talk you into it," he murmured.

A strange feeling, almost a flutter, rippled over my skin and through my body. He was right. He usually instigated any sort of intimacy between us, even the casual touching of hands or a hug. I hated that I behaved in such a way to make him feel unwanted, but also marveled at the power I held over such a strong vampire, to surprise him with a simple kiss.

I lifted up on my toes again and kissed each of his cheeks gently. Then I rested my mouth against the base of his neck, right where his collarbones met. Finally, I mirrored his earlier action and lifted his hand to my mouth, placing another kiss on his knuckles.

A fine tension left his muscles, so minute I almost didn't see the release, but I definitely felt it. Despite his confident demeanor, Finn still hadn't been sure of me.

Looking into his beautiful amethyst eyes, I could no longer deny that the connection we shared was rare and precious. I'd never been the type of woman to scream or throw things when arguing with my lovers. When we were together, the emotions Finn evoked were sharper and clearer than any I'd ever experienced before. Everything I felt when I was with him, I felt it deeply, down to my very soul. If he wasn't someone special, he wouldn't induce such a strong response.

Somewhere in my chest, I felt something click into place, as though a missing part of my heart had finally been returned. For the first time since Finn began his pursuit, I considered letting myself be caught, despite the numerous reasons I shouldn't.

Chapter Fifteen

FTER OUR CONVERSATION over breakfast, I was surprised when Finn showed me into a sunroom attached to the back of his home. I gaped as I took in all the herbs and plants any skilled witch would need in their garden. It was eerily similar to my own.

There was a table set up in the middle of the solarium and books were stacked on one side. I walked closer and realized that all the books on the table were mine. There was even a notebook and several pens and pencils. There was a potting bench against the back wall with a large hutch above it. It contained not only gardening tools, but glass jars for potions and dried herbs, empty amulets, a crock full of wooden utensils, and bundles of herbs tied together with twine that were hung to dry. Beneath the bench sat planting pots, copper cooking pots, and several different sizes of mortars and pestles. Next to the potting bench was a small gas stove. Though it was antique, the appliance was in pristine condition and sparkled.

"What's this?" I asked.

"It's my sunroom. While I usually do my reading and research in the library, I make potions, amulets, and cast spells out here. After I saw your study and solarium yesterday, I thought this would make you feel more at home."

His consideration surprised me, though it shouldn't have. He cooked for me the last two days and taken care of me yesterday when I could barely function. Despite his tendency to take control and try to boss me around, he made my comfort and care his priority. I would be lying if I said I didn't find that incredibly attractive.

"Thank you. This is perfect," I replied.

He continued to surprise me. "I have some things to take care of, including getting you a burner phone. Donna threatened to come get you if she couldn't at least call you on a daily basis."

That sounded like Donna. I smirked at him. "Are you scared of her? She's just a little thing."

He grinned. "Of course. I can't make her behave."

I laughed because the idea of Donna behaving was amusing.

"I have some things to do in my office this morning. Are you going to be okay out here alone?"

I rolled my eyes. "Yes. I'm a big girl, I can handle a few hours of solitude."

Finn cupped my face and kissed my forehead. "Okay. I'll come get you when lunch is ready."

"Wow, you made me breakfast *and* you're going to feed me lunch. I could get used to this."

He stepped back. "I'm counting on it."

The smile on my face faded as he left the room. With everything that had happened in the last few days, I hadn't had time to dwell on the repercussions of my deepening connection to Finn. When it was all over, I would have a relationship with him, no matter what the coven rules were. The longer we were together, the clearer it became that he was special to me and my feelings for him were deeper than I'd been willing to admit just a few days ago.

Now was not the time to worry about it. The coven and the entire supernatural community was under attack. I'd deal with the consequences if I survived.

✧　✧　✧

THREE AND A half hours later, I was ready to tear my hair out. When I sat down at the make shift desk Finn set up for me, I wasn't sure where to begin, so I started by rereading the prophecy.

One will live
Two will die
Three will return the Fourth to life
Together the Five will right the past,
Create the future and hold it fast
All hold keys to power untold
And will find their Fate as evil grows bold
Five may live
Five may die
Five may love
Five may fall
Should this come to pass
Then ten will save Creation
Or lose that which they have found at last

Once I exhausted all the possible meanings and clues I could think of, I began to research the legend surrounding the prophecy of the Five.

Despite the fact that it was only considered a myth by a majority of the witch population, there were still many over the years that researched and speculated about what it meant, what it foretold.

The general belief was that the prophecy was somehow related to the end of the supernatural races.

I read through page after page of research and citations, cross referencing text after text until my brain held so much information I thought it would overheat. I took notes and grouped books according to theory, dates, and other minutiae. I hadn't done so much reading since college, and even then only when cramming the week before finals.

Finally, at twelve-thirty, I threw down my pen. The pages were nothing but a blur of black and white and I had a crick in my neck from sitting with my head down for hours.

"Fuck." I stood up, rubbing the tense muscles of my neck and shoulders.

"Problem?"

I flinched, whirling around to see Finn leaning against the door jamb, his arms crossed over his chest. He looked like a GQ model, only a lot sexier and a little scarier.

I rolled my shoulders, trying to loosen up the cramp in my neck. "Yeah, I don't know what in the hell I'm looking for. I don't even know where to start. For most of my life, I believed this was only supposed to be a myth. Now, it's a matter of life and death."

He straightened, walking over to me, his hands taking over the restless massage I'd been giving myself. I let my head fall forward against his chest as his fingers both relaxed my muscles and made me wince.

"What do you need from me?"

"I don't know what I need," I sighed. "I wish my mother was here. She always gave the best advice and she was the calmest in a crisis."

Finn's warm hand cupped the back of my neck, squeezing rhythmically. "Would it help if you spoke to Belinda?"

"Maybe. She's always been more scholarly. My mother encouraged me to do more reading and research, but I never listened. Until it was too late."

He tilted my face back. "I have a feeling that having a vast amount of raw talent had a lot to do with that attitude."

Since he was right, I shrugged. Spell casting and the making of amulets, potions, and charms had always come easily for me. "Maybe. But raw talent won't save the coven, or the vampires or the werewolves. We need a successful plan and we also need the knowledge in order to develop it."

He stepped back. "Well, then I guess it's a good thing that I invited Belinda over for lunch. Lachlan and Calder are both here." He paused. "And so is Ricki, though she doesn't appear to be particularly happy about it."

Despite my concerns, I had to grin. It seemed Calder was putting an end to Ricki's tendency to run away, whether she liked it or not. Though she would probably kick me for thinking this, I was glad she'd finally found a man that wouldn't leave her. Now, he had the difficult job of convincing her that he was hers forever.

"Okay. So, what are we eating?" I asked.

Finn threw an arm around my neck and pulled me out of the solarium. "Beef stew and cornbread."

"Wow. What else do you cook?" I asked. "Anything gourmet? Because I'd like to place an order for dinner."

He squeezed me tighter for a moment. "Unfortunately, I'm at the end of my repertoire. You'll have to cook dinner."

"Bummer. I hope you like all your food extra crispy."

He chuckled.

We entered the kitchen where I was immediately accosted by Ricki. She moved quickly, grabbing my arm.

"Kerry! Thank God. Can I talk to you for a minute?"

In my peripheral vision, I saw Finn bite back a smile. Obviously, something was going on that I wasn't aware of. "Sure."

She pulled me away from Finn and out in the hallway. When Calder moved to follow us, she stopped and snapped, "No! Bad dog. Stay!"

I had to cover my laugh with a cough at the expression on Calder's face. It was an interesting mix of pained and annoyed. He growled under his breath at her and she flipped him off.

Dragging me behind her, Ricki stomped down the hallway to Finn's empty study. She yanked me inside and shut the door behind us before releasing her grip on my arm. Ricki paced around the room, looking at the shelves of books, the paintings on the walls, and even at the knick knacks on the mantle, yet she never once looked at me.

"What's wrong, Ricki?" I asked.

She whirled around, throwing her arms up in the air. "Everything!" She stopped and took several deep breaths. I could tell she was trying to calm down. "Do you know what *he* did?" she asked. She didn't wait for my answer. "*He kidnapped me*!!" Her voice was loud enough that I knew every supe in the house heard her.

I crossed the room and grabbed both her biceps, stilling her restless movements. "Ricki, calm down. Now, why are you saying Calder kidnapped you?"

"Because he fucking DID!"

Okay, so Ricki wasn't ready to calm down just yet. I wanted to find a flyswatter and smack the crap out of Calder's behind. If he had just been clear in the beginning, this entire mess between them could have been avoided.

"It will be all right, Ricki. Just calm down and tell me what happened."

"Okay, so when Shannon and I left your house yesterday, he rode with us, remember?"

I nodded.

"Well, when we got to my house, there were vampires and werewolves waiting for both of us. The vamps were Conner's men, I think. Anyway, they went with Shannon to her house to help her get her stuff together and then Calder and his pack mates stayed with me. After I packed a couple of bags, I thought they would take me to Conner's house. That's what Donna said should happen. Instead, he brought me out to the compound where Lachlan and Belinda are staying and he wouldn't let me leave! I tried to call Donna but he stole my phone and unhooked the fucking landline in his cabin. And *she's* been there. Fuck, she came with us here today!"

"Who?" I asked, confused.

"The woman I saw him with at the party after we…after he…" She stopped speaking and cleared her throat. "She was in her underwear. I know you said he probably wouldn't have sex with someone else after he marked me, but all I could think about was Craig and my dad and how they swore time after time that they weren't screwing around…."

Goddess, Calder was fucking this entire situation up. If it didn't stop, it would be beyond his ability to repair and their relationship had to work. It was instrumental to fulfilling the prophecy. Clearly he'd forgotten the golden rule: if your mate is human, you better explain anything and everything explicitly so there would be no misunderstandings. What humans viewed as a deal breaker was considered normal behavior for wolves. Like keeping an endangered mate close, whether they liked it or not. Or expecting a female to understand your very serious intentions just because you bit her and marked her permanently.

I hated to do it, but I was going to help Ricki get away from the compound and into the safe house with Donna and Conner or Lex and Ivie. Otherwise, she'd never be willing to give Calder another chance. If I thought for one minute the wolf honestly intended to hurt her, then prophecy be damned, I wouldn't help him get her back.

"We'll fix it right now, Ricki. Just take a couple of deep breaths. We'll get this mess straightened out and have some lunch, okay?"

She nodded and did as I asked. I could see that there was more to her vehement insistence than just anger. She was hurt. I really, really wanted to smack that fucking werewolf. He should have reassured her about all this by now.

We walked back into the kitchen together. Belinda and Finn looked amused but they were trying desperately to hide it. I noticed that Chloe was leaning against the wall and realized that Ricki had been referring to her. Now, I wanted to laugh because, even if Calder was interested, Chloe was more likely to kick his ass than kiss him. She was tough, strong, and just as dominant as Lach. Calder wouldn't be alpha enough to mate her and they all knew it.

When she saw my gaze on her, she rolled her eyes and winked, letting me know she understood exactly what was happening. I didn't know her that well, but I was pretty sure she was enjoying watching Calder squirm.

Lachlan looked annoyed and resigned and Calder appeared pissed.

"Finn, could you please call Conner and find out if Ricki should come to his house or Lex's? She's very uncomfortable with her current situation."

"No fucking way," Calder snarled. "She stays with me."

Ricki moved closer to me, though she stood up for herself. "No, I'm not." I could tell that she was struggling to maintain her composure.

"Yes." Calder's voice dropped an octave, so deep it sounded as though it were being dragged from the depths of his soul. His green eyes flashed, their shape shifting slightly.

Oh shit. Was he losing his grip on his control?

A long growl filled the room, loud and so low that it almost hurt to hear it. In a flash, Lachlan was in Calder's face, snarling. To my surprise, Calder didn't immediately cower at his alpha's show of dominance, as most betas would do. He stood his ground.

"She's mine, Lach," he growled.

The MacIntire alpha made a sound I'd never heard before and it made every hair on my body stand straight up. Then there was a blur of motion and Calder was lying flat on his back, his face bleeding, and Lachlan towered over him.

"I told you that you had twenty-four hours to straighten out any misunderstandings and that I wouldn't allow you to keep a woman at the compound against her will. It makes her a liability," Lach stated, the echo of his wolf in the rasping growl that escaped his throat as he spoke.

Calder tried to rise but Lach put his foot on his chest, slamming him back against the ground. Ricki flinched behind me. Though she was angry with him, I could tell that it upset her to see Calder hurt. Maybe the situation would be salvageable after all. With a little help.

Though I suspected I'd regret it, I spoke up. "Lachlan, may I speak to Calder privately for a moment?"

Ricki's body went rigid at my words. "What are you doing?" she whispered.

I glanced over my shoulder at her. "I'm going to explain some things to your werewolf."

She scowled at me. "He's not my..." At my arch look, she trailed off and continued to give me a death glare, crossing her arms across her chest.

I faced Lachlan to find him studying me with a surprised expression. I kept my back straight and met his gaze head on. If the coven was going to have a relationship with the pack, he needed to see me as a leader, an equal. Right now, Belinda was the High Priestess but she wouldn't be forever. He needed to respect me as her successor, just as he expected his allies to respect Calder as his beta.

"Very well," he murmured, moving his foot off Calder's chest.

Calder rolled to his feet, his expression pained. I was certain his ribs were at the very least bruised.

"Follow me," I commanded before I left the kitchen and went back to Finn's study. I guessed it was my day to fix everything.

Once we were behind closed doors, I rounded on Calder. "What the fuck are you doing?" I asked.

He blinked at me, obviously shocked by my tone. Then he frowned. "Listen, witch, I don't need a lecture from you."

"You're right," I agreed. When his frown faded, I continued, "You need me to turn your ass into a toad."

He growled at me so I zapped him. Damn, why couldn't I do this before now? There were quite a few ex-boyfriends in my past I would have enjoyed shocking when they were acting like jackholes.

"Hey!" he yelped.

I moved closer, getting into his face. In the wolf pack, that was a definite act of aggression. I knew it would get his complete attention. As a beta, he wouldn't be able to back down from the challenge. "You listen to me, dumbass, and you listen well. Despite your behavior, I think you're a good match for my friend, so, if you want to keep your mate, you're going to listen to me right now and do...Every. Fucking. Thing. I. Say."

His eyebrows rose at my words. "I'm listening."

"Ricki is human, Calder. You can't treat her the way you do the bitches in the wolf pack."

"I know that," he snarled.

"Do you?" I asked. "Because, from what I've seen, you aren't treating her any differently."

"We're at war."

I rolled my eyes. "It doesn't matter! If you don't start talking to her and explaining what your mark means for you and for her, you will lose her. Do you want that?"

He shook his head.

"Good. Now, there are two things you must do if you want to convince her that you are her mate. First, you need to woo her. And I don't mean the way wolves woo by jumping her ass every chance you get. I mean, you need to do things for her, say nice things to her, treat her as though she's special to you."

"How in the hell do I do that?" he asked.

"Do you think she's pretty?"

"She's fucking gorgeous," he snapped.

"Tell her that." I bit my lip to keep from laughing at his expression. Wolves were not the most verbose supes by nature, but compliments and sweet talk were words that were really not in their vocabulary. "If you notice that she likes certain things, be sure to bring them to her. Like her favorite foods or if she likes to read mysteries or romances or watch movies." Though I knew her likes and dislikes, Calder needed to learn for himself. I knew he would pay attention if I told him it was important. Werewolf males were notorious for taking excellent care of their mates, catering to their needs without being asked. Unfortunately, they were controlling as hell and sometimes a little thick-headed, so werewolf females often fought courtship and mating every step of the way.

"Okay, I can do that."

"And be affectionate without sexualizing it." This time I did laugh at his blank expression. "Hold her hand, hug her, and kiss her without trying to get into her pants," I explained.

"What?" he snapped.

"Calder, human women enjoy non-sexual attention just as much, sometimes even more, than they do sex. It makes them feel as though you care about them as a person instead of seeing them as a walking vagina with a nice rack."

He nodded as though my explanation made sense. Then he smiled. "So, you're going to help me?" he asked.

"Yes." I leaned closer, poking the center of his chest. "But know this. If you fuck this up and hurt my friend in any way, I'll castrate you and make you eat your own testicles." Then I let a little surge of power flow down my arm and out my fingertip, giving him a nice little shock. "Understood?"

With a new light of respect in his eyes, Calder nodded. "I understand."

"Good, let's go eat. I'm starving."

Chapter Sixteen

LUNCH WAS AWKWARD. Ricki looked close to tears and Calder resembled a kicked puppy. He kept staring at her with a hang dog expression on his face. Everyone else looked as though they were trying not to laugh.

While I didn't think that Ricki's obvious upset was funny, it was entertaining to see Calder at a loss for how to charm his way through problems with the opposite sex. Most of the females of the wolf pack might not want to mate him, but they rarely turned away a romp between the sheets. Also, they would never go out of their way to avoid him as Ricki was doing.

Finally, after an hour of strained silence interrupted with small talk, Conner arrived to collect Ricki. He and Calder conversed briefly and I saw the werewolf smile and nod before Conner left with his wayward mate.

Coming up behind him, I asked, "So what did Conner say?"

Calder grinned. "He told me to bring by Ricki's bags tonight and that my usual room was available should I need it. He also mentioned that her room was next to mine."

It seemed that all of us were playing matchmaker when it came to Ricki and Calder.

"Well, I guess we'll know where to find you," I teased.

He shrugged. "It depends on what Lach says."

"For fuck's sake, go. You're pitiful. Worse than any lovesick pup I've ever seen," Lachlan yelled from the next room. "In your condition, you're worthless anyway."

Completely unfazed, Calder sauntered back into the kitchen where Finn, Lach, Chloe, and Belinda waited. "Well, I'll hang out here for a bit. Gotta give her time to miss me before I show up again."

Shaking my head, I followed him. A little levity was a relief after the stressful events of the last few days. It seemed the hits were coming hard and fast and it felt nice to take a break and remind ourselves exactly what we were fighting for.

Unfortunately, my semi-relaxed state was short-lived. Belinda stood when she saw me.

"Kerry, I think we need to discuss a few things."

I stifled a sigh. Just when I thought I would have a moment's peace. "Okay. Why don't we go out into the solarium? I have all my books and notes out there and I need to discuss the research with you."

She nodded and followed me through the house to the sun-room. Her eyes widened when she saw the large, bright area. "This is beautiful."

"Yes, it is. Finn brought my things out here because he thought it would remind me of my study at home."

The High Priestess smiled serenely. "You have a good match there."

I fiddled with some of the papers on my desk, my hands restless. "Do you think so?"

"Of course."

Our eyes met. "But I don't think the coven will," I murmured.

"I'm sure there will be some in our community who will think that consorting with vampires is a bad idea, but most of them are the elders. The younger generation, *your* generation, doesn't seem to take the antiquated attitudes towards vampires and werewolves as seriously as the older witches. I think you'll be able to bring them around, eventually." She paused and said something totally unexpected. "And if not, well, they're getting up there in years, so they'll die of old age soon anyway."

I snorted, my laugh taking me by surprise. Belinda rarely said anything even remotely sarcastic or snarky. "I guess you're right."

She walked back to the table and leaned a hip against it. "Don't worry about it, Kerry. Even if they don't approve now, they'll soften to the idea once it's revealed that the vampires can be trusted."

"Do you think they can be?" I asked.

Belinda arched her eyebrows. "You don't?"

I groaned. "I know several that I would trust with my life and the lives of my friends, but my experience has been limited to them or the ones that want to kill me or kidnap and use me. I don't know what I believe."

"The world is rarely black or white, Kerry. You know this already. Just as there are good humans and bad humans, there are good and evil witches, vampires, and shape shifters. You can't judge the entire species on the actions of a few. Just as you can't be judged by the actions of your parents."

She was absolutely right. If I was to be judged by the actions of my family, well, I would be the darkest of dark. My father saw to that before he died. Refusing to dwell on the bad memories, I shook my head. "You're right."

Belinda patted my hands. "Don't let past sorrow dictate your future happiness, my dear. And don't let those old bitches in the coven decide it for you either."

I snorted, once again taken aback by my High Priestess' words. "Yes, ma'am."

"Now, let's get to work on this prophecy and see if we can't figure out what it means and if there is anything we can do to keep the supernatural apocalypse at bay."

✧   ✧   ✧

"OH MY, WHAT time is it?"

Belinda's question interrupted my concentration. "I'm sorry, what?"

"What time is it?" she asked again.

I looked at my phone. "It's after seven."

Now that I was no longer wholly focused on the texts in front of me, I realized my back was screaming at me to stretch. Moving stiffly, I straightened my back and felt the vertebra in my spine pop as I lifted my arms over my head.

We hadn't made much headway in the stack of books and notes on the table, largely because many of the texts contradicted one another in some way. We were slowly making our way through the similarities and differences, trying to figure out what the prophecy meant. Divination of this sort was always told in some form of riddle or puzzle that must be solved. The purpose of prophecy was enlightenment.

Unfortunately, we didn't have time to achieve enlightenment. There was too much at risk.

"It's time to stop for the night, Kerry." Belinda's quiet voice broke through my rapidly swirling thoughts.

"I just feel like I'm missing something important," I responded.

"We'll figure it out. Now, I've already spoken to Finn. He will bring you to the coven meeting tomorrow at eleven. I need to announce you as my successor before we discuss the meeting that we attended with the Council and the pack."

"Can't you just stab me with something? Maybe in the eye? I think it would be less painful."

Belinda shook her head. "I'm sure it won't be that bad."

I gave her a look.

"Okay, so it won't be the best meeting in the history of our coven, but we'll get through it."

"You better bring a whip," I quipped. "You'll need it."

"Kerry."

"What? You know I'm right. The elders in the coven are going to have a shit fit when they realize that you've chosen me as the next High Priestess. Between my black warlock father and my progressive, free-thinking mother, I'm lucky I'm still even allowed in the coven. Then, you announce our alliance with the vampires and shape shifters? They're going to think you've lost your fucking mind."

"Enough with the swearing, Kerry." Belinda's voice whipped through the solarium, sharp and clear. "I know this won't be easy and I'm sure that there will be some things said tomorrow that will hurt, not only you, but me as well. We have to weather it. This isn't about me and it isn't about you or your lineage. This is about the future of the entire supernatural community and we need to make them realize it. Holding the position of High Priestess isn't the easiest job in the world. You have to put the welfare of the coven before your own. And you have to be impartial and open-minded. Honestly, I think you are the only witch strong enough to hold the position and wise enough to do a good job. When things get heated or uncomfortable tomorrow, show the other witches of the coven why I chose you. Handle it with dignity, grace, and a firm but gentle hand."

"I will, Belinda."

She nodded. "Good. Now, I'm sure Lachlan is climbing the walls by now. He hates being away from the compound with the situation being what it is."

I followed her out of the solarium and into the den where Lachlan, Calder, Finn, and Chloe were all watching a movie.

Lachlan was on his feet as soon as he saw Belinda. "Ready to go?"

She smiled. "Yes, please. I'm hungry, tired, and in desperate need of a hot bath."

He ushered her out of the den and into the foyer. The rest of us followed. As Lach helped Belinda with her coat, Chloe and Calder shrugged into their jackets as well.

Just as they were getting ready to leave, I called out to Belinda. "Are you sure you can't just stab me with something pointy and painful instead of making me go tomorrow?"

"Eleven, Kerry." Belinda looked at Finn over her shoulder before she started down the steps of the front porch. "Make sure she's there."

"I will."

As the werewolves and my High Priestess climbed into the car, I elbowed Finn lightly. "Traitor."

He didn't respond, merely wrapped an arm around my shoulders and guided me out of the cool night air back into the house.

Then he asked me a question guaranteed to put me in a better mood.

"How about a long, hot bath and a massage?"

Belinda was right. Vampire or not, he was a keeper.

Chapter Seventeen

AN HOUR LATER, I emerged from Finn's luxurious bathroom, damp and red all over. I'd taken a very hot bath, with scented oils, and drunk a glass of wine. Now, I was staring at the master bedroom, which was only lit by the flames in the fireplace and a few candles set about the room.

Several ornate glass bottles sat on the side table next to the bed and Finn was standing in front of the fireplace in nothing but a thin pair of pajama pants that clung to his ass quite nicely. The fit also led me to believe he wasn't wearing any underwear.

My blood suddenly felt like syrup moving through my veins, thick, sensuous, and slow.

He turned, smiling slightly when he saw me wearing nothing but a huge robe and my hair in a haphazard pile on top of my head. "You look a lot more relaxed." He gestured to the bed. "Let's see if we can make that even better."

I walked to the bed and hesitated, my hands clasping the belt of the robe. Finn didn't speak. Instead he came up behind me and untied my robe, sliding it off my shoulders and down my arms.

"Lie down," he commanded softly. "I just want to help you relax."

I sucked in a deep breath and climbed into the center of the bed, lying face down on the mattress with my hands stacked beneath my cheek.

I heard the soft clink of glass and knew he was pouring oil into his palm. The light floral scent of lavender candles surrounded me. I gasped lightly when his incredibly hot palms cupped my shoulder blades, slowly spreading oil on my skin. The oil smelled of jasmine and vanilla, warm and sensual.

At first, I felt myself melting beneath his touch, the tense muscles of my back and neck releasing under his ministrations. Then, as his hands traveled to my lower back and buttocks, the syrupy feeling returned to my blood. I was suddenly very aware of the rough glide of his callused fingertips on my skin, the cadence of our breathing, and the cinnamon and vanilla scent of Finn. With each stroke and press of his fingers, an ache began to grow between my thighs.

I almost moaned in disbelief as his hands stopped touching my lower back and buttocks. He couldn't stop now when it was beginning to feel so good. I jumped a little when his fingers closed around my ankles, more oil on his palms. Slowly and methodically, he began to massage my calves in long strokes, lightly at first, then more deeply. Then he moved to the backs of my thighs. With each pass of his hands, which cupped the backs of my legs, his thumbs drew perilously close to the place where I ached for his touch the most.

Shifting restlessly, I parted my legs a little more, inviting him to touch me. I groaned softly as one of his thumbs brushed my labia. The steady movement of his massage paused for a moment before he resumed. On the next pass of his hands up my thighs, both of this thumbs met briefly over my center, causing my hips to flex and my nipples to tighten.

Without speaking, Finn used his hands to spread my legs, pushing my knees up and out so that I was lying on the bed on my stomach with my knees bent even with my waist. He trailed a hand down my spine, pressing and stroking. As he reached the base, he reversed the direction of that hand while the other slid up my leg to cup the ache between my thighs.

Firmly, he rubbed his entire palm against me, spreading oil from my clit down to my entrance. Then he removed his hand and I felt a stream of cool air as he blew lightly over my pussy. Suddenly, everywhere he'd spread the oil began to tingle and heat under his breath. The gentle throb between my thighs became a hot need that I'd never experienced before.

"Ahhhh." I couldn't form words, only unintelligible sounds.

The steady stream of air stopped just before two of Finn's fingers circled my now swollen clit. My entire body jerked at the intensity created by that simple caress. He increased the pressure of his hand, stroking me with small, firm movements. Within a few minutes, I hovered on the edge of release, my lower body trembling with the need to come.

"Finn," I whispered, attempting to press myself more firmly into his hand.

His other hand moved over my back in a soothing motion, sliding down over my spine and my ass until he reached my aching center. I held my breath as he traced a finger around my entrance, the oil on my skin warming under his touch. With excruciating slowness, he slipped first one finger inside me, then another. I felt my muscles clench around him and my orgasm shimmered, ready to explode, yet just out of reach.

I moaned as he used his finger tips to press firmly on a spot inside of me that felt uncomfortable at first, then intensely pleasurable. Goddess, the g-spot wasn't a myth after all. Under his dual assault, I began to pant, on the verge of one of the best orgasms of my life.

"Finn, please," I begged.

As if he had been waiting for those very words, he increased the pressure on my clit and my g-spot and I detonated. There was no other way to describe it. I felt as though my skin was too fragile to hold the shockwaves of bliss that obliterated every thought or emotion I had. I was nothing but a mass of physical sensation, writhing in the throes of agony and ecstasy in equal measure.

Just as slowly as he built my climax, Finn brought me down from the peak. My body shuddered and quivered as he drew out the orgasm until the final contraction of my muscles passed and left me a boneless mass on the bed.

He leaned over me, kissing my shoulder and neck lightly. "Do you feel better?" he asked, his voice rough.

My eyelids fluttered open and I arched my back, stretching like a cat. "Much." My ass brushed his erection, still covered by his pajama pants. "But I think there's one part of you that needs some attention."

He smiled slightly. "That was for you, sweetheart. You needed to relax."

I hummed in the back of my throat. "Well, I'm not quite re-laxed enough to go to sleep," I teased. "I think I need at least one more orgasm before I'll be too tired to keep my eyes open."

When he shook his head, I sighed. "I want you inside me, Finn."

His deep purple eyes flashed at my invitation and I saw the tips of his fangs extend to peek out from beneath his upper lip. "Very well." When I began to roll over, he stopped me with his hands on my hips. "Don't move. Stay exactly as you are."

I complied, resting my cheek on my hands. I heard the rustle of fabric then felt the mattress shift as Finn moved between my thighs. His thighs touched mine and I felt the hard flesh of his erection rest against my ass. His skin was fiery in its heat.

I felt a drizzle of oil hit the skin of my lower back. I turned my head so that I could see what he was doing. I watched as Finn placed the bottle back on the nightstand and used his other hand to rub the oil into his cock. It was incredibly sexy.

When he saw my eyes on him, he shook his head. "Lie back down and relax. If you move too much, I'll stop."

I went back to my earlier position, with my cheek resting on the backs of my hands. I gasped when his fingers ran through the oil pooled at the base of my spine and slid them to my ass, grazing over the tight ring of muscle. He pressed lightly, coating the area with oil. When I lifted my hips toward his touch, he hummed in the back of his throat and moved his hand.

Before I could protest, the head of his erection nudged my pussy and he thrust inside me with one smooth slide. I sucked in a sharp breath at the sudden sensation of being filled. He moved languidly, as though he weren't desperate for release, as I knew he had to be. With each long stroke, I felt him hit my g-spot. He shifted and changed the angle of his hips until he found a place inside me that made me gasp. Then he was relentless, thrusting against that spot over and over again until every muscle in my lower body was coiled tightly, clenching in anticipation of another orgasm.

I protested when he slowed, causing my climax to recede slightly. Finn merely pressed against my knees with his hand, moving my legs so they were straight and he straddled my thighs. In this position, he felt huge and each thrust seemed to go deeper than the last.

His slick hands grasped the cheeks of my ass as he moved faster. The arousal that had waned when he slowed grew quickly, once again bringing me to the edge of a mind-blowing orgasm.

Finn brushed my hair away from the curve of my neck and leaned forward, placing his mouth against my ear and sank his teeth into my earlobe, eliciting a gasp from me.

He kneaded muscles in my buttocks, his thumbs meeting at the top of the crevice between them. His mouth remained on my ear as he whispered, "I love your ass, Kerry. Has anyone ever fucked it before, sweetheart?"

I whimpered as he placed his thumb over my asshole and put a light pressure against it. "No." The sensation he evoked with his touch making my toes curl with pleasure.

"Would you let me be the first?" he asked, his thumb caressing me teasingly, testing me.

"Yes," I choked, arching my back at his touch, craving it and fearing it in equal measures.

Finn's mouth latched onto my neck, sucking lightly, as he pressed his finger inside me. The oil coating his thumb created a tingling burn that I reveled in. He moved his cock and hand in tandem, pulling back and thrusting forward simultaneously, wrenching a cry from my throat.

I had to come. I *needed* to come. The ache inside me was almost unbearable and a fine tremor ran through my limbs.

"Please let me come." I heard the plea in my voice but didn't care. If I had to beg, so be it. I couldn't stand it any longer.

Finn sank his teeth into my neck and the climax that I craved crashed over me. My entire body seized, my vision fading and my ears filled with the thunder of my own pulse. I heard a high, keening cry and realize it was coming from my throat.

Finn groaned against my neck, pounding into me hard enough that I knew I would bruise, but I didn't feel pain. He shuddered against me, his thrusts growing uneven and gradually slowing as he sucked at the wound on my neck.

Finally, he stopped moving, his cock buried deep so that his hips pressed against my ass, where his thumb was still inside me. I shivered as his tongue traced the bite on my neck to help close the wound. Slowly, he removed his finger and I shuddered at the sensation. Finn draped his body over mine, his softening erection remaining within me.

I felt spent, utterly relaxed and slightly scandalized. No one had ever touched me the way Finn had or given me an orgasm so strong that I'd gone blind, deaf, and dumb. If his thumb felt that fantastic, how would his cock feel inside me? I shivered in anticipation at the thought.

Finn pressed a kiss to the side of my neck where he'd bitten me and withdrew from my body, using his pajama pants to clean me gently. I rolled my head to the side to watch him disappear into the closet, nude. He came out moments later, a clean pair of pants in his hand and walked into the bathroom.

I didn't move as I heard water running for a brief moment before it shut off. When Finn re-entered the bedroom, he was wearing the clean pajama bottoms. He paused at the end of the bed, studying me with a satisfied expression on his face.

"You look like you're about to fall asleep."

"More like lapse into an orgasm coma," I mumbled.

Finn chuckled in response. "Do you want pajamas?" he asked.

There it was again, Finn taking care of me. My heart melted a little. "Just a t-shirt and underwear."

He went back into the closet and returned with one of the huge t-shirts I liked to sleep in and a pair of my panties. He helped me into them then yanked the blankets down the bed.

After we settled down into the mattress, Finn pulled the covers back over us and rolled me into his arms.

I felt surrounded, consumed, and cherished. Throughout the day, Finn had done everything in his power to see to my needs. It was a lovely feeling, to be taken care of so thoroughly. I felt….loved.

As I began to drift into sleep, I whispered, "Thank you for taking care of me today."

His arms tightened around me. "It was my pleasure."

I smiled as I sank into slumber. There were no more nightmares or visions as there had been the last two nights. My sleep was deep and dreamless. Because of Finn.

Chapter Eighteen

THE NEXT MORNING, I woke up early and felt more refreshed than I had in days. Sometime during our sleep, Finn had turned over and was lying partially on his stomach. I had draped myself over his back, resting my cheek against his shoulder.

When I moved away, he sighed in his sleep, but didn't stir. It seemed that my vampire was exhausted.

I stilled. Somehow, I'd begun to think of Finn as belonging to me, despite my attempts to keep him at arms' length. I held my breath and crept from the bed into the closet. I pulled on a pair of flannel pajama pants covered in penguins.

I used the powder room in the downstairs hall instead of the master bath, hoping that Finn would get some much needed rest. As I washed my hands, I realized that sometime yesterday, between the breakfast he'd cooked for me and the massage with a happy ending, I had subconsciously embraced my relationship with Finn. The obstacles in my path no longer seemed as large or as important as being with him.

Confusion and contentment fought for supremacy in my head and in my heart. I found my cell phone charging on the kitchen counter and realized that Finn must have plugged it in for me last night. He managed to find yet another way to take care of me.

My throat tightened when it finally sank into my brain. I'd accused him of trying to take over my life and control me when, in reality, he only wanted to tend to me in a way that modern men rarely did any longer. It may have been old-fashioned, but it was something I would have appreciated from any other man I'd dated in the past. I felt like a heel. I'd characterized his actions in the worst possible light when he'd done nothing to deserve it. Well, maybe he was arrogant and pushy, but I never would have given him a chance to show me who he truly was if he hadn't pursued me so intensely.

My mind was in turmoil. So many thoughts and emotions swirled inside me that I couldn't focus. I took a slow, deep breath and decided to take it one day at a time. My entire life was in shambles and all of us were in peril. The only thing I could do now was try to return Finn's considerate behavior. In fact, I wanted to do for him what he'd done for me, not because I felt obligated but because I genuinely cared.

With that thought in mind, I set the coffee maker to brew a pot of coffee and got to work making a breakfast casserole. I fried crumbled sausage, peppers, and onions and layered them on the bottom of a baking dish. Then I beat several eggs with cream before stirring in some shredded cheese. After a dash of salt and pepper, I poured the eggs into the baking dish with the meat and veggies and put the whole thing in the oven to bake.

Finn still wasn't awake when I placed the casserole in the oven, so I decided to wait until it was ready before taking a cup of coffee upstairs for him. I had several hours before the coven meeting at 11 a.m., so there was no rush and he deserved the rest.

I poured myself a cup of coffee, adding creamer and sugar, and carried my phone into the solarium. When I checked, I saw that Donna had called me three times last night. Concerned, I tapped her name and put the phone to my ear.

"Why in the hell haven't you been answering my calls? I was worried sick until Conner called Finn and he explained that you were working with Belinda."

Okay, so she was angry. "I'm sorry, Donna. I meant to call yesterday, but it was...stressful."

She paused before blowing out a breath. "You're forgiven. But don't scare me like that again."

I had to smile at her grudging acceptance of my apology. She talked a tough game, but Donna really was a softie at heart.

Her voice softer and full of concern, she asked, "Are you doing okay?"

My throat tightened. "I'm fine. Nothing a day at the spa and killing a warlock won't cure." She was quiet for so long I thought we'd lost connection. "Donna? Are you there?"

"Why do you do that?"

I winced at the hurt in her voice, though I wasn't exactly sure what she was talking about. "Do what?"

"You distance yourself from others with humor or sarcasm. Why?"

"No, I don't."

She sighed again, and it sounded sad rather than frustrated. "You do, Kerry. I've known you for years and every time I bring up your father, you avoid the discussion with jokes and self-deprecation. There's so much about your history that I don't know. And you're even more aloof with others, like Lex or Belinda. I watched you and listened to you at the party a few nights ago. You do and say things to put others on the defensive, even those that want to be your friend. I don't understand it."

I wanted to deny it, but she had a valid point. For years, I did things to purposefully annoy Belinda and other coven members, using the excuse that it was all in good fun, and I considered my slightly hostile banter with Lex to be his doing since he tended to be moody. In reality, I instigated it all.

Some of my actions were meant keep my friends from knowing certain things about me. It hadn't occurred to me that they weren't like the coven elders and members. They wouldn't look at me as though I were tainted just because of who and what my father had become and they wouldn't care if I was the most powerful witch in the universe. To them, I was still Kerry.

"You seem dead set on remaining alone and it breaks my heart," Donna whispered. "I'm here for you. So are Ivie, Shannon, and Ricki." She paused. "Finn would do anything for you. Please don't push us away anymore. You don't have to be alone."

Finn had said something similar all those nights ago on my front porch before my world had descended into chaos. I took a shaky breath when I realized that he understood me with the same depth that my closest friends did. He knew me, every part of me, and he still came after me and cared for me.

Once again, something inside my chest shifted, settling into place as though a part of me had been waiting for this moment.

"Goddess, I think I'm falling in love with him," I breathed.

"What?"

Damn, I hadn't meant to say that out loud. Unfortunately, it was too late.

"You love Finn?" Donna asked. "How is that possible? Just a couple of weeks ago I overheard you threaten to turn him into a lobster and have surf and turf for dinner."

I chuckled at the memory. My threat had only worked for a couple of days before Finn had gone right back to his sneaky ways.

"There's a lot I haven't told you and I said I *think* I'm falling in love with him," I answered.

"Apparently," Donna quipped, obviously irritated at my closed-mouthed responses. "Wait! You did it again! Here I am trying to be sensitive and tell you that I'm here for you and you change the subject."

I couldn't help but smile. "I didn't mean to. Would it make you feel better if I told you something you said helped? So, thank you."

Donna stammered for a few seconds before answering, "Well, you're welcome. Don't you think for a single second that I'm letting you off the hook, Kerry. I want the whole story, every tiny detail of it, the next time we see each other. Understood?"

"Yes, ma'am."

"Ugh. Don't call me ma'am."

"As you wish, bitch," I retorted.

"Oh, bite me."

Smiling, I said, "I love you."

"I love you too."

I glanced at the clock and realized the casserole would be done soon. "Okay, I have to go. I made breakfast for Finn, so I need to go wake him up."

"Ooohhh, you have fallen hard. Usually you're out the door before the guy can get up to pee and now it's all, *I made breakfast for Fiiiinnn.*"

"Shut up."

She laughed. "I'll talk to you later."

"Bye."

I disconnected the call with a huge grin on my face. Somehow, my conversation with Donna made me feel as though a heavy weight had been lifted from my shoulders. I hadn't realized how much of a burden those thoughts and fears had become or how much I'd isolated myself from my friends.

I rose from the chair I'd perched on and turned to leave the room. I yelped when I saw Finn leaning against the doorway, his arms crossed over his bare chest and his hair rumpled from sleep.

But it wasn't how sexy he looked that caught my attention, it was the expression on his face as he looked at me.

He straightened as I got closer to him, looping his arms around my waist, pulling my lower body into his. I stared up into his amethyst eyes and my heart leapt. There was tenderness and something more in their depths.

Finn leaned forward and brushed his nose alongside mine in a sweet, affectionate gesture that made my knees weak.

"Good morning." His voice was still sleepy and rough.

"Morning."

"Thanks for making coffee and whatever is in the oven. It smells delicious."

I pulled out of his arms. "Shit. I forgot about breakfast."

I heard him chuckle as he followed me back into the kitchen and, for the first time since my mother died, I didn't feel lonely or afraid of what the future might hold.

Chapter Nineteen

◣◥◣◥◣◥◣◥◣◥◣◥◣◥◣◥◣◥◣◥◣◥◣◥◣◥◣◥◣◥◣◥◣◥◣◥◣◥

FINN AND I walked into the office building hand-in-hand. The coven meeting was to be held in one of Conner's office buildings. The coven elders hadn't wanted to go to his or Lex's home and had refused any vampire or pack presence in our usual meeting place, so a compromise had been reached.

With the exception of his security detail, most of Conner's employees were human and the coven elders were convinced that any nefarious deeds that the vampires or wolves had planned would be foiled by the presence of humans.

Honestly, I thought they were kidding themselves. A powerful vampire like Finn could easily control the few mortals on the floor and wipe their memories when the time came. If the vampires wanted to harm the coven, then a semi-public venue wouldn't stop them.

It seemed that the centuries in which witches had avoided vampires made us weak when it came to defending ourselves against attack. Because of the prejudices the coven instilled, many of our members had very little understanding of vampires and their abilities and even less knowledge of how to defend themselves. My mother had ensured that I knew about all the supernatural species, though many of the coven elders thought it was sacrilegious.

Finn squeezed my hand gently, taking me out of my thoughts. We rode the elevator up to the tenth floor, still holding hands. He didn't even release me when we entered the designated office for our meeting.

He seemed to know where he was going, so I let him lead me down several hallways until we reached a door that was labeled, Conference Room 2. Finn opened the door for me and let me enter first, never releasing my hand. My feet hesitated for a moment when all eyes turned to us. All of the coven elders were present and so were quite a few of the regular members, both men and women. Belinda was seated at the head of the large conference table, an empty chair next to her. Along the wall behind her, Lachlan, Donna, and Conner were sitting and conversing among themselves.

I tried to ignore the stunned stares from my fellow witches and the disgusted expression that each of the elders wore. I'm sure Belinda received none of this when she entered with two vampires and a werewolf because she wasn't the tainted one. Despite the fact that my mother had been greatly respected among the coven, I carried my father's blood, the blood of a warlock that practiced the most forbidden magic. Donna wanted to know about that part of my life, but she would be horrified if she did.

I kept my head held high as we walked to the front of the room, my face impassive, and refused to look away when someone met my eyes. Finn tightened his grip on my hand for a moment before he released it and moved to sit with the other vampires and werewolf.

Belinda's face held approval when she saw the gesture of affection between Finn and I and she smiled slightly at me. The High Priestess radiated confidence and strength. I wished I felt half as self-assured as she appeared.

"We will begin soon," she whispered as I took the seat next to her. "Are you ready?"

I glanced over at her. "Not really."

She patted my arm gently, her demeanor reminding me a great deal of my mother. "You'll do fine."

"Is it too late to change my mind about this whole successor thing?"

She barely managed to stifle a sigh and I bit back a grin. I loved giving her a hard time. Some of my amusement faded when I realized that, once again, I was pushing her buttons and thus creating distance between us.

"Thank you for believing in me, Belinda."

She seemed surprised at my words. "You're the best choice for the next High Priestess. I don't care what anyone says about your mother or your father. They won't be leading this coven, you will, and I think you will do a damn good job."

As it had been for years, Belinda was the only one in the coven who had any faith in me. I nodded and she stood and called the meeting to order. I could see both the speculative and disapproving looks I was getting. Most of the elders looked as though they'd just bitten into a Lemonhead. The rest of the coven seemed curious and maybe a little uneasy.

Belinda began by saying that this was an emergency meeting and normal protocol would be suspended. Though I hadn't thought it possible, two of the elders faces' became even more pinched and annoyed. Still, no one objected until she mentioned me.

"With so much upheaval in the underground community of Dallas, I decided that I should choose my successor as High Priestess. I have selected Kerry Gayle and would like the ritual to be completed today."

Several of the coven members objected, most notably Janice March. She was the newest of the elders and a few years older than Belinda. She'd also wrongly assumed that she would be the next High Priestess.

"Absolutely not!" Sharon Greene, Janice's mother, jumped to her feet. "She isn't fit to be a member of this coven, much less the leader. I'd rather see you choose a High Priest than her," she hissed.

I tried not to flinch. I knew what they all thought about me, but this was the first time that anyone had said it so bluntly. Most of the time, I endured thinly veiled barbs and backhanded compliments. High Priests were rare, not that male witches were rare, but likely because the men knew better than to take on all the drama that came with the job.

Sharon glared at me, her eyes shimmering with actual loathing. She had always been the most toxic of the elders, despising me since I was little more than a child. She also tried to push her daughter, Janice, on my mother as the next High Priestess, but my mother had chosen Belinda, which meant I was even more hated.

"I concur." This was from Beatrice Donaldson, another elder who'd disliked me for most of my life.

Their vehement objections fueled other coven members.

Constance Stern also stood, her hands fisted to her side. She wasn't an elder, but likely would be in another ten to fifteen years. She was five years older than me and even bitchier than I was, which was saying something. "You can't do this!" she exclaimed. "The coven has a right to object to any successor the High Priestess chooses."

Belinda raised her hands and their voices died away. "You may. But the only way for another witch to take Kerry's place is if she challenges Kerry and wins. However, it is my right to perform the ritual and declare the successor of my choosing, then, and only then, can your choice be presented as challenger."

It was an archaic rule, one that hadn't been enforced in centuries. If enough of the coven disagreed with the High Priestess' choice of successor, they could vote on their preferred candidate and the two would engage in a contest of knowledge and power. The victor was given a choice at the end of the contest; they could allow the loser to leave without punishment, banish them from the coven, or kill them. Most often, the losers were left alone or banished, but I had a strong hunch that, if I was challenged and lost, I was a dead woman.

The elders bombarded Belinda with arguments, their voices getting louder and louder. The witches in the room who were not involved merely sat in their chairs, staring at each other with wide, frightened eyes.

"She sent Saundra Abrams to her death!" cried Beatrice.

I vaguely heard Sally, Saundra's sister, gasp before other voices drowned her out. I'd accepted my part in Saundra's death, and would always regret it, but Beatrice made it sound as though I'd purposefully hurt someone I considered a friend. I felt anger building within me at the ugliness spewing from the mouths of the women around me.

"Everyone knows her father practiced black magic and tried to kill her. Evil begets evil. He turned and so will she."

My skin went ice cold when Sharon spat those words at Belinda. Instantly, I was reliving the moment I killed the vampires at my cottage and the dark pleasure I felt at their deaths. But, after, when I was no longer riding the hard edge of raw power, I'd felt regret. Until I'd found out what they'd done to Saundra. I felt a niggling sense of doubt in myself. Was Sharon right? With what I would need to do in the coming weeks and months, would I turn as my father had?

Clear as a bell, I heard my mother's voice and the words she'd said to me the day I turned sixteen, "Every witch's soul holds good and evil, Kerry, but we each have a choice to make. Some are weak and cannot resist the evil inside. Others skirt the line by saying and doing cruel things under the guise of righteousness. Then there are those that are too afraid to take risks, so they limit their experiences and power, ensuring that they will never grow as witches or people, yet they will remain pure. A wise witch recognizes her strengths and her weaknesses and constantly questions if her actions and choices do more harm than good. She takes risks, but does not endanger others. Always strive to be a wise witch, my girl, careful but not fearful and forever in search of knowledge."

I looked up and saw that Belinda was staring down at me and I knew why I was hearing my mother's voice. No doubt she'd shared that same speech with Belinda when she'd named her as successor. Though she didn't say it aloud, she told me what I needed to know.

Show them why I chose you, Kerry. Be the wise witch.

Several witches were shouting now, offended at Belinda's obvious inattention to their objections. I could feel anger building in the corner from the vampires and werewolves seated there and knew I needed to do something before one of them snapped.

Slowly, I stood and took a deep breath. Then I whispered an incantation. When the spell was complete, I clapped my hands once. The sound reverberated around the room like thunder and everyone fell silent, staring at me with hostile or fearful eyes.

I projected my voice so that it would carry without requiring me to shout. "That is enough." When several elders started to interrupt, I lifted a hand. "You have had your say. It is time for me to have mine."

Everyone who was standing sat and I felt every pair of eyes in the room riveted on me. My nerves felt frayed, but I swallowed them back and tried to project the same serenity that Belinda did.

"Let me address Sharon's accusation first," I stated, staring the elder in the eye. "Yes, my father was a warlock who practiced the dark arts. However, my mother was a witch you all respected greatly. I carry both of their blood, just as we all carry good and evil within us. Where we stand is based on the choices we make. We have all made mistakes, I'm sure, but we choose to do the right thing afterwards. That's what separates us from black witches and warlocks. I'm sure if each of you investigated your ancestry you would find at least one or two practitioners of the dark. Should you be held accountable for their actions?"

There were murmurs throughout the room, but no one spoke up.

"Secondly, I do feel responsible for Saundra's death. At the time, I didn't understand what we were dealing with in regards to the Faction. Now that I do, I regret what happened to a witch I considered a dear friend. I have tasted the power of the vampire warlock in their ranks and he is strong. I will not underestimate him again."

"You have no place at the head of this coven," Janice sniped.

"A week ago, I would have agreed with you," I responded.

Once again the room fell silent, almost preternaturally so.

I continued. "A week ago, I would have told Belinda in no uncertain terms that I had no desire for the position of High Priestess. Now, I think that's exactly where I need to be."

"Even if your lineage was of no concern, you are not powerful enough to be High Priestess." Sharon's voice rang out, full of hate.

Belinda answered before I could. "Kerry is more powerful than all of us, even me. She alone will have the strength to overcome the Faction's warlock."

There were scoffs and exclamations of disbelief.

"I don't believe you," Beatrice argued.

Then, to my surprise, Belinda snapped. "I have always been a fair and impartial High Priestess and I have always tried to respect your opinions, even if I didn't agree with them. You dare to call me a liar?" she asked. "Since you think so little of my word, why don't we allow Kerry a chance to demonstrate? Or do you think I lied when I said that she killed four vampires completely unaided?"

There was an uncomfortable silence before Janice responded, "I don't think you intend to be deceptive, Belinda. It's just difficult to believe that Kerry is so powerful when none of us have seen her cast in years." Though her words were carefully selected to seem respectful, I could see the malice sparkle in her eyes.

"I see." Those two little words from anyone else would seem innocuous. From Belinda, they sounded like a warning. "And how would you like Kerry to demonstrate her abilities?"

From the back of the room, I heard a voice. "Let her share power. Only the strongest can disperse to a group of this size. In fact, in our recorded history, the only witch who could share power with more than fifteen witches was her mother and she barely managed eighteen. If Kerry can do more than that, then this argument ends for today. Will the elders agree to that compromise?"

Everyone turned and Sally Abrams stood up. She had been the one speaking. Shocked, I wondered if it was because she was angry with me over Saundra or because she knew I could do it. As one, the elders gave her their backs, and she met my eyes. Though her expression was sad, she nodded to me. She supported me, despite what had happened.

I tilted my head.

Crossing her arms over her chest, Sharon spoke first. "That's fine. If Kerry can share power with, say twenty-five of us, then I am willing to forgo the elders' right to present a challenger as the successor." She glanced at the rest of them. "Do you all agree?"

One by one, each of the ten elders agreed, even Janice and Beatrice, which didn't surprise me. They didn't think I could do it or they never would have agreed to this. Over the years since my father's death, I'd withdrawn farther from the coven. I hadn't casted a spell in front of anyone but Belinda since my mother's burial rites, which had been four years ago.

I glanced at Belinda out of the corner of my eye, but her expression was serene and unconcerned. She knew what I was capable of but nothing on her face gave away her thoughts.

"Very well." Her voice was just as calm as her appearance. She turned her eyes to me. "Kerry, are you ready?"

I nodded and stepped back from the table, surveying the forty or fifty witches crowded into the room. I didn't have an exact head count, but I knew that if I could disperse magic to each of the witches here, then there would be no question about my strength and ability to lead the coven.

Taking a deep breath, I closed my eyes and began to recite the basic incantation used for a witch to give power to another. It was intended to help practitioners who were in danger and in need of a boost. The strength and breadth of the spell would expand based on the amount of magic I filtered through my body. It would require a great deal of control and skill to do this without injuring myself or someone else.

As it had the night of the attack on my cottage, it was as though the power was waiting for me to call upon it with words or even will alone. I drew it into myself with each breath, gathering more. As it built within me, I continued to chant the spell. Then I reached out. First to Belinda, then the elders, one by one, giving them parts of the force that surrounded me.

I felt my hair lift from my shoulders as though I were standing outside in the wind. The magic solidified in the room, rubbing against my skin as though it were corporeal. I heard gasps from the elders as the power spread to them in turn and knew they were feeling what I was; each hair on their body standing at attention, the blanket of magic like a physical caress on their skin, while a pressure built from within.

As I unraveled braids of magic, directing it to the rest of the witches of the coven, something happened, just as it had before. It was growing almost beyond my control. If I didn't release more, I felt like I might explode.

Still whispering the words of the spell, I opened the dam within me wider, the power no longer a small stream, but a turbulent, fast-moving river, rushing over the entire room. Someone cried out as more filtered through me.

Suddenly, I could no longer hold it back. A shockwave originated from my body and ripped through the group, knocking over several witches, including me.

When my body hit the floor, the impact severed the spell and the connection. Magic still hummed along my skin and I watched with wide eyes as small silver and gold starbursts danced in the air as the residual power began to fade.

I looked around and saw most of the coven members lying on the floor as well.

"Oh crap," I whispered. "What did I just do?"

Belinda, who was stretched out next to me, turned her head, a smile on her face. "You made them eat their words. You just shared your power with all fifty-five witches in this room, as well as all the vampires and werewolves on this floor."

Lachlan appeared, hovering over Belinda. "Are you okay?"

She nodded and took his hand, allowing him to help her to her feet. Then he aided me. I glanced over my shoulder to find Conner helping Finn and Donna off the floor as well, all of them wearing triumphant expressions.

Are you okay? Finn mouthed.

I nodded. I appreciated that he was standing back and letting me handle this situation, something I would tell him later. For now, I needed to focus on coven business.

When I faced the rest of the witches in the room, I saw shock, awe, and a healthy dose of fear, even from the elders.

Belinda waited for the room to settle before asking, "Is everyone all right?" She completely ignored the fact that it was my loss of control that knocked everyone on their asses. Then again, she probably thought I'd done it on purpose.

There were nods and murmurs of agreement. Since I could feel the residual magic in the air, my skin tingling, I realized many of them were still shaky.

Then the High Priestess fixed a steely stare on the row of elders seated in front of us. "Are there any more questions about Kerry's abilities?"

Seven of them shook their heads immediately. It was no surprise that Sharon, Beatrice, and Janice were stubbornly silent and still.

"Beatrice?" Belinda prompted.

"She has the strength to lead." Her voice was muted and a little petulant.

"Janice? Do you agree that her demonstration will suffice?"

Janice refused to speak, only nodding her assent.

Finally, Belinda met Sharon's eyes. "Sharon? Do you concur that the conditions of our agreement have been met?"

Though I could tell she would rather bite her tongue than answer, the elder said, "The conditions have been met. Kerry will be your successor."

But when Sharon looked at me, I knew with absolute certainty that she was lying and that this wasn't over. As long as she was able, she would do everything in her power to prevent me from becoming the next High Priestess.

Perhaps it was time to purchase a copy of *How to Win Friends and Influence People*.

Chapter Twenty

TWO WEEKS LATER, Belinda and I were sequestered in Finn's solarium, arguing over the prophecy and the coven. After days and weeks of fruitlessly searching for some tidbit of information that would help me decipher the prophecy of the Five, I was ready to call it quits. Obviously it existed and it was coming to pass. However, none of the books I'd found regarding its foretelling seemed to have any suggestions or spells to help us win the coming war.

Belinda disagreed, saying we had to keep reading and searching, that the answers we needed were out there. The only thing I'd managed to find of any interest was the spell that linked the life-forces of two people. The High Priestess was not as excited about it because, historically, it had been used by black witches to control other witches, vampires, and werewolves. Still, something about the spell intrigued me, so I tucked it away in one of my notebooks for further study. I was certain there were positive uses to be found. Though she wore an expression of tight-lipped disapproval, Belinda didn't stop me.

Once it was settled that we would continue researching the prophecy, the High Priestess began my training as her successor. While I suggested we had plenty of time and perhaps should wait until we were safer, she seemed determined. Her intensity was disconcerting. Belinda was the most composed person I knew and yet she was sometimes impatient and snippy with me, which rarely happened over the years, even when I tried jerking her chain.

During the coven meeting two weeks ago, she had performed the ritual which would clearly name me as the next High Priestess. Though it was merely for show, it was an important part of the process as it demonstrated her faith in my abilities to do the job well.

Once the meeting was over and she and I were on our way back to Finn's house to discuss the next step, I suggested that perhaps she should rethink her choice. At the time she didn't respond. However, I mentioned it again today and Belinda became agitated.

"It's too late to back out, Kerry," she insisted. "Even if there was another suitable candidate, there's no time to train anyone else."

"But it's obvious that the elders don't want me as the High Priestess. They'll fight me tooth and nail and likely ignore any suggestions I make or treat me with complete disrespect. This isn't going to work."

Belinda rubbed her forehead absently as though her head ached. "You can make it work, Kerry. I never said this would be easy. You'll have to deal with initial mistrust and weak confidence, just as most new High Priestesses do. Be patient and start with the younger witches. Many of them grew up with you and don't give the rumors about your father much credence. You can work your way up to the elders." She paused, seemingly gathering her thoughts. "I don't think you'll have as much trouble as you expect, though. There are at least three elders in the coven who have admitted I made the right choice after your display at the meeting."

"Really?" I asked.

"Yes, really. Now, we need to discuss what actions will be taken to establish civil relations with vampires and werewolves. I know that much of this wasn't resolved in the meeting after your demonstration, but we need to have something to present to the coven in regards to our future."

After several more long hours, Lachlan came into the study as the sun was setting. "We need to leave," he stated abruptly.

Belinda began to argue. "I'll only be a minute-"

"No. You're tired and Kerry's tired. This discussion can be continued another day."

"Lach, I said just a minute."

Glowering at her, he growled, "One minute. I'll wait outside."

After he left the room, I smiled tiredly at Belinda. "He's right. We're both exhausted and stressed."

She sighed. "I know, I know. It's just that there's not much time and I want you to be prepared."

I cocked my head to the side. "That's the second time you've said that today. Why do you think we're running out of time?"

Her expression shut down, blocking me out and making it impossible to tell what she was thinking. Woodenly, she answered, "When the fighting starts, you need to be able to do everything that I do, Kerry. You will need to be able to take over without a hitch should anything happen."

"Nothing will happen," I insisted.

She touched my hand lightly. "In war, you never know what tomorrow will bring."

Belinda seemed to shake off her pensive mood and started gathering her things. She left several ritual and spell books that outlined the ceremonies that were performed on the Sabbats, equinoxes, and solstices. Then Lachlan came back into the room, a stern expression on his face, and she was gone.

Feeling vaguely unsettled, I wandered out of the solarium and went in search of Finn. I found him in his study, stretched out on the sofa in front of his fireplace with a glass of red wine in his hand.

I paused in the doorway and just stared at him for a few moments. In the last weeks, Finn and I had fallen into a pattern. We usually got up around the same time every morning and took turns making breakfast. Then we each spent a few hours in our respective offices before meeting in the kitchen for lunch. Sometimes I would go back to the solarium to practice spells or read the texts that Belinda had given me or I would carry the spell books and rituals into his study and read on the couch while he worked at his desk. Then we would eat dinner together, watch television or make love, and then fall asleep together. It was idyllic and exactly what I used to imagine my future marriage would be. Though I'd never thought I would end up falling for a vampire.

One afternoon a few days after the coven meeting, I paused in my reading and looked over at Finn, who was studying something on his computer screen.

"I just realized that I have no idea what you do for a living."

He glanced at me and laughed. "Well, after so many years of working and trading stock, I don't really have a job except managing my money and investments, which keeps me busy enough."

"But Conner and Lex own businesses and work every day. Shit, forget I said that. That's not how I meant it."

He was still grinning at me, completely unfazed by my awkward statement. "Well, I doubt Conner or Lex work as much as they used to now that they have found their mates. Also, the Council has kept me busy enough for the last few decades."

He did have a point there.

The amusement faded from his expression. "It can be daunting, to see the centuries stretching out before you and never knowing if you'll always be so lonely."

Feeling slightly saddened, I rose from the sofa and went over to his desk, sitting in his lap. I wrapped my arms around his neck and rested my cheek on top of his head. "I didn't know that you felt that way." I threaded my fingers in his rich brown hair. "I'm sorry." And I was. I was sorry for everything; his solitude, what he'd had to endure as a newly turned vampire, and the horrible way I'd treated him for so long.

Finn hugged me closer. "Don't be. I won't be lonely any longer."

Since that afternoon, our relationship lost a great deal of its turbulence, mostly because of me. I stopped fighting my feelings and began to relax my guard. Each day was easier than the last. He still irritated me with his bossy behavior and I frustrated him when I wouldn't fall in line, but we managed.

Now, I stood in the doorway to his study, watching him stare into the fire, a peaceful look on his face. He looked happy.

"Are you going to stand there and stare at me all night or come sit?" he asked without turning his head.

I wandered over to the sofa and stretched out on the cushions with my head resting on his thigh. I sighed in contentment as he began to run his fingers through my hair in slow, steady strokes.

"You do that quite often, you know," he murmured.

"Do what?"

"Stand in doorways and stare at me. It's a little creepy."

He jumped and chuckled when I pinched his leg. "Whatever. You love it."

"The way you look at me? Yes, I do love it."

We sat in silence, enjoying each other's company, until my stomach growled loudly. I felt my cheeks heat as Finn laughed and patted my hip.

"I think that's my cue to feed you dinner," he joked.

I sat up. "That's promising. What are we having?"

"Steak, baked potatoes, and broccoli."

"Sounds perfect."

We made dinner and ate together, mostly in comfortable silence. Finn wasn't the sort of person who spoke unless he had something to say and I found myself mirroring his behavior, which was probably a good thing. I had a tendency to say things without thinking about the consequences. Perhaps he was a good influence on me after all.

After dinner, we washed the dishes together.

When we were done, I couldn't resist teasing Finn. "So, what's for dessert?" I asked.

"You." He charged me and I may have squealed before trying to run.

Laughing, he caught me before I'd gone more than two steps and carried me up the stairs so quickly I was dizzy.

I shrieked when he stopped at the end of his huge bed and tossed me toward the center of the mattress. I couldn't stop giggling as he pounced on me. Straddling my hips with his legs, Finn stripped his shirt over his head and did the same with mine. I tried to wiggle away when he moved off of me in order to unbutton and unzip my jeans.

Chuckling, he rolled me onto my stomach and gave my ass a playful smack. "Stay still."

Before I could crawl away or even turn over, Finn whipped my jeans and underwear down my legs, leaving me in only my bra. When I tried to get up on my hands and knees, he pushed me back down with a hand between my shoulder blades. In a blink of an eye, he'd unsnapped my bra.

As soon as he released me, I scrambled up the bed and sat with my back against the headboard.

Eyes bright, Finn shoved his pants and boxer briefs down his legs. "Get back here," he ordered, smiling.

I shook my head, crossing my arms over my chest to hold my bra in place. My eyes moved over his body, starting at his shoulders and moving down over his chest and tight abdomen, finally resting on his hard, thick cock.

With a low growl, he lunged forward and wrapped his fingers around my ankle, dragging me across the bed so that I was sprawled on my back. Still laughing, I tried to shove his hands away as he pulled my bra from my body.

As Finn began to take teasing nips at my neck and breasts, I gasped, "That tickles!"

He grinned and continued to torment me, completely ignoring my squeals and the wild thrashing of my body. This was the first time I'd ever laughed with a lover during sex and I was surprised at how much fun it was.

When he lowered his head to my nipple and sucked, I twisted both of my hands into his hair and yanked. My skin felt overly sensitized and the sensation of his mouth was almost too much. Finn lifted his head, grinning at me, and grabbed both of my wrists, pinning them to the bed by my head. Then he continued to lick and suck at my nipples while I writhed beneath him, begging him to stop yet unsure if I truly wanted him to.

Without releasing my wrists, Finn used his knees to nudge my thighs apart and slid his cock inside me. Every nerve ending in my body felt as though it had been touched by a live wire, overwhelming my ability to process what I was experiencing. My back arched when he slid his tongue over my breast and I could swear I felt it in my clit.

"Finn!"

His response was to slide almost completely out of my body and thrust forward. My vision clouded over as Finn stretched my arms above my head, transferring my wrists to one hand. With the other, he tilted my chin up and to the side, baring my neck to him.

Placing his lips to my ear, he whispered, "I'm going to take you hard and fast, and there's nothing you can do but lie here and take it."

His words had the same effect on me as a physical touch. All amusement was gone now and only the desperate desire for climax remained. As Finn plunged inside me, my knees hooked over his widespread thighs, I felt my body tighten unbearably. I jerked beneath him as his mouth moved from my ear to my throat, burning like a brand against my skin.

My body felt taut, suspended just beneath the peak. Muscles trembling, I tried to move my hands, to lift my hips, anything to help relieve the ache between my thighs. Then, at last, Finn sank his fangs into my throat, releasing me from the terrible tension. I cried out as the orgasm slammed into me, helpless beneath the force of my climax and Finn's restraining hands.

As the orgasm slowly receded, I lay beneath him, panting, with my hair draped across my face. I realized that Finn had released my hands and I wrapped my arms around his torso, cradling him closer while he ran the tip of his tongue over the bite on my neck. Though he was heavy, I tightened my grip on his body when he tried to roll away.

"Stay with me for a little while," I whispered.

Tucking his face against my neck, Finn pressed a kiss to my throat and slid his arms beneath my body to hold me closer. Together, we basked in the afterglow, exchanging kisses, touches, and softly spoken thoughts.

Much later, after I pulled on panties and a t-shirt, Finn pulled me into his side, running his fingers through my hair. Not for the first time in the last two weeks, I realized how much I would have lost if Finn hadn't kept up his relentless pursuit over the past few months. Something about him, about his very essence, brought me a sense of peace, as though I finally had another person in my life who would remain there unconditionally. I hadn't felt that since my mother died four years ago.

I let the deep contentment wash over me as I drifted to sleep, letting go of the last vestiges of my defensive walls. I was safe with Finn.

Or so I thought.

Chapter Twenty-One

THE ROOM WAS dark when I awoke and I was alone in the bed. I shifted, reaching an arm out for the lamp, but encountered only empty air. I suddenly realized that the sheets beneath me felt different, silk rather than high quality cotton. And Finn's distinctive vanilla and spice scent was absent.

I froze, frantically searching my memory. How did I get here, wherever *here* was? My blood turned to ice as the sound of someone breathing reached my ears. I desperately wanted to ask who was in the darkness, but some instinct told me I really didn't want to know.

A low, masculine voice uttered a single word, so softly that I couldn't catch what he was saying. A single candle flared to life on a table across the room, then, in a slow wave, more candles were lit around the perimeter of the room. Lastly, in a small fireplace to my right, a log began to crackle merrily as it burst into flame.

My eyes searched the shadows, looking for the man who'd spoken. Gradually, his shape was revealed as he moved forward from the corner and sat on a chair next to the table that held the first candle. I stopped breathing when I realized I was face-to-face with the black-eyed vampire who had killed Saundra.

My first impulse was to spit out the strongest, nastiest spell I could muster, but I managed to control it. The soft, unfocused quality of the candle light and the lack of any other sounds or scents in the room told me I was asleep and likely still snuggled up to Finn in his bed.

So we stared at each other, his onyx eyes glittering blankly in the light, until he smiled. I felt chills crawl up my spine when I recognized that the gesture didn't touch his cold eyes. He was dead inside, so filled with evil that its presence was the only thing keeping his body moving and his heart beating.

"Good evening, Kerry."

I didn't respond to his greeting, not even a blink of my eyelids.

The practiced smile fell from his lips as he continued to study me. "It's rude not to return a greeting," he chastened.

"It's also rude to invade another witch's dreams without permission or invitation," I responded, keeping my voice evenly modulated. He wanted me to feel as though I were at a disadvantage and off balance. Though it was working, I'd had years of pretending that ugly whispers and attempts to make me uncomfortable didn't exist. I had plenty of practice at hiding my true feelings.

"Touché." He leaned back in the chair and crossed his legs. He put out his hand, as though he were reaching for something on the table and I watched in surprise as a high ball glass appeared in his grasp. He sipped the amber contents, watching me carefully over the rim.

Striving to appear as relaxed as he did, I bent my legs, resting my elbows on my knees, and folding my arms on top of them. "I assume you brought me here for a purpose. Would you mind telling me what that reason is?"

He tilted his head. The gesture, combined with his emotionless eyes, reminded me of a bird of prey just before it swooped in on its next meal. "I have an offer for you, from my master." When I didn't respond, he continued, "He would like you to consider joining us and he's prepared to pay you handsomely for your help."

I arched my eyebrows. "What sort of payment? Money? Gold? Jewels?"

He sipped his drink again before answering. "Yes, as well as immortality and power beyond your wildest imaginings."

"I'm sure," I muttered, knowing I would likely be killed as soon as I no longer served a purpose or forced to commit atrocities for centuries until I went mad from the blackness that would eat at my soul. I took a deep breath, making every effort to project the calm self-assurance that Belinda seemed to possess. "You may tell your....master that I thank him for his offer but I will have to respectfully decline."

For the first time, his small smile reached his eyes. "That sounded very much like a *fuck you* wrapped up in pretty language."

I shrugged. "Take it as you will."

He laughed, the sound rich and resonate. "You are a great deal like your father, Kerry Gayle. He too had fire and spirit."

I couldn't hide my shock at his words. "You knew my father?" I tried to wipe all emotion from my face but knew I failed miserably.

He inclined his head. "Yes. It was my intention to turn him, but he died before my plans came to fruition."

I frowned at him. "What is your name?"

"Ah, finally, you ask for my name. I was beginning to feel hurt at your oversight." He set his glass on the table before folding both of his hands in his lap. "You may call me Dante."

Something about that name jogged my memory, but I couldn't quite place where I'd heard it before. Maybe from my mother or father or perhaps somewhere else.

"So, is this the fifth circle of Hell?" I quipped, trying to hide the fact that I was searching my brain for any hint as to where I'd heard someone mention a warlock named Dante.

His eyes narrowed. "Anger? No. Perhaps the seventh."

"Violence?" I queried.

He smiled again, once more seeming genuinely amused. "You know Dante."

I didn't respond. My knowledge of the *Divine Comedy* extended to the excerpts we read in school and the Cliff Notes I'd bought to help me comprehend what I was reading because I was lazy as a teenager and tried to get by putting forth as little effort as possible.

"Please consider my master's offer, Kerry Gayle. You are the first person in twenty-five years to make me feel sincere amusement. I would find it distasteful to harm you."

Ah, here was the threat I'd expected upon awakening in this place. "Harm me? I thought your master merely wanted to ask me if I was interested in joining his ranks. I've politely refused, so why would anything more be necessary?"

Dante's face once again fell into the cold mask he usually wore. "You know why."

"I'm sorry, I'm afraid I don't," I lied.

His eyes flashed, glowing like obsidian in the candlelight, a sure sign I was digging down into a place of his soul that I'd believed to be dead. It seemed it had merely been dormant and there was more to Dante than his obvious impassivity. "Don't pretend ignorance, dearest, it doesn't become you."

"I'm sure I don't know what you mean."

It seemed all the years of practice I'd had at pushing Belinda's buttons and irritating the coven elders was coming in handy now. Dante's eyes veritably sparked with ire. "Do not toy with me, *witch*, you will not win."

I leaned forward, savoring my final dig. "I'm sure I would, *bloodsucker*, because I did before. Or have you forgotten the vampires you brought to my cottage who are no longer in your ranks?"

Before he could respond, I reached down and pinched my inner thigh hard enough to bring tears to my eyes. Sticking around after such an inflammatory remark would be a colossally bad idea.

Gasping, I jerked awake, the tender skin of my upper thigh stinging viciously. I was in Finn's bed, his large body spooning me from behind. I panted as my eyes scanned the dim room nervously, half afraid that Dante had somehow followed me back here.

Finn shifted behind me and the warm glow of the lamp filled the room. He rolled me over to my back.

"Did you have another nightmare?" he asked, concern and tenderness in his gaze.

I swallowed hard and shook my head, not trusting my voice just yet. Despite my bravado when faced with Dante, my heart was racing with fear and it would take me a few moments to gain my composure. I cleared my throat, but I still sounded hoarse when I spoke. "He came to me in my dream."

Finn went rigid as he leaned over me. "Who?"

"The vampire warlock who killed Saundra and came for me. He calls himself Dante. He invaded my dreams."

"That's not possible. The wards and protection on this house are almost impenetrable. Only a witch as strong as you could break them and, even then, it would take a great deal of time. Enough that I would have time to stop them."

As my body and mind calmed, an idea came to me and I hated to think it was a possibility. "Not necessarily," I whispered.

He looked down at me, his purple eyes burning. "What do you mean?"

"There may be a way around the wards, but it requires black magic." I paused. "However, it means that I've been betrayed by one of my own people, because the only way the witch could have gotten around the spell was if I brought the talisman into your home."

"Talisman? As in a Hangman's Talisman?"

I nodded. A Hangman's Talisman was created using the hair and skin of a person who recently died and it could link a witch to whomever carried it. They could be found at any time or place by the witch that enchanted the talisman. The closer to the time of death, the stronger the magic. It was called the Hangman's Talisman because, in centuries past, black witches and warlocks often harvested the hair and skin of those who were hung or drowned during the witch hunts.

Considering talismans were meant to be a protection against evil, I thought that whoever named the spell had a dark sense of humor or a well-developed sense of irony.

I sat up, throwing my legs over the side of the bed. "We need to find it and destroy it."

Finn followed suit.

"Let's start with the bag I carried to the meeting. I would have found it if it had been tucked into my clothing."

We hurried downstairs to the sun room and I removed everything from my bag, even checking the lining and stitching. There was nothing there. I hadn't left Finn's house since the day of the coven meeting and only a few people had come and gone in the last two weeks.

Frustrated, I slammed my bag down on the desk and my eyes fell on the stack of books that Belinda had brought to me. Some of them were from her personal library, but a few were housed in the coven's library. I very much doubted that the High Priestess would betray me, but any of the witches in the coven would have had access to a few of the books.

I grabbed one of the library texts and began to page through it, checking the front cover and between the paper to see if a talisman had been tucked inside. I turned the book upside down and shook it. Nothing. I ran my hands over the binding and the inside and outside of the hard cover but it didn't seem as though it had been tampered with.

I moved on to another coven library book. Still nothing. However, as I went through the third, I felt my fingertips tingle and knew that the Hangman's Talisman was somewhere inside. It wasn't pressed between the pages, but, when I smoothed my hand over the inside of the back cover, I felt the tingles sharpen into a sting as my fingers brushed small raised bumps beneath the paper that lined the inner cover.

I found a letter opener and gently began to pry the liner away from the hard cover. Whoever had inserted the talisman hadn't glued the paper back very well, so it pulled away easily. There, lying along the bottom edge of the book cover, was the talisman. Strands of hair, preserved skin, and herbs were twisted together in a small braid. I felt my stomach heave at the sight, but forced myself to study the nasty little piece of magic. My heart stopped beating as I recognized the shade of the hair and the slightly wavy texture.

"Dear Goddess," I breathed. "They used Saundra's hair and skin."

Unable to control the nausea any longer, I dashed to the powder room down the hall and collapsed on my knees in front of the toilet. Though there wasn't much of anything in my stomach, I emptied the bile and continued to dry heave for long minutes. When the painful expulsion finally eased, I realized that Finn was crouched behind me, holding my hair back and pressing a cool, damp cloth to the back of my neck.

When I calmed, he handed me the cloth so I could wipe my face. He helped me to my feet so I could rinse out my mouth and splash my face with cold water.

Once I finished, I leaned against the sink, meeting Finn's eyes in the mirror in front of me. "I have to call Belinda immediately. If someone managed to get a Hangman's Talisman to me, I'm sure they would have attempted to do so with her as well."

Finn helped me into the kitchen and sat me at the kitchen table as though I were aged or infirm. Then he went upstairs to retrieve my burner phone and brought it back down to me. "I'll make some tea while you call Belinda."

I nodded absently as I selected her name from my speed dial list. The phone rang and rang until I thought it was going to be picked up by voicemail. At the last moment, the line clicked and I could hear breathing on the other end.

"Belinda?" I asked. "Can you hear me?"

Instead of the High Priestess' voice as I expected, the low, smooth tone of a man came through the speaker. "Thank you for calling, dearest, but Belinda is indisposed at the moment." Then he ended the call.

I stared at Finn from across the room, horror filling me. "It's too late. Dante has Belinda."

A split second later, Finn's phone rang. His eyes narrowed when he checked the Caller ID. "It's Conner." He lifted the phone to his ear. "Hello?" He paused, listening to whatever Conner was saying. "We'll be there soon."

Finn hung up, already moving in my direction. Helping me to my feet, he said, "One of Conner's men turned. He and Donna are fine, but Ricki and Shannon were injured. Conner said..." he hesitated, "Conner said that Shannon's injuries seem minor but

Ricki is likely dying. He said that there isn't much he can do short of changing her and Calder is resisting. I need you to gather whatever healing spells, herbs, and potions you have here. You'll need them." His eyes were worried. "Hurry."

I felt adrenaline and terror flood my veins. The prophecy was coming to pass. Ricki was seriously hurt, probably dying. I ran from the kitchen, hoping like hell we wouldn't be too late.

Chapter Twenty-Two

THE DRIVE TO Conner's house would have been a great deal more hair-raising if I hadn't been consumed with worry about my friends. Finn drove as though the hounds of hell were on his heels.

When he screeched to a halt in front of Conner's home, I was out of the car before he had a chance to put it in park. I sprinted up the front steps and into the house. When I entered the foyer, I realized I didn't know where to go, so I started yelling.

"Donna! Conner!"

Donna's pale face appeared over the railing at the top of the stairs. "Oh, thank God you're here. Ricki's in the guest room. She's lost a lot of blood and…and." She didn't have to finish the sentence for me to understand her meaning.

I dashed up the stairs and followed her into one of the spare bedrooms. I felt like I'd taken a punch to the gut when I saw the blood. So much blood.

Calder was kneeling on the bed next to Ricki, but he was staring Conner down as though he were moments away from trying to rip out his throat.

I moved to the bed, removing herbs, potions, and other things I would need to cast healing spells. "What's are you two doing?" I asked.

"He wants to turn her into a vampire." Calder growled the words.

"It will save her life," Conner snapped. "Would you prefer that she died?"

I saw Ricki's eyelids flutter and wondered if she could hear what was happening.

"Why don't you two back up and let me look at her?" I suggested. "I may be able to help without resorting to changing her."

Though they were still eyeing each other with thinly veiled hostility, Conner and Calder moved back enough for me to squeeze beside the bed. I looked down at Ricki. Her face was pale and there was a streak of blood on her jaw.

"Hey, Ricki. How you doin'?"

Her eyes opened slowly. "Kerry," she rasped. "What happened?"

I gently pulled away the cloth that Conner had been using to apply pressure to her wounds in an attempt to stop the bleeding. I struggled to keep my face from showing what I was thinking when I answered her. "There was an attack at Conner's house and you were hurt. I'm gonna help you out here, okay?"

She took a shallow breath. "Okay."

I looked over at Conner and whispered, "Have you tried vampire blood and saliva to start the healing process?"

He nodded. "It's the only reason she's not dead now," he answered, keeping his voice low enough that she wouldn't hear.

I felt my heart plummet. There was very little I could do for such serious wounds. Even with my abilities, I couldn't bring back someone so close to the brink without using forbidden spells. "Maybe we should call an ambulance."

Conner moved closer. "We can't. You know we can't. Even if we managed to adjust the memories of all the humans involved, there would be records, both electronic and hard copies. It's too risky."

"So we just let her die?" I hissed. "Or you change her?"

His face said it all.

"No." Calder crowded into the group. "If she changes, she will be a wolf. She's my mate, it's my decision."

Donna saved me from stepping in when she snapped, "No, it's not your decision, Calder." Then she turned to Conner. "And it's not yours either. It's Ricki's. We should ask her what she wants to do."

Conner scowled. "She's too weak to endure a werewolf bite right now. The transition would kill her."

Donna didn't respond, instead going back to keep an eye on Ricki.

Something tugged at my mind, like a memory that remained just out of reach. I focused on it, but it slipped away. Still, Conner's words struck a chord with me in some way.

"Maybe not," I murmured.

Calder's intensity was instantly on me. "What do you mean?"

I dug in my bag. "There's a spell. I found it in a book Belinda brought me. It might be useful."

I found my notebook and pulled it out. The paper I'd copied the spell on was still tucked in the back. I read it carefully, because I wanted to be sure that I understood what I was doing. It might work. By connecting them, Calder's strength would help Ricki survive the transition.

Looking at Calder, I asked, "Are you willing to tie your life force with Ricki's?"

"If it will save her, I would give my own life, so, yes."

I drew in a deep breath. "Okay, I want to ask her what she wants before we proceed." Gesturing for them to remain across the room, I went to the bed and brushed my fingers over Ricki's forehead. Her skin was clammy and her breathing was rapid and shallow. We were running out of time.

"Ricki," I murmured. "I need you to wake up for a second, okay?"

She moaned softly but didn't open her eyes.

"Ricki, you need to look at me," I insisted, my voice firmer.

Her lids cracked and she gasped deeply, shuddering, but her eyes opened wide and fixed on me.

"You're badly injured, Ricki, and I need you to make a choice for me."

Her voice was nearly inaudible. "What do you mean?"

I stroked her forehead and wrapped my hand around hers gently. "If we don't do something drastic, you're going to die."

Her body shivered again and she gasped, the pause between her next breath so long I was afraid she wasn't going to take another. She stared at me, waiting for me to continue.

"Conner can turn you or-" I paused. "I can bind your life force with Calder's. You'll have to ingest his blood and you'll become a wolf like him. If I do this, then you two would be irrevocably linked. If he is killed, you would die also. If you die, so does he."

She tried to speak, but her voice cracked. When Ricki cleared her throat, it sounded painful. "And if Conner turns me, what then?"

"You live the rest of your very long life as a vampire."

I watched as she processed what I said. Her eyes drifted over my shoulder and I knew she was looking at Calder.

So softly I almost didn't hear it, she asked, "Did you mean what you said to me yesterday? About the mark and everything else?"

I could practically feel Calder's intensity radiating at my back. "Every fucking word."

Her eyes closed and something changed in her face. Ricki didn't open them again, but said, "Do the spell."

I watched as her chest barely rose and fell with every tiny breath and I knew I had to hurry. Quickly, I began to lay out everything I would need. The spell only required a few herbs and blood, but I wanted to be sure I did everything perfectly. I would only have one chance to perform this incantation. With a spell this important, I would have preferred the chance to practice mixing the herbs in the correct ratio and reciting the words several times before performing it. I didn't have that option now.

"I need a sharp knife and a bowl," I commanded over my shoulder. "Quickly."

Conner disappeared from the room in a blur of motion.

To Donna, I said, "I need a candle. White if you have it."

She nodded and left the room as well.

Calder moved back to his original position of kneeling on the bed next to Ricki, cradling one of her hands in both of his. I tried not to let panic overwhelm me as the pauses between her breaths grew longer.

Conner returned with the bowl and the knife.

"Sterilize them with alcohol and add just enough water to cover the bottom of the bowl," I ordered and he carried them into the connecting bathroom.

When he returned, I took the bowl and placed it on the night stand, laying the knife neatly across the top of the bowl. Murmuring the first set of words in the spell, I began to add the dried herbs into the water.

Donna returned with the candle, which I took from her and set it to the left of the bowl.

Glancing at Calder, I asked, "Ready?"

"Yes."

His voice was clear and filled with resolve, which was excellent. Ricki would need that resolve to help her come back from the precipice.

I began the chant and lifted the knife, a spark of power flaring in my belly. In my other hand, I extended the bowl to Calder, who cupped it in one hand. I took his other hand, extending his index finger over the bowl. As I recited the second part of the spell, I pierced his skin with the knife and squeezed a few drops of his blood into the herb and water mixture. When the blood hit the mixture, I felt a surge of power. As I lifted Ricki's hand and repeated the process, the magic began to grow.

Normally, I would have cringed at using the knife on both of them, but they were about to drink a few drops of the other's blood in a moment, so it didn't matter.

I took the bowl back from Calder and set it back on the table. Then, I lifted the candle. With a small amount of their mingled blood on the tip of the knife, I began to carve symbols of unity and healing on the candle, beginning the third part of the spell. The building magic pressed in around the bed, creating a connection between the three of us. As I placed the base of the candle on Ricki's chest, I recited the passage that brought the flame to life on the wick. I brought one of Calder's hands to clasp it in place, then did the same with Ricki's.

Her eyes were glazed, but focused on me as I worked. For a moment, I felt panic trying to creep up my spine, but I forced it back.

Repeating the third and final paragraph in the spell, I put aside the knife and lifted the bowl to Calder's lips. He sipped it, but I gestured for him to drink a bit more until he took half. Grimacing, he helped me lift Ricki's head enough to get most of the liquid in her mouth. She winced as she swallowed what had to be a bitter mix of dried herbs, water, and blood.

"As I will it, so mote it be."

When I uttered the closing words of the spell, the power increased until I felt as though I would be crushed beneath it. Calder and Ricki both gasped, their bodies becoming rigid as one, and the final link between them snapped into place. It was done.

As the magic receded, I heard Ricki make a sound, part cough, part moan. Then she stopped breathing. In horror, I watched as Calder collapsed on the bed next to her, clutching his chest. I couldn't allow this to happen. I couldn't sit back and watch someone I loved die, not again.

I felt for a pulse in her neck and found nothing. Then, I realized that if I could muster enough energy to stop someone's heart, then I could use it to restart one as well. Praying to the Goddess that it would work, I placed my hand over Ricki's heart, focusing on what I wanted to happen. If I could visualize the spark forcing the organ to begin pumping again, it would be more effective.

Sucking in a deep breath, I let the power flow down my arm, forming a ball of energy just behind my palm. As I released the air, I released the energy in the form of electricity. Ricki's body jerked. I checked her neck for a pulse. Nothing.

Once more, I laid my hand on her chest, refusing to let a shred of doubt enter my mind. I would save her. I repeated the process, watching as Ricki's body arched again.

When I put my fingertips to her neck, I felt a weak, steady pulse. I started to position her head for mouth-to-mouth, but she took a loud, gasping breath on her own. Terrified that she would stop again, I stood by the bed, trying to ascertain her condition.

Within a few minutes, her chest began to rise and fall more steadily and her face was no longer as pale. Calder seemed to be fine as well, although still unconscious.

Hesitantly, I lifted the blood-soaked cloth that had covered her wounds. Already, the accelerated healing process had begun, a sign that Calder's blood had worked and she would begin her first change sometime in the next thirty-six hours or so. Unfortunately, it wasn't an exact science, so I couldn't be sure.

Suddenly, exhausted, my ass hit the bed beside Ricki and tears of relief trickled down my face. A light touch on my shoulder startled me and I looked over my shoulder to find Finn staring down at me.

"I'm glad you were able to save her," he murmured, using his thumbs to gently wipe my tears away.

"Me too."

Unfortunately, it was time to focus on the other woman who needed my help; Belinda.

Chapter Twenty-Three

TWENTY MINUTES LATER, we were all in the library except for Calder, Ricki, and Donna. Donna was upstairs, removing Ricki's bloody clothes and washing her skin. Conner and Finn were speaking softly in the corner, while Shannon and I sat on the couch.

One of Conner's men, I wasn't sure of his name, was attempting to clean and dress Shannon's injuries. Mostly she was bruised, but her forehead was bleeding and there were several lacerations on her arms and hands. Unfortunately, Shannon wasn't impressed with his fawning.

"I'm fine," she snapped, trying to dodge his hand. "I'll wash up in a few minutes."

"Sit still and let me clean your wounds," he insisted.

Her eyes narrowed. "I've already killed one vampire tonight, let's not make it two."

The vampire's hands froze, hovering over her skin. I had to stifle a laugh at the shocked expression on his face. I doubted any other human woman he knew would have had the gumption to speak to him like that. I reached out and took the cloth from him.

"She doesn't mean it. Blood always makes her a little snippy, especially if it's her own. I'll take care of her."

He nodded.

"Thanks for your help." I nudged Shannon with my elbow.

She flinched. "Yes, thank you."

I turned to her, using the gauze to wipe away the excess blood on her face. "You should be nicer to the vampires. They're a lot stronger than humans, you know."

"Strength isn't everything," she muttered.

The sliver of amusement I felt faded away, replaced by worry. "What happened?" I asked, grabbing a fresh piece of gauze and putting a bit of alcohol on it.

Shannon hissed when I went back to cleaning the wound on her forehead. "It seems one of Conner's men worked for the Faction. He let several other vampires into the house and they tried to kill us. Calder told us to go downstairs in the basement, but we got cut off. We hid in Ricki's closet, but they found us." Her breath hitched when I got a fresh piece of gauze and began to clean the blood from her forearms and hands. "I thought we were going to die. He moved so quickly that I could barely see him. I couldn't get a shot off. It wasn't until he started...." she swallowed. "It wasn't until he started...that I could get a clean aim. I shot him in the head."

I nodded as I finished cleaning her cuts. "You did what you needed to do. If you hadn't killed him, he would have kept coming."

"I just wish I'd stopped him from hurting Ricki."

Finn brought over a glass with an inch of clear liquid in it. I assumed it wasn't water. I took it and lifted it to Shannon's lips, urging her to take a sip with the hopes that it would calm her nerves.

She coughed a little and took another drink. Then she pushed the glass away. "That's enough."

Finn set the glass on the heavy coffee table and sat down on it so he was facing us, elbows to knees. "I have news about Belinda and Lachlan."

Something about the way he said Belinda's name sent a shaft of fear through me and my heart began to pound.

"Lachlan was severely injured." He reached out to take my hand and that's when I knew what he was going to say. "Belinda didn't survive. I'm sorry, Kerry, but she's gone."

I wanted to scream and cry but I felt as though I'd been encased in ice. Since my mother's death, Belinda was one of the few women that I felt I could turn to. While my friends were wonderful, there were a lot of times I couldn't confide in them because of what I was. She had always been there, never letting me push her away with my bitchy behavior.

Now I understood why she'd been so insistent that we begin my training immediately, despite what was happening around us. She was more than a witch. As a Seer, she had the gift of foresight. Belinda knew she was going to die.

I forced myself to breathe and push past the feelings that threatened to overwhelm me. I had to keep it together. There was too much at stake. While most of the coven would look to me for answers, I doubted the elders would do anything to help and I had strong suspicions that one of them had possibly betrayed us.

"What's next?" I asked.

Finn glanced at Conner and some unspoken thought passed between them. "You said you believed someone at the coven meeting would have to have helped the Faction track you down. Do you truly think that is the case?"

"I know it is," I whispered. "How else would Dante be able to connect to me in a dream or find Belinda? We were both carefully hidden and I know Belinda would have cast spells or set wards to prevent someone from ascertaining her location through the usual magical means."

Finn clasped my hands a little tighter. "I don't like the plan I'm about to propose to you. Actually, I loathe it, but we need you in this war and I can't deny it any longer." He glanced at Conner one more time, his expression stiff. "The coven will want to perform the traditional rites for Belinda and we think it would be an excellent opportunity to find the traitor amongst your people. It's clear that there are few people we can trust, even among those closest to us."

I thought their idea was a good one. "It could definitely work. But I think it would be better to do this at the emergency meeting I'm going to call tomorrow morning to announce my ascension to High Priestess. Everyone will be on their best behavior at Belinda's rite, but I believe they will be more honest and maybe even outright hostile at the meeting. It will be easier to get a read on them while their guard is down."

Conner nodded. "Excellent suggestion. Where will you hold the meeting? One of my offices?"

I shook my head. "No, we'll have it at the coven library."

Finn studied me, a slight frown on his face. "I thought the elders refused to allow the werewolves and Council members access to the Coven House."

I arched an eyebrow. "What better way to bait someone who obviously despises the Council and the pack than to invite those they hate to our sanctuary?"

Conner's eyes were speculative as he appraised my suggestion. "That's an excellent and cunning idea."

Finn was silent, but he nodded in agreement.

I squeezed his hands before releasing them and standing. "Well, I have some calls and arrangements to make. This needs to stop before anyone else gets hurt."

None of us slept much that night. The elders were surprisingly subdued when I contacted them. In fact, all of them readily agreed to help me notify the rest of the coven of Belinda's death.

Shannon grumbled about being useful for things other than acting as a glorified receptionist, but she made coffee and tea for us and pitched in whenever anyone needed help. Finn and Conner were busy working out the logistics of security for the meeting and, once I finished my phone calls, I had plans of my own to make.

Around three, Finn came over to the table, took the pen from my hand, and pulled me to my feet. "You're half asleep and probably not thinking clearly. Let's get some rest."

"But, I have to finish-"

He picked up the notepad I'd been scribbling on and turned it around, pointing to the bottom of the page. "The sentence that you were writing here?"

I glanced down and realized that I'd been writing nothing but a bunch of gibberish. "Well, shit."

He threw the pad down on the table. "Let's get a few hours of rest and then you can get back to work."

After a quick check on Ricki, who was still sleeping though she was nearly healed, I let Finn lead me into a guest room, help me out of my clothes, and into a t-shirt he'd found somewhere. I settled onto the bed and he climbed in next to me, pulling the duvet over us.

Finn tucked me close. "Sleep, Kerry. You can be strong in the morning."

To my surprise, I was barely able to hold my eyes open. Within minutes, I was asleep.

As I slept, I saw myself at my mother's cottage in the country. I sat at the kitchen table with her and Belinda, drinking hot tea, and playing Scrabble. I felt a pang of longing at reliving the memories I'd almost forgotten. In the years since my mother's death, I'd been so busy trying to avoid Belinda that I lost sight of how much time we spent together during my teen years. In hindsight, I realized that she treated me as a sister, with equal parts love and exasperation.

The scene shifted and, this time, the three of us were seated around the table in the solarium, a bowl in the center. Candles were lit around the room and the smell of burning herbs tickled my nose. This wasn't one of my memories.

"What's happening?" I asked.

Mom and Belinda were chanting, eyes shut, and we were all holding hands. When I tried to pull away, they tightened their grip on me.

"What the hell?"

Mom's eyes popped open. "Don't move," she commanded firmly.

I stopped moving and she and Belinda continued the incantation. A light, warm breeze filled the solarium, gaining strength and speed. Soon it grew into a hot wind that somehow didn't touch the flames of the candles, which barely flickered.

"As we will it, so mote it be." My mother's voice and Belinda's rang out together and the fiery wind died away.

They released my hands and opened their eyes.

"I have to be dreaming," I muttered. "That's the only explanation."

"Is it?" my mother asked.

I rolled my eyes. She always loved to try to undermine my certainty of things, to force me to question everything. She said it would build my character. Honestly, I think it was her way of getting back at me for my attitude during puberty.

"She hasn't changed much," Belinda told Mom dryly. "Still sarcastic and stubborn as always."

"You know, there are several other things I'd prefer to dream about, like Jason Statham and I lost on a desert island. Or Tom Hiddleston taking me on a picnic at the beach. Or-"

"Shut up, Kerry," my mother sighed. "The past four years have been so peaceful that I forgot how quickly you push my buttons."

Belinda and I grinned at each other. I felt relaxed and happy, no longer weighed down by my grief and pain.

Mom placed her hands over mine, bringing my attention back to her. "There's something you should know." Her face was serious as she spoke. "Don't be fooled by what you see of the Faction. They are older and far more powerful than the Council realizes and their spies are everywhere."

I didn't tell her that I'd already learned that hard lesson, especially with Belinda looking at me with gentle, sad eyes.

Mom stood up. "It's time to go."

"Can't you stay longer? Please?" My voice was small, as though I were once again a child. I felt like one, lost and frightened. After four long years and the insanity of my life over the last few months, I craved the comfort of my mother's embrace and her scent.

Hugging me close, she kissed my cheek. "I love you, my sweet girl. I'm proud of who you've become." She pulled back and smiled at me. "And you picked a winner for your mate."

I stared at her, surprised. How did she know about Finn? Then I remembered this was a dream, probably created by my subconscious.

Belinda hugged me as well, whispering in my ear, "I'm sorry I won't be there to help you when the time comes, Kerry, but you are the strongest, brightest witch I know and you will be fine." She kissed my cheek. "Tell Lachlan I'm sorry. Don't let him give up and try to help him move on from me."

Before I could ask her what she meant, Belinda released me and stepped away.

"I love you," I whispered to my mother, watching as she and Belinda faded into the shadows.

When my eyes opened to the bright light of day, I lay in the circle of Finn's arms and let the bittersweet ache of seeing my mother again wash over me. I also felt calm, almost serene. Though they were likely a figment of my grief-stricken mind, seeing my mother and Belinda whole and happy brought me a measure of peace.

I just hoped that I could maintain that peaceful feeling today. I would need it when dealing with the elders of the coven, especially after they found out that I had allowed vampires and werewolves into the Coven House.

I heard the cadence of Finn's breathing change and knew he was awake. It was time to get up and scare the shit out of a traitor.

Chapter Twenty-Four

THE MOOD IN Coven House was somber when Finn and I entered. I could hear muted voices coming from the meeting hall but there were no men or women loitering in the halls, joking and gossiping. Though I was thirty minutes early for the meeting, there were witches here before me. I was almost certain I knew who they were, too.

Sure enough, Janice and Constance appeared in the open double doors that led from the foyer to the meeting room. They stopped so abruptly I thought they were going to topple over like a pair of dominoes.

They quickly hid their surprise and displeasure at my appearance.

"Kerry, how are you holding up?" Janice asked me, her voice sickeningly sweet and soft. She came forward, arms extended, and with an expression that she must have thought was appropriately sympathetic. She was wrong. From five feet away, even I could see that she wasn't sincere.

I grabbed her hands before she could wrap her arms around me and squeezed them. "I've been better, Janice. How are you doing?"

She tried to muster up a fake tear, but wasn't successful. Instead she settled for sniffling as though it was a valiant effort to hold back her sobs. "It's just awful. Absolutely horrible."

I nodded in agreement. It was horrible, but it was likely that Janice or one of the other elders here today were responsible. I looked at Constance. "Hello, Constance. Thank you for coming early to help prepare for the meeting. I appreciate that."

Constance opened her mouth to respond, but obviously had no clue what to say and shut it just as quickly. After clearing her throat, she answered, "No problem."

Janice wrapped her hand around Constance's wrist. "We were just on our way into the kitchen to make a pot of coffee. Can I bring you a cup?"

While I was tempted to say yes just to see if she would try to poison me, I declined. "No, thank you. I'll grab something to drink later."

She nodded and dragged Constance out of the foyer toward the kitchen.

Finn leaned down and whispered in my ear, "That was almost painful."

I tried not to snort. This wasn't exactly a laughing matter, but he was right. Janice's overly sensitive facade was almost comical.

"Why didn't you let her hug you?" he asked, still speaking so softly only I would be able to hear him.

Tilting my head back, I put my mouth to his ear. "I'm pretty sure any hugs she gives me will be so she can figure out which two ribs she needs to stick the knife between when she stabs me in the back."

He shook his head. "You say that as though it were a joke, but I think it's frighteningly close to the truth."

I shrugged. "It is the truth and there's nothing I can do about it until she openly defies me."

I tapped the truth amulet on Finn's wrist. Since I hadn't had the tools or time to create a new one, I thought it was somewhat poetic that I would use a truth amulet Belinda made to find the witch who had betrayed her. Since I wasn't sure who I could trust in the coven, I was glad that Finn possessed the power needed to use it.

"Just remember to tap your wrist if the amulet turns orange when a witch is speaking."

Finn tilted his head in acknowledgement.

I took one deep breath to steel myself for the confrontation that was soon to come. Finn laced his fingers with mine and, immediately, the calm I felt lying in bed with him this morning returned.

"Ready?" I asked.

"If you are."

"I guess we'll find out soon enough," I murmured.

We walked through the open French doors into the meeting room and my eyes were instantly drawn to Sharon and Beatrice, who were the only other witches there. It seemed that the other seven elders were not as eager to undermine me so quickly after my ascension.

"Hello, Sharon, Beatrice. I appreciate you both arriving so early." Since my polite words seemed to unnerve Janice a few minutes ago, I decided to continue with the same serene, politically correct attitude I'd often envied in Belinda.

Sharon didn't bother with niceties. "What is he doing here?"

"Do you mean Finn?"

I had to bite back a smile when her mouth pinched tightly as though she were making every effort to control her response. Damn, maybe Belinda had been more like me than I thought, only instead of using sarcasm to irritate people, she killed them with kindness. This was going to be fun.

"Yes," Sharon hissed.

"He is attending as an envoy of the vampire council."

"You brought a vampire *here*, to Coven House?" Beatrice gasped.

"Yes. Actually, several more will be here later."

"You can't do this!" Sharon exclaimed. "You didn't even ask the elders for approval."

Okay, this was becoming less fun and more of an annoyance. "It may not be approved by the elders, but it is happening." Maybe it was time to throw out some bait and see who bit. "A lot of people I care about were hurt or killed last night and someone in this coven is responsible."

Beatrice gasped and Sharon's face grew ashen.

"Are you suggesting that a witch betrayed the coven?" Beatrice asked, aghast.

"I'm not suggesting it, it's a statement of fact. I found a Hangman's Talisman in a book that Belinda obtained from the library in Coven House. Though I haven't had a chance to examine her belongings, I'm certain I'll find another somewhere among them. The Faction wouldn't have been able to track us otherwise."

"Dear Goddess," Beatrice whispered.

"Surely you can't think that one of the elders would do such a thing?" Sharon asked, her voice a great deal more subdued than it had been a few moments ago.

I studied her, unable to determine if I was seeing guilt or shock in her expression. "Until I find the traitor, I'm not taking any chances."

Finn shifted beside me, turning slightly away, but I remained focused on the two witches in front of me.

"An elder would never do such a thing," Sharon insisted. "Right, Beatrice?"

"Absolutely not."

Something in Beatrice's tone caught my attention, but, before I could decipher what it was, she sighed and spoke. "Let's go check on Janice and Constance in the kitchen. I'm sure they're making the coffee too strong."

They skirted around Finn and me. I listened until the sound of their footsteps faded away, then asked Finn, "Did you notice anything strange?" I asked him.

He moved me further into the room, glancing over his shoulder to ensure we were alone. "I'm not sure if it was both of them or only one, but the amulet turned orange when they were speaking to you."

A chill ran up my spine. It was very possible that I'd been standing a few feet away from the women responsible for Belinda's death. The icy dread was engulfed by a surge of rage and power. I wanted to lash out and destroy the witches that I'm sure were huddled in the kitchen discussing ways to get rid of me. A part of me wanted to luxuriate in that dark impulse, to imagine all the ways I could hurt them and make them pay for what they had done to Belinda and to me. The realization filled me with fear. Was this what my father felt before he fell to the temptation of black magic?

Finn's hand came up to rest on my shoulder. "Kerry, you need to try to calm down. You're eyes are glowing."

I closed them and focused on slowing my breathing. I had to maintain control. This wasn't the time or place to unleash hell on the traitor. I needed to be patient, bait the trap, and let the witch who betrayed us fall into it.

When I had a firm grip on my emotions and my powers, I opened my eyes. "Let's get this done."

While I got my things set up on the table at the front of the room, Finn called Conner and they discussed the best areas to place the vampire and werewolf security. With Lachlan out of commission, Calder should have been here, but he was still drained from all the energy that healing Ricki was taking out of his body.

Chloe stepped in to represent the pack until Calder was back on his feet. I assumed the male wolves would give her trouble, but they seemed positively cowed by her presence. I sensed there was a story there, but I would have to wait until things were calmer to get it.

Conner, Lex, Finn, and Gabriel would all be in attendance at the meeting. I had purposefully left out the fact that the entire vampire Council would be here when talking to Sharon and the other elders earlier. Just as I had neglected to tell them that some of the werewolves were coming as well. I wanted to get a reaction, a strong one. If they were angry or off balance in another way, then the traitor was more likely to make a mistake and reveal their perfidy.

Fifteen minutes before the meeting was scheduled to begin, men and women began to trickle in. Though attendance wasn't required, it was considered bad manners to miss the first meeting with a new High Priestess after her ascension.

Last night, I assumed a great deal of the coven members would refuse to come to the meeting. Over the years, many of them had fallen on a spectrum in regards to their treatment of me. Some pretended I didn't exist or demonstrated polite tolerance. Others were outright nasty.

However, I was surprised at the turn out. By my count, at the 10 a.m. start time, all but five witches in the coven were there, almost ninety of them. As everyone shuffled to their seats, chatting quietly or even crying almost silent tears, I noticed three more women arrive.

Though Belinda often started the meetings promptly at their scheduled time, I decided to wait five minutes for people to settle and compose themselves. Finn moved to the back of the room where I could clearly see him from my position in front of the members.

I lifted the bell used for rituals and meetings and rang it three times, signaling to the coven that it was time to begin the meeting.

Before I spoke, I muttered a spell to help my voice carry throughout the room so I wouldn't have to raise my volume.

"Thank you all for coming. I am here with a heavy heart, as I know you are as well, at the loss of our fallen High Priestess. Because of the circumstances of her death, I'm afraid we cannot allow ourselves to grieve today as we usually would. There is something we must discuss as a coven and it was Belinda's wish for our future. I'm sure you all know that she was working to achieve a peaceful relationship with both the vampires and werewolves in this area. Unfortunately, she could not bring this to Coven House before her death. As her successor, she shared with me how beneficial she felt this would be for our people and I agreed with her." I paused to take a breath and allow this to sink in.

Someone near the front of the room muttered, "Only because you're going to bed with one of those bloodsuckers."

I felt my brows lift. "Excuse me?"

It didn't surprise me in the least when Janice March rose to her feet from her place with the elders. "You are blatantly violating coven edicts. Just because you are the High Priestess doesn't mean you can do whatever you want."

I reminded myself to breathe rather than imagining her bursting into flames where she stood. In my current emotional state, it was a dangerous image to consider. It was also tempting.

"I agree that, as High Priestess, I should not expect to break coven law with impunity. However, I know many of the witches here agree that several of our laws and rules are outdated and need to be changed. If we establish a relationship with the vampires and werewolves, I don't see how my choice in mates would matter."

The room fell completely silent. I couldn't even hear anyone breathe. Then I realized what I said and felt my heart start pounding. My eyes flew to where Finn was standing at the back of the room. He was leaning back against the rear wall, a small, satisfied smile on his face. Well, at least he didn't look like he wanted to run away.

Murmurs began at the back of the room, moving forward, bringing my attention away from Finn. Conner, Gabriel, and Lex were entering the room with Chloe.

"You dare bring them into our sanctuary!" Sharon screeched.

I lifted my hands and the room began to calm except for Sharon, Beatrice, and Janice. Though I expected Constance to be outraged, she looked confused rather than angry.

"Please quiet down for a moment," I requested. "I think you'll find the terms that Conner and the MacIntire pack have offered to be fair and unobtrusive."

Finally, even the elders stopped yammering as the vampires and werewolf made their way up the center aisle to the table where I stood.

"This is Conner Savage, one of the Council members. All I ask is that you listen to what he has to say and carefully consider his words. Most of you know how Belinda felt about healing the rifts between our communities, but I'm sharing with you my feelings as well. It is time to put aside all the anger and frustration of the past centuries and work together. Even though Belinda and I had the support and protection of the vampires and wolves yesterday, our High Priestess was lost. If we, as a coven, remain separate, I fear we won't be able to protect ourselves from whatever plans the Faction has for us."

For a moment, I thought I had gotten through to them. Most of the younger coven members were nodding in agreement as I spoke, but, as soon as I shut my mouth, the elders and several of the older witches began shouting objections as one.

I stared at them and wondered if I could generate enough power to cast a spell that would make them all shut up for a few minutes. Or maybe even for a month or two.

I sighed and met Finn's eyes. He looked as exasperated as I felt, but also amused. Unfortunately, because so many people were speaking at once, there was no way for him to use the truth amulet I'd given him. In regards to finding the traitor, this meeting was a waste. Maybe, at the very least, I could get a majority vote from the coven agreeing to an alliance with the vampires and shape shifters.

I pushed up my mental sleeves and waded in.

Chapter Twenty-Five

“I'M SO GLAD I'm a werewolf,” Chloe stated as she drank from her beer. “None of that, let's take a vote shit. As beta or alpha, I tell them what's going to happen and, if I'm feeling generous, I might listen to their politely worded concerns. If some pup threw a tantrum the way that Sharon woman did today, he would have needed a trip to the infirmary and a few days to recover.”

I snorted, staring into my own glass of wine. “Goddess, if only it were that easy. I can imagine the response if I tried to implement that kind of leadership. It would turn into a bloodbath.”

After my introduction of Conner, the meeting had gone downhill quickly. Finally, it had been Sally Abrams who forced the vote over the elders' strident disagreement.

“My sister died at the hands of the Faction, or have the elders forgotten that?” she asked, her eyes glittering with anger and unshed tears. “You stand there and argue about coven laws that are five hundred years old rather than listen to someone who could help us. Our fallen High Priestess is dead and you carry on these petty, small-minded arguments because you don't like her choice of successor. What's more important to you? The rules or the members of this coven?” She paused, her chest heaving with each breath. “If your answer lies with laws and tradition, perhaps you should consider stepping down from your position. Elders are supposed to be advocates for the other members of the coven."

It was then that the elders fell silent. They had to. If they continued to argue, they looked exactly like the catty women they were. Conner spoke for ten minutes and answered questions for another thirty. Chloe chimed in with what she could, explaining that the alpha of the MacIntire pack had been severely injured while protecting Belinda. That alone probably earned enough votes from the coven for a majority agreement to an alliance with the vampires and werewolves.

Finally, forty-five minutes after the uproar, it was put to a vote. Of the ninety-three remaining members of the coven, only fifteen voted against the proposed changes. Unexpectedly, several elders voted for the changes rather than against.

After the vote, plans for Belinda's funeral rites were made. The coven had a private cemetery on my mother's land in Farmersville and we would have to bury her tomorrow as Wiccan rites usually didn't include embalming or any type of preservation. During the ritual, her body would be wrapped in fabric, buried, and returned to the earth as soon as nature allowed.

Two hours after it began, the meeting adjourned. Though I was upset that I hadn't been able to seek out the witch who'd turned against us, I was relieved that I would no longer have to fight the coven over a relationship with vampires and werewolves. The younger witches seemed very open-minded. Though the older witches disliked the idea, I figured I'd only have to listen to their bitching for ten, twenty years max, before they croaked.

"Kerry, are you okay?" Chloe asked, breaking me out of my memories of the meeting that morning.

"Yeah, I'm fine," I mumbled before draining my wineglass. "It's late and I think I'm going to head up to bed."

She nodded, sipping her beer. When I was almost to the door, her words stopped me. "You did well today. Belinda would have been extremely proud."

I felt my eyes burn. "Thank you," I whispered. Then I left the room before I cried. I'd done enough crying the last few weeks to last a lifetime.

Conner insisted that Finn and I stay at the house he shared with Donna. Strength in numbers, he said. Considering how often he had guests, I was beginning to wonder if he just used any excuse to have company. I went up the sweeping staircase in the front of the house and walked down the hall to the room where Ricki was resting.

Late that afternoon, Calder awoke, hungry and thirsty. Ricki came to not long after that, still disoriented and weak, but surprisingly well. I expected her to begin the transition in the next day or so. Calder must have agreed with me because he asked Conner if they could move down to the basement later that night. Calder was downstairs right now, preparing the apartment.

I knocked and stuck my head into Ricki's room. She was sitting in bed, leaning back on a stack of pillows, her hair damp from the bath she'd insisted on taking. Though I'm sure it was painful and difficult, I couldn't blame her. Dried blood was not exactly comfortable on the skin.

"Hey."

Her head came up at my greeting. "Oh thank God, a real, live person that isn't going to treat me like a complete invalid."

I grinned. "Calder driving you nuts?"

"Yes! And Donna. And Chloe." She paused, running her finger over the embroidery on the duvet cover. "Donna told me what you did for me. I don't remember much except you asking me if I wanted Calder or Conner to change me."

I walked over to the bed and sat down, my hip next to her. "Can I ask you why you chose Calder?"

She didn't answer at first and I felt my stomach start to sink, worried that she was regretting her choice. "I'm not sure what you said to Calder that day at Finn's house, but he was...different after that. He stopped being so bossy. Then he started doing all these nice things for me. He brought me my favorite ice cream and talked about how beautiful he thought I was. It was wonderful. Then, the night before the attack, he told me that I was the only woman he would ever be able to love, that I was his mate. I lost my mind. I mean, you know how many times my father said the same thing to my mom. Then she would take him back and everything would be great until a few months later when he cheated again. I told him he was full of shit and to leave me alone." She swallowed and a tear trickled down her face. "I was so horrible to him, Kerry, but he gave me a couple of hours to cool down and found me. He, he explained about wolves and how they mate for life, unless their other half dies. He also told me that not every wolf gets a second chance."

She blinked rapidly and I could tell she was trying to keep from breaking down. I took one of her hands and laced our fingers together.

"He actually dropped to his knees and begged me to give him a chance, just a chance, to prove that what he said was true."

I felt my eyes widen. Werewolves didn't beg unless they were weak, and, as the beta of the MacIntire pack, Calder was anything but weak.

"Right?" Ricki asked. "I told him to give me a day to think about it. We were outside in the back yard and he left me there. Chloe must have been listening because she sat down next to me and told me that I would be a fool to turn him away again. Then she told me more about how the pack works. She said that she's never seen a male wolf beg a female the way Calder begged me. I planned to tell him that I would try the night we were attacked."

I stroked Ricki's hair as she wiped away a couple of stray tears. "So you don't regret it?"

She shook her head. "No, I don't."

I squeezed her hand. "Good. Now, has Calder explained to you what happens next?" I asked.

She nodded. "He said it might be painful at first, but he would help me every step of the way."

"That's great. I think Finn has some books on medicinal herbs for werewolves, I'm sure there is something in there about how to ease a new wolf's first change. I'll help Calder make it as comfortable for you as possible."

"Thank you," Ricki sighed, her head falling back as exhaustion overtook her. She blinked and lifted her head, which swayed. "I'm sorry. I'm just so tired."

"It's the changes happening in your body and all the healing," I answered. "You sleep. We'll talk in a few days when you're feeling better."

"Okay," she whispered, her voice barely audible.

I watched her eyes drift shut and released her hand. Satisfied that she would be okay, I left her room and walked down the hall to the room Finn and I would be sharing. It was empty.

Unsure if I was relieved or frustrated by Finn's absence, I walked into the bathroom and turned on the taps to the huge tub. I poured in some bath salts and lavender oil. Last night and today had taken their toll on me and a long, hot bath sounded perfect.

After I stripped out of my clothes and pulled my hair into a messy knot on top of my head, I slid into the hot water, hissing at the temperature. Then I collapsed against the back of the tub, let the heat soak away the tension in my sore muscles, and tried not to think about the fact that this was just the first in many hard days to come.

A whisper of sound caught my attention, then I smelled him. I opened my eyes to find Finn sitting on the edge of the tub, fully dressed.

"Is it helping?" he asked quietly.

"It sure as hell doesn't hurt," I responded.

He flicked a little water at me and I grunted.

"Yes, it is helping a little." I smiled at him. "Care to join me? That might help a lot more."

Finn reached out and ran his fingers along my cheekbone. "Whatever you need."

When he cupped my cheek, I put my hand over the back of his and leaned into the touch.

"I need you." And I did. I needed him to hold me, to touch me, and to help me forget the loss and fear that dogged my steps today.

Finn stood and removed his clothes quickly. I sat up in the water so he could slide in behind me. Once he settled into the water, I leaned back and let my back rest against his chest, my head on his shoulder. He twined our fingers together and wrapped his arms around me, bringing mine with them. I sighed and let the undemanding embrace soothe my frayed nerves.

After several long minutes, Finn released my hands and reached for the wash cloth I'd left on the edge of the tub. He lathered it up with soap and began to wash my body. As the cloth brushed over my nipples, I felt the first stirrings of desire. His other hand followed, smoothing the soap over my skin, the slick sensation contrasting deliciously with the texture of the cloth.

He leaned forward, raising me to a seated position and lifted my leg so that my heel rested on the edge of the tub. Slowly, he moved the cloth over my calf, past my knee, and up my thigh.

Then he lowered it back into the water and repeated the process with my other leg. Only this time, the cloth didn't stop on my upper thigh. He gently rubbed the cloth over my pussy before slipping his other soapy hand down to clean me more thoroughly.

Though his touch was light and almost clinical, I felt my blood stirring. His hands felt so good on my skin. When his fingertip brushed my clit, I couldn't control the small motion of my hips, the impulse to lift my body so he touched me fully.

"What do you need from me, Kerry?" he asked, his voice sounding slightly strained.

"I need you to touch me." I didn't hesitate because my words were absolutely true. The feeling overwhelming me wasn't passion, it was uncontrollable and as necessary as my next breath.

Once again, his finger drifted over me, grazing over the places that needed more intense attention. "Like this?"

I shook my head. "No. More."

"Tell me," he whispered, nudging my head to the side so he could gently bite my neck without breaking the skin.

"Make me come," I demanded, my voice ragged. "Please."

He rewarded my words by pressing two fingers firmly against my clit and rubbing in sure, strong circles. His other hand tugged at my nipples. Though it hurt a little, the pain transformed into pleasure almost immediately. Somehow, he knew exactly how to touch me to keep me balanced on the edge of bliss and agony, never going too far. I lifted my hips into his hand, grinding my lower back against the hard ridge of his cock.

Finn's mouth latched onto my neck, nipping and sucking without drawing blood. His lips lifted to brush my ear. "I want you to come for me, Kerry."

When the first wave of the climax washed through me, I gasped. My body arched and I moaned as Finn continued his steady, firm strokes over my clit. Just as the pleasure waned, edging toward pain, he slowed his rhythm, bringing me down a little at a time.

As the last shudder wracked my body, I tilted my face back toward him, wrapping an arm around his neck to pull Finn's mouth to mine. Though his hand left my clit, he still toyed with my breasts, cupping and stroking the flesh, rubbing his palms over my nipples.

Despite my orgasm, arousal still hummed beneath my skin. Without breaking the kiss, I turned, getting to my knees, then straddled his lap. Finn grabbed my hips, fitting my body into his. I rocked against his erection, humming in my throat as my clit slid over his silky skin. Slowly, I began to sink down on the hard length of his cock.

When he filled me completely, I took a moment to revel in the sensation. This wasn't going to be a race to orgasm, or a wild ride. I needed the connection of not only our bodies, but our hearts. I ended the kiss and looked down into his eyes, running my fingers through his hair.

Finn pressed his lips to my throat. "I love you, Kerry."

At his words, my eyes closed and I was swamped with emotion. Though our connection, the thing that made us *soul mates*, intimated love, he'd never said the words to me before.

"I love you too," I whispered into his hair.

Finn wrapped his arms around my waist, holding me close for a moment longer, before he lowered his head, laying small kisses along my chest until his lips rested over my heart.

His hands drifted down to my hips, urging me to move, and I began to rock slowly against him. Our movements were unhurried and sensual. Finn's mouth closed around one of my nipples, the tips of his fangs pressing against my skin as he sucked.

I took him deep and circled my hips, my legs going so weak I could barely move. As I gradually climbed toward the peak, Finn bit the inner curve of my breast, his fangs breaking the skin. I gasped as the orgasm overtook my body. As he drank, he held my hips against his, using his thumb to press and roll my clit while I shuddered against him. A moment later, I felt his body grow rigid and his breathing sounded slightly labored. I squeezed him with my internal muscles, wanting to prolong his pleasure as he had mine.

The last tremor of release left me and my body curved over Finn's head, my limbs feeling too heavy to hold me up any longer. Though it hadn't been as forceful as our usual lovemaking, there was a new intensity, something more profound than just shared pleasure.

I shivered as Finn's tongue slid over the bite on my breast, helping the wounds to heal.

The last of my worries and fears about my relationship with Finn vanished under the tenderness that filled my heart. Whatever happened in the coming weeks and months or even years, it would be easier to handle with him by my side.

Chapter Twenty-Six

OVERNIGHT, THE TEMPERATURE plummeted. The cloudy, gray sky and bitter cold wind suited my mood and the air held the promise of icy rain, maybe even a light snow. The trees had finally lost the last of their leaves, so bare branches danced in the wind.

As Finn and I drove away from the coven cemetery, the gray sky and brown grass of the countryside looked as barren and lost as my heart. I felt almost adrift, with only Finn's hand in mine to keep me anchored. I allowed myself the luxury of feeling sorrow and rage while I was with him. In front of my coven, I'd had to be strong and sure, but, here in the car with him, I didn't have to put on a show.

Belinda's burial ritual had been one of the most difficult experiences of my life. Only the death of first my father, then my mother, could surpass the emotional upheaval I felt. The entire coven turned out for the burial rite.

As High Priestess, it was my responsibility to begin the ritual by calling the Four Corners and the elements they represented. North and the ancient earth, East and the icy air, South and the fire that burned, and West, which represented water. As soon as I completed the call, a soft rain began to fall, warmer than I expected considering the temperature of the air around us. It felt as though the Goddess herself were crying hot tears for the loss of one of her daughters.

We performed the chants and wrapped her body in white fabric. Once the ritual was completed, the elders that were strong enough, along with a couple of other witches, lowered her body into the grave. Every witch in the coven walked to the side of the grave and replaced one shovel full of dirt. I wasn't even sure where the custom originated from, since it wasn't in any of the funeral rites I'd read about, but it felt like the closing of a circle.

After the earth that had been displaced was returned, we chanted one more incantation and the rite was complete. I spoke to every witch in the coven, one at a time, until only the elders remained. With the exception of Janice, they all acknowledged me with either words or a touch of their hand. They were also mindful not to mention the vote that had taken place at the meeting yesterday.

Janice, it seemed, didn't get the memo about appropriate funeral behavior, because she approached me as soon as the other elders departed.

"We need to talk." Her voice was tense and slightly shrill.

I tried not to wince. "About?"

"What happened in the meeting yesterday. I don't think you know what you've done."

We had been standing in the rain for over an hour, which was rapidly turning from warm to freezing drizzle, and I was tired down to my bones. I didn't have the energy for another argument.

"Janice, if you are unhappy about what was decided yesterday, draft a formal complaint and present it at the next meeting as stated in coven law. I didn't make that decision alone. Your fellow witches had something to do with it as well."

She appeared even more agitated, grabbing my arm and squeezing so hard, I yelped.

"You don't understand, Kerry,"

Suddenly, a large angry vampire wedged his body between us. "I'll thank you to take your hand off your High Priestess." Finn enunciated each word slowly and clearly, his tone razor sharp. "Whatever grievances you have can be dealt with tomorrow. Right now, Kerry needs to get warm and dry before she becomes ill."

He didn't even wait for her response before turning and wrapping his arm around me, steering me quickly toward the car. I glanced over my shoulder as I climbed into the passenger seat and saw Janice standing in the place I'd left her, her hands crossed at her waist to cup her elbows. She looked upset and frightened rather than scornful.

I decided I would call her later that night.

It would be far too late when I discovered that I made the wrong choice when I turned my back on her.

✧　　✧　　✧

THOUGH I'D TAKEN a bath the night before with Finn, I desperately needed a hot shower when we returned to Conner's. Even with the car heater on full blast during the hour long drive back, I was still shivering from the cold.

Finn urged me to go upstairs and get out of my wet clothes while he went into the kitchen to make me some chamomile tea. I felt no urge whatsoever to argue and dragged myself up the stairs to the guest room. After kicking off my shoes, I stripped off my coat, sweater, and slacks, leaving them wherever they landed. My undergarments hit the bathroom floor on my way to the big, glass-walled shower. I reached inside and turned the water on hot. While I waited for the water to warm up to the scalding temperature I desired, I took my hair out of the knot I'd twisted it into and combed the unruly mass. The damp weather had turned it into a frizzy explosion.

I hissed when I stepped into the shower and the hot water hit my chilled skin. Gradually, I adjusted to the temperature and sighed in pleasure as the heat seeped down into my skin and bones. I let my head fall back so that my hair was soaked before briskly rubbing shampoo into my scalp. By the time I'd rinsed out the lather and conditioned the strands, I finally felt warm.

Though it was tempting to stand beneath the shower for the rest of the day, stretching out in the comfy bed in the next room was an even more enticing picture. Unfortunately, I had too much to do, so sleep would have to wait. I used a bath pouf to soap up my skin and quickly washed it off.

When I turned off the water and opened the shower door, I saw Finn standing on the other side, a steaming mug in one hand and a huge towel in the other. Smiling, I took the towel from him and briskly dried off my skin before wrapping the damp material around me.

I sipped the tea, humming at the perfect balance of herbs and honey that warmed my throat and belly. "Hmmm. This is exactly what I needed," I told Finn.

He leaned over and kissed my forehead. "What's next?"

"A nap," I joked.

"You should sleep for a bit," he agreed.

I chuckled and shook my head, sipping my tea again. "I would love to, but there are things we must do."

"Nothing that can't wait a couple of hours. Dry your hair and get some rest."

My limbs felt heavy from exhaustion, my body in vehement agreement with his suggestion. "Okay."

Finn smiled and took the mug from my hand. "I'll put this on the night stand for you to finish before you sleep. Go dry your hair before you get sick."

After ten minutes of using the blow dryer, I decided enough was enough. My hair was still slightly damp, but I could barely keep my eyes open. When I wandered into the bedroom, I saw that Finn had laid out a warm pair of pajamas and underwear for me, though he was no longer there. I dropped my towel on the bench at the end of the bed, dressed, and climbed into bed, pulling the covers up to my chin.

I spied the cup sitting on the side table and drained the last bit of warm liquid. Lassitude and peace washed over me and I felt the prick of concern. Though I'd been tired before, this felt different. Suspicious, I lifted the cup to my nose and sniffed.

Valerian, chamomile, and something else. That sneaky vampire has slipped potion into my tea to help me sleep. The cup clattered on the night stand as I tried to set it down so I could get back out of bed.

Finn appeared above me, taking the mug before it fell to the floor.

"You..." I couldn't seem to find the insulting word I wanted to use, so I settled on, "jerk. You drugged me."

He smoothed my hair away from my face. "You need rest, Kerry. Even you have to admit that the last month has worn you down. It won't last long."

Somehow I found the strength to keep my eyes open. "It's wrong. You can't just go around slipping me potions and herbs when you think I need them."

Finn smirked. "Well, if you weren't so damned stubborn, I wouldn't have to."

I sighed as another wave of lethargy washed over me. "Maybe you're right." When I realized what I'd said, my eyes opened wide and I struggled to focus on him. "Wait, that's not what I meant. Dammit, Finn, I can't think straight." I blinked to clear my vision. "Just know, when I wake up, your ass is mine," I mumbled.

He touched my nose with the tip of his finger. "I look forward to that. Does that mean I should schedule a Claiming ceremony?"

"What?" I had no earthly idea what he was talking about.

"Well, if you want to put your stamp on my ass, I should be able to do the same to yours."

"Huh?"

Finn chuckled at my confusion. "We'll talk about the Claiming ceremony when you wake up too."

"Wait, Claiming? No, no, no. Not…"

I fell asleep before I finished my sentence, blind to the hurt and anger on Finn's face in my stupor.

Chapter Twenty-Seven

SOMETIME LATER, I awoke with a gasp and sat straight up in the bed. It took a few moments for my head to clear and memories of my conversation with Finn to return. A quick glance at the clock showed me I'd slept for nearly three hours.

Throwing back the duvet, I marched into the closet and dressed in jeans and a sweatshirt, tucking my phone in my pocket. My head felt surprisingly clear and my body no longer felt as though it weighed more than I could carry. Still, a certain pushy vampire and I needed to have a conversation about boundaries. Right. Fucking. Now.

I checked the living room, Conner's study, and the kitchen and still no Finn. The irritation I felt upon waking was rapidly morphing into me losing my shit. Finally, I found him in the library upstairs, only a few feet down the hall from the room I'd woken up in.

He was stretched out on one of the sofas, one leg straight out and the other bent so his foot touched the floor. An open book rested on his chest and his eyes were closed. In repose, I could see the dark circles beneath his closed lids and the slight pallor of his skin. Just like that, all the anger washed out of me. Looking at him, I wanted him to continue sleeping because he so obviously needed it and I understood why he'd done what he had. That didn't mean we wouldn't be discussing boundaries, but it definitely wouldn't be now.

I took a step back from the couch, intent on sneaking away so he could finish his nap, but Finn's hand lashed out and wrapped around my wrist. I jerked and made a sound that was half scream, half squeak. He turned over on his side and pulled me down to sit beside him.

"Are you going to lecture me now?" he asked, his voice husky with sleep.

I shook my head and brushed his hair away from his eyes.

"Why not?"

"Because I would have done the same thing to you if I had taken a moment to look away from my own problems and notice how exhausted you are." I smiled when he chuckled. "That doesn't mean we won't have a talk about it later. That's not how you treat your mate, even if she is a stubborn, pain in the ass witch."

Finn's body tensed beside me and I suddenly felt uncertain about my words.

"Am I?" he asked. His eyes were serious and slightly sad.

Confused, I responded, "Are you what?"

"Your mate."

I frowned, disliking how off balance this conversation felt. "You said, I mean, I thought that you wanted that. Did I misunderstand?"

He shook his head. "No, but I'm wondering if you did."

"I don't understand."

Finn shifted, sitting up so we were eye to eye. "I want to Claim you, Kerry."

"I want that too," I responded. "Though I think we should wait a few months, maybe even a year before we have the ceremony. It will be a difficult transition for the coven to accept you as my mate, more so if you Claim me."

Suddenly, Finn moved and I was in his lap and he was kissing me fiercely.

When he finally released my mouth, I whispered, "What was that all about?"

He laughed, but it didn't sound as though he found anything truly funny, and rested his forehead against mine. "Earlier, before you fell asleep, you were quite insistent that you wouldn't be my Claimed."

I rolled my eyes. "See, this is one of the reasons why you don't drug your woman. I wasn't saying no to the ceremony, just no to doing it *immediately*. Now that I'm the High Priestess, I have to weigh all my actions carefully, especially with the prejudices and fears the other witches have toward vampires and werewolves."

"I understand," he answered.

He tilted his head so that our lips met. The kiss was gentle, sweet, and expressed several emotions, all of them achingly beautiful.

Dimly, I heard the doorbell, but ignored it. After a few seconds, Finn withdrew and sighed.

"We need to go downstairs," he muttered.

I leaned forward, wanting to continue where we left off. "Why? I'm sure it's for Conner or Donna."

His mouth tightened. "No, it's not. The visitor is here to see you."

I cursed and Finn helped me stand. We walked down the hall to the stairs. I glanced over the railing and saw Sharon Greene standing in the foyer, staring defiantly up at Conner.

"I need to see her now," she insisted stridently.

"Then you should have called her. It's been a difficult day for her and she's resting," Conner responded firmly.

"You have no right to prevent me from seeing her. As the High Priestess, it's her duty to see me."

I rolled my eyes and started down the stairs. She noticed my approach and smiled smugly at Conner.

Keeping my face impassive when I reached the last step, I stated, "I may be the High Priestess, but I don't recall seeing anything in coven edicts requiring me to accept an audience with an elder any time they wished."

Her eyes narrowed and sparkled with malice as her face flushed red. She scowled at Conner when he coughed, probably to cover a laugh. Then, her gaze returned to me. "I wouldn't be here if it wasn't of dire importance."

"Fine. Conner, may we use your study?" I asked.

"Feel free," he answered. "Should I have Donna bring in some coffee?"

Other than the fact that Donna would probably break the coffee pot over his head for making such an offer without talking to her first, I didn't particularly want Sharon to stick around long enough to drink a beverage of any kind.

"No, thank you. We'll be keeping this visit short. I know there are many things to be decided today." I turned toward the short hall that led from the foyer to the study. "Sharon, if you would follow me."

She stopped short when Finn fell in step behind us. "I refuse to have this conversation with *him* in the room."

I glanced over my shoulder, arching my brows. "*Him?* You mean Finn?"

Sharon's eyes moved nervously over to my mate but she nodded. "Though the coven may have agreed to an alliance with the vampires, there are certain things in our group that should remain private," she answered stiffly.

She had a point so I nodded at Finn. "It's okay. We'll only be a few minutes."

He didn't look pleased but I widened my eyes, giving him a pointed stare. Not five minutes ago we'd been discussing my responsibilities as High Priestess and he was already resisting that boundary.

Finally, he grunted. "I'll be in the kitchen with Conner." Then he walked away.

Sharon watched him go and seemed to relax in relief when he was out of sight. She turned back to me. "Thank you."

That was probably the first time the woman had thanked me for anything. I shrugged, leading her into the study. "You should try to get used to being around vampires. With all the changes in the coven, the witches will be interacting with them more and more."

She didn't answer, merely came into the room and shut the door behind her.

Deciding to leave that argument for another day, I moved to the sofa on one side of the room and sat. I gestured to the seat beside me.

Sharon settled beside me, her expression revealing a mixture of emotions; fear, anger, resignation, all tinged with excitement. It put me on edge.

"What can I do for you?" I asked, folding my hands in my lap and crossing my ankles in a very lady like pose. Two days on the job, and I was already emulating Belinda's mannerisms. Though she would have at least offered a guest some water, so maybe I wasn't quite as well-mannered.

Sharon put her hands over mine, her face melting into an earnest expression. "I'm begging you to reconsider this alliance with the Council and the MacIntire pack. There are reasons that witches stopped interacting with them all those centuries ago. Now is not the time to make these changes."

I tried to slide my hands away from hers, but her grip was painfully tight. I spoke in a low voice, hoping to talk her down from
this ledge she seemed to be on. "Sharon, you know I can't do that.
It's time for the entire supernatural community to move into the
new millennium. The Council and the pack agree with that
assessment. They are willing to compromise in order for this to
work. We have to be as well."

Her face tightened, a malicious gleam filling her eyes. "I knew
you would say that," she mumbled.

I felt a shaft of fear, wondering not for the first time if Sharon
intended to do me harm in order to have her way. I opened my
mouth to cast and tried to yank my hands free, but she seemed to
have bone-crushing strength in her hands.

I cried out in pain as I felt something in my wrist give way.

Sharon grinned maniacally, reaching into her coat pocket and
pulling out a small potion bottle. Just as the study door flew open
to reveal Finn and Conner, she smashed the bottle to the ground,
the rancid scent of herbs and rot filling the air. She shouted an
invocation and I watched in horror as the room began spin and
fade.

Then there was nothing but blackness encasing me. The suffo-
cating darkness seemed to last for minutes rather than a few
seconds before a room began to form around us. My heart
stopped beating when I recognized it from the dream I'd had just
two nights ago.

I heard a door open to my right and turned my head. Dante
stood there, dressed in a black shirt and slacks. He looked cold and
dangerous, like a snake coiled prepared to strike.

"Hello, darling," he crooned. "I'm so glad to see you made it
safely."

Before I could say the spell on the tip of my tongue, Sharon
threw a handful of something in my face, using a one-word

invocation. My entire body locked. I couldn't speak or move. I could breathe and felt my heart beating hard and fast behind my ribs. Then I realized what she had done and was torn between the intense desire to scream and laugh simultaneously.

The powdery substance coating my burning eyes was graveyard dirt mixed with something else. I couldn't even blink away the sting. The traitorous bitch had cast a binding spell on me.

My eyes cut to the side, where Sharon hovered in my peripheral vision, a smug smile on her face. Though I'd never killed anyone except in self-defense, I decided in that moment that I would be the one to end her. In coven law, the punishment for treason was death, though the entire coven usually gathered together to brew the poison that the convicted would drink. Death was quick and painless.

Looking at her, knowing that she was the reason Belinda was dead, death by poison sounded too easy. Burning at the stake seemed a great deal more appropriate.

Under my unblinking stare, Sharon's smile began to fade and Dante laughed. The sound froze the blood in my veins. It was actually quite beautiful to hear, deep and rich, but completely empty, devoid of any sort of true amusement or enjoyment.

"I'd say your days are numbered, witch," he said gleefully. "I can feel her hatred from across the room. Having seen her in action, it almost makes me sad to do this."

My eyes wheeled in their sockets, focusing on him instead of Sharon. In a motion so quick that I couldn't register more than a blur, Dante lunged across the room and plunged a dagger in her heart.

I tried to feel pity when her head lolled, our gazes meeting. As I watched the light fade from her eyes, I only felt satisfaction and it scared the shit out of me.

Chapter Twenty-Eight

FTER KILLING SHARON, Dante carried her body from the room. I strained against the binding spell, hoping that Sharon's death would have weakened it but it was futile.

A few minutes later, the vampire warlock returned to the room, carrying a wet cloth in one hand and a towel in the other. Every cell in my body wanted to quail as he approached me, but the spell held me fast.

Unexpectedly gentle, he wiped the dirt away from my eyes with the damp cloth and then produced a bottle of eye wash from his pocket. Holding the towel beneath my eyes, he washed the fine grains of dirt from my eyes with the solution, then blotted them dry. I still had dirt on the rest of my face and in my mouth, but I knew he wouldn't clean it off. There was something in this graveyard dirt that made the binding especially strong.

Dante never spoke a single word as he tended to me. When he was satisfied with his ministrations, he laid the towel, cloth, and eye wash on the table by the chair he sat in during my dream. Stepping back, he lifted a finger to his chin, tapping it as he studied me.

I despised feeling like a sculpture left out for his approval. Bound as I was, there was little I could do to save myself. I felt the hard lump of my cell phone vibrate once in my pocket and felt a surge of hope. Conner and Finn could trace my location using my cell. Hopefully, that would be the first thing they would do. As long as Dante hadn't heard the subtle sound of my phone shuddering in my pocket.

"So much strength contained in such a meek looking package," he murmured. "Yet, here you are, bound completely before me."

His taunt pierced my chest, making me forget all about the pain in my wrist, as well as my possible rescue, and released the rage in my heart. It flowed like hot lava through my veins, bringing with it the darkest sort of power. He turned away and I blinked at his back.

Then I realized I *blinked*. Just minutes ago my eyes felt as though they were frozen open and now I could control my lids. Perhaps I had a way to counteract the spell holding me in place.

Quickly, I fixed my eyes open when Dante turned back toward me.

"The Slayer has been waiting for his opportunity to speak to you. He thinks perhaps I was too....insistent with my last proposal." He must have sensed my confusion since I couldn't change the expression on my face. "My master is the Slayer."

It was probably a good thing I couldn't move or speak because I really wanted to snort. His *master's* name was Cornelius. I'm not sure how he obtained the name of The Slayer, but it was likely a moniker he'd chosen himself, just like the cocky guys in high school.

The door opened once again, and one of the most beautiful men I'd ever seen entered the room, and that was saying something since every vampire on the Council could be a GQ model. I caught myself before I could blink in shock.

Unlike Finn, his beauty was ethereal, almost androgynous. He looked like an angel, with short platinum hair clipped close to his head and incredibly bright blue eyes. They were a shade darker than Conner's, but no less arresting. His brows were perfectly arched and, like his eyelashes, a few shades darker than his hair. His face was narrow but made striking by his high cheekbones, slightly hollow cheeks, and sensuously curved mouth. He had the type of face that would have been beautiful to behold no matter his gender.

He smiled serenely at me as he came abreast of Dante. When he looked away, I felt as though I'd been holding my breath for a long time and had just taken a full one. Without his appearance and the weight of his gaze to distract me, I could sense something different in him. He was a vampire, but he was also more. His very essence seemed to expand around him and it felt ancient and powerful.

Cornelius looked at me again, his ocean blue eyes snaring me, pulling me in. They seemed to offer me anything and everything I could ever want. All he needed in return was my undying devotion, my very soul.

As he came closer, I fell deeper into his thrall. Warmth and contentment rose within me and I would gladly give him anything he demanded to continue to bathe in the peace he offered.

Cornelius lifted a hand and stroked my cheek. "Such a pretty little witch," he murmured. "I'm glad you finally came to see me."

It was his attempt to gloss over what Sharon had done that helped me separate from his enchantment slightly. Though his words were welcoming, they didn't ring true.

I let myself slide along the leading edge of his power, testing it and tasting it, trying to figure out exactly what he was. Then I recognized him and fear crashed through me like a squall on the ocean, uncontrollable and shrieking.

I had underestimated my enemy. Cornelius had earned the title of The Slayer countless times over. He was the last of the soul eaters.

The soul eater was cursed to devour the souls of others in order to continue their eternal existence. They were extremely difficult to create and most had died out centuries ago. They were the one supernatural entity, other than demons, that preyed on humans, vampires, werewolves, and witches alike.

The Slayer's smile was angelic. "You know what I am now, do you not?" he asked.

I couldn't respond because of the binding spell, but he seemed to intuit my response.

"Do you fear me, little witch?" he asked, leaning forward so our cheeks brushed and his lips were beside my ear. "You should."

The fear that cascaded through me waned slightly. I realized that he needed me for some reason. If he didn't, he would have just killed me. If the Faction knew about the prophecy, than taking any one of us out of the equation would be all it took to turn the tide their way.

The knowledge calmed me somewhat. I was still wary of him, but knew that my death wasn't in the immediate future. I cautiously drew at my power, pushing at the spell that bound me. My toes flexed slightly within my shoes.

Cornelius turned and spoke to Dante. "I would like to hear what she has to say when I ask her questions."

The warlock nodded. He spoke a few words and my head was suddenly free of the invisible vise holding it still.

"Tell me, Kerry, what do you know of your father?"

I forced down the angry response that crawled up my throat. I still hadn't regained complete control of my body and I didn't want to antagonize him until I could protect myself. "Not much. He died when I was eight."

Cornelius tilted his head, his eyes earnest. "How did he die?"

If this asshole wanted to torture me, he was doing a good job. I never talked about my dad or his death. I hadn't even brought it up with Finn. It was too painful and a strong reminder that I had both good and evil sharing space within my body and soul.

"He died when a spell went awry."

Cornelius clucked his tongue at me. "Now, now, I think you're omitting some very important details. I mean, one doesn't usually die performing a typical spell, do they?"

I shook my head. I felt my pinkie twitch as I subconsciously fought the hold the spell had on me. All I had to do was talk about the darkest day of my life for a little longer until I was free.

"So, how did he die?" he asked again. "Tell me the truth this time."

I took a deep breath and released it slowly, anger, regret, and resentment swirling inside me. It wasn't directed completely at Cornelius. No, a great deal of it was reserved for my father. "He was casting a black spell. It was meant to kill me."

The Slayer lifted his hand again, touching my cheek. I had to forcibly control my flinch.

"Are you sure?" he asked, his voice full of understanding and sympathy.

This was what made soul eaters so dangerous. Even knowing that they would devour you from the inside out, you wanted their attention, their comfort, their love. You went willingly into the jaws of death.

I didn't answer.

Cornelius looked over his shoulder at Dante. "You were there, were you not?"

My eyes flew to the warlock in surprise. I didn't remember him. My memory of that night was muddled due to the trauma of watching my father seizing in agony as his body tried to fold upon itself. He nodded.

"Tell Kerry what happened," The Slayer insisted.

Dante came forward, his stare never wavering from mine. "He was casting a spell to siphon off your power, not kill you. But you were frightened and crying. He changed his mind. He didn't want to hurt you or traumatize you so he tried to call back the spell but the power had to go somewhere. Your father knew that, but he did it anyway. For you."

On the edges of my mind, the memory floated by, my father looking at me with apologetic eyes, my sobs, and then his final words to me, "I'm so sorry, Kerbear."

I felt tears fill my eyes. After the events of the last two days, I could no longer hold back the grief inside me. Even though I knew he was toying with me, I couldn't contain the sadness.

"Why are you telling me this?" I asked. "To hurt me?"

"Ah, no, dearest. Never to hurt you," Cornelius whispered. "I want you to understand who your father truly was. He was a man that loved you."

His words were further proof that he was trying to manipulate me. Despite my anger toward my father, I'd always known that he loved me. While she was alive, my mother insisted that he'd taken the wrong path and made mistakes but he had never, ever stopped loving me.

Believing that he was getting under my emotional armor, the soul eater moved in for the kill. "Black and white is a myth, Kerry. In our world, there are infinite shades of gray. Some dark, some light, but never truly pure." When he saw that I was listening, he continued. "My people aren't evil. We want what you want; unity. However, with the world as it is today, the strong must be in control in order to maintain that harmony. A firm guiding hand is exactly what both the humans and the rest of the supernatural creatures need."

"Humans?" I asked.

He smiled. "Yes. Humans. Why should we hide what we truly are in fear that they will attempt to destroy us? Even with their weapons and numbers, we are superior. They are our food source and one does not invite a pig to eat at the dinner table. Especially not when ham is on the menu."

Somehow I managed to hide my disbelief. This guy was batshit crazy. Either that or he'd been hiding under a rock for the last hundred years. The humans might not wipe us out if we were discovered, but they damn well would corral us into 'testing facilities'. I'm sure the rest of my days would be spent in shapeless scrubs with daily injections and blood draws. No doubt, the U.S. government would see our value and attempt to replicate our strengths without any of the pesky side affects like turning furry once a month, drinking blood, or drawing down the moon.

"Why do you want me?" I asked, trying desperately to sound weak and vulnerable. It would be difficult to pull off the act, as I was accustomed to saying exactly what I thought.

"Do you honestly think the witches are the only side with a prophecy of their future? I have been waiting and preparing for you for centuries. It was foretold among the sin eaters that a witch of unimaginable power would rise, birthing a new era for our people. With each new generation of witches and vampires, I've selected those who will be most beneficial for the cause and groomed them. Twenty-five years ago, I thought that witch would be your father. Then you came into your power and I knew you were the one my people were waiting for." He pressed his lips to my forehead and I fought the urge to gag. "You will be the mother of the new soul eaters and our descendents will rule."

Dear Goddess, he took the prophecy literally. Had none of his advisors explained to him that prophecy must be deciphered? It was rarely as straightforward as that. Foretelling of the future was meant to bring enlightenment and prevent irreparable mistakes from being made. If they were basic instructions, then the profound understanding brought by the riddles in prophecy would be missed. One was supposed to reflect upon the words, look deeper than their superficial meaning.

I cleared my throat, still trying to sound timid. "What if I'm not the witch? I don't think I can be what you need or want."

Cornelius' eyes changed. They hardened into two chips of blue glass. "Then I suppose I'll have no use for you after all."

In other words, I would be a dead woman.

I closed my eyes and prayed to the Goddess that I would either escape my binding spell or Finn and Conner would arrive with the cavalry before it was too late.

When I finished, I lifted my lids and gazed levelly at the soul eater and warlock in front of me. "Tell me more."

Chapter Twenty-Nine

T MY WORDS, a satisfied grin spread across The Slayer's face, but Dante watched me with hooded, suspicious eyes. Neither of them gave any indication they would free the rest of my body from the spell, so I took that to mean that they still didn't trust me.

I waited for one of them to speak, cautiously pushing back at the binding spell, looking for weakness. It was difficult to maintain focus on the two vampires in front of me while using magic right beneath their noses.

Before Cornelius could continue, I cleared my throat. "Pardon me, but would it be possible for you to release me from the binding?"

He considered me momentarily. "I'm afraid that I can't, Kerry. I'm not entirely convinced that you are on our side."

I licked my lips. "Okay, I understand your concern, but I'm very uncomfortable and Sharon injured my wrist before we came here. Is there any way you can move me into a seated position?"

Though I could tell he wanted to say no, he wanted to convince me of his benevolence. Denying a simple request wouldn't exactly make him look like a good guy. The Slayer looked to Dante, who nodded slowly. "Very well," Cornelius sighed. "Dante would you please get Kerry a chair?"

The warlock did as he asked, walking around behind me to position the chair. I only hoped that my baggy sweatshirt covered the bulge of my phone in my back pocket.

Apparently, it did, because Dante recited the incantation and my body relaxed. I knew that they would be expecting me to make my move to escape in the next few seconds. Though I wanted to, I knew it would be suicide. Instead, I focused on the momentary weakness in the spell, poking and prodding with magic, stretching the parameters a bit.

The warlock pulled me down into the chair and my limbs became heavy again. I concentrated on moving my knee after he repeated the spell and it shifted slightly. I was gradually regaining control over my body, despite the binding.

My cell phone was a hard lump against my backside. I wanted to shift so that it wasn't digging into my flesh, but I couldn't. It would give me away.

I tilted my head back to look up at Cornelius. "Thank you."

He nodded.

Suddenly, Dante's head came up as though he heard a loud noise. If he did, he was the only one. My skin tingled as magic shimmered in the air and I realized what had happened. One of the warlock's protection wards had been broken. I felt the corners of my mouth twitch. Finn and Conner must have found me.

His head snapped around, his black eyes narrowing on me. "Where is it?" he asked.

I widened my eyes and tried to look innocent. "What?"

He snarled. "The charm, amulet, whatever they used to track you."

"I don't have anything like that." I knew he would believe it was the truth because, technically, I wasn't lying. I didn't have a charm or amulet to help them locate me. All I had was my cell phone. Perhaps if Dante thought more like a modern witch than an archaic one, he would have checked.

Cornelius glided toward the door. "You stay here with Kerry. I'll take care of our unexpected guests."

I tried to ignore the slimy fingers of fear that trailed down my spine. Finn wasn't weak or inexperienced and I knew he and Conner would have brought men. Cornelius left the room, silence in his wake.

I glanced at Dante, but he was staring at the wall, his eyes unfocused as though he were looking off into the distance. While he seemed distracted, I concentrated on flexing my power, trying to shrug off the spell. I squirmed in my seat, my limbs still heavy, but now under my control.

The floor shook slightly, bringing the warlock out of his trance. His dark eyes fixed on me. "You do realize that you can't win, don't you?"

"Pardon?"

He smiled coldly. "You may have fooled Cornelius for the moment, or at least given him the hope that you can be swayed, but I understand you better than you think, Kerry. A few kind words and playing to your resentment and love toward your father won't change your mind about your loyalties. Especially after we killed your friend, Saundra, and the High Priestess." His eyes gleamed. "I really must get the spell you used to hide your location. It was very effective. Otherwise, we would have been having this conversation last night over the dead body of your lover."

I gritted my teeth, desperately wanting to choke the life out of the smug bastard, but I couldn't give away the fact that the binding spell was weakening. Still, I filed away that information for later. Finn would be relieved to know that the location of his home had not been compromised. "You couldn't find me? Are your powers so weak?" I asked, arching an eyebrow at him. "Perhaps that's why The Slayer wants me....to replace you."

"You'll never abandon your coven. You're too pure at heart. My master doesn't understand that because your father wasn't difficult to turn, especially after he got a taste of the dark." He cocked his head to the side, reminding me of a bird of prey eyeballing its next meal. "I don't see that in you. Even after you took the lives of my men, you didn't seem as affected as your father was after he took his first life."

I would bite my tongue in half before I admitted to Dante how tempted I had been by the enjoyment I felt after the death of his minions. I'd fought the shadow of my father's descent into darkness my entire life, with the coven and with myself. I might have felt satisfaction at defending myself and my home from invasion, but I didn't seek out that feeling again. I didn't crave it or even wonder if I would ever feel it again.

Cornelius had been correct in one thing; the world was rarely black or white. Even the purest of hearts held a kernel of weakness, a fatal flaw. Be it envy, greed, or pride, any witch was susceptible.

Dante came closer to the chair where I was seated. "Perhaps I should just kill you now and save my master the trouble of trying to talk you into joining us when you obviously have no intention of doing so."

I tried one more time to play innocent. "I don't know what you're-"

He snapped his fingers in my face and I stopped speaking. I kept my eyes lowered, using my eyelashes to hide the fact that I wanted to grab those fingers and break them.

Dante squatted down in front of me. "You and I both know you will never give in."

I heard the door open and looked up. My eyes widened in shock when I saw Janice March slip into the room.

The warlock stood and turned. "Ah, the daughter of the traitor. Have you come to join your mother?"

Even I could see the sheer terror in Janice's eyes and I knew she had come to help me, not her mother. I realized that this was the reason she wanted to speak to me after Belinda's funeral ritual.

She squared her shoulders and tried to project confidence. "No. I'm here for my High Priestess."

"Then you'll join your mother in death," Dante replied.

I could see that the words affected Janice like a physical blow. Without warning, she lashed out at the warlock.

He laughed and deflected the spell. "You know you'll lose, yet you attempt to fight anyway. Perhaps I'll keep your suffering to a minimum before you die."

Knowing he was about to hit Janice with something nasty, I pulled power from somewhere deep within me and practically shoved it into her. Dante lifted a hand and his voice rang out in a single word incantation. Miraculously, my wild effort to protect Janice worked.

Her head fell back and she shrieked as I funneled a massive amount of magic into her body, murmuring a protection spell as I did so. Dante's attack manifested into an explosion of light when it hit Janice.

When he understood why his strike was ineffective, the warlock turned on me. I didn't have long. Desperate, I pulled back the power I'd thrown at Janice and began to fight the binding spell in earnest.

Staring into the burning black eyes of the vampire, I saw my death. I had waited too long and now I was out of time.

His hand lifted, appearing to move in slow motion, and I heard his voice boom like thunder. I braced for excruciating pain, which never came. In horror, I watched as Janice sprinted across the room and threw herself between us.

I cried out when her body collapsed at my feet, my shock and rage giving me enough strength to finally break free of the binding spell. I flung out my hand and Dante was lifted off his feet and thrown across the room. As it had the night of the attack on my cottage, my power was responding to my wishes without verbal invocation. The magic pressed in on me, growing claws that raked across my skin. It was more power than I'd ever felt before.

It seemed that Dante had found my breaking point. I no longer gave a damn about good and evil, right and wrong. All I cared about was destroying him. I wanted to remove all evidence of his existence from the face of the earth.

I called up the power, relishing in the sharp pain it brought me. That pain meant death to the enemy.

I watched in satisfaction as Dante's eyes grew big as he felt the ebb and flow of magic emanating from me. Then I held up my hand, palm up, and curled my fingers into a fist, whispering words that I didn't understand. It was a spell that I had heard only once before as I sat around a table with my mother and Belinda in my dreams.

I smiled as Dante's body decayed rapidly before my eyes, his skin thinning and turning dark before it cracked. His mouth opened in a silent scream before the flesh of his lips disappeared, leaving only a grinning skull behind. His bones disintegrated, leaving only a pile of dust where he once stood.

I turned my hand so that my palm faced the floor and slowly spread my fingers. The dust of Dante's remains seemed to melt into the floor, returning to the earth as nature required of all dead things.

The power within me gloried in the destruction of my enemy and demanded to be released again. For one frightening moment, when I tried to call it back, the magic fought against my hold, reaching out, searching for another enemy to obliterate.

Determined, I took control and commanded the magic to disperse. When it finally faded away, I released the breath I'd been holding. I needed to find Finn, but first, I had to check on Janice.

I walked over to her crumpled body and crouched down. Placing my fingers at her neck, I waited, hoping I would feel at least a faint pulse. There was nothing. Just by touching her skin, I knew she was dead, but I still hesitated. Perhaps I could bring her back the way I had Ricki. I moved my hand to her chest, feeling for her heart, but I could sense that it was damaged beyond repair.

I removed my hand. Though she had been hostile toward me for most of my life, Janice had given her life to save me.

In that moment, I had an epiphany. While I could accept that every white witch could carry the seed of darkness, even those who weren't perfect could perform the most selfless of sacrifices. It came down to their choices.

I touched Janice's forehead. "Thank you for saving me," I whispered, half hoping she would open her eyes and answer me.

I straightened and went to the door. I cracked it and looked out into the hallway. I opened it wider and looked quickly to the left and right. It was empty. I stepped out of the room and tried to get a better view of what was on each end of the hall. There seemed to be stairs to my right, so I pressed my back to the wall and crept toward them as silently as possible. I frequently glanced over my shoulder to be sure that no one was behind me.

As I reached the top of the stairs, I peeked over the railing just as a man appeared below me. I froze until I realized that it was Finn.

"Finn," I whispered.

His head twisted at the sound of my voice. "Thank the Goddess," he murmured.

I was already rounding the railing at the top of the stairs, moving as fast as possible, when he leapt up and landed on the steps in front of me. I didn't hesitate before I threw myself into his body, wrapping my arms around his neck.

"Are you all right?" he whispered in my ear. "Are you hurt anywhere?"

I shook my head, my hair brushing his cheek. "I'm fine. I just want to go home."

Cradling me close, Finn answered, "Let's go."

Chapter Thirty

IT SEEMED I missed one hell of a fight while I was dealing with Dante in the upstairs bedroom. From what I understood, my rescuers were surprised by the number of vampires on the premises. All their current intel suggested the Faction was a small group, but what they encountered on their way into the house was a great deal more than that. If they only knew.

Somehow, in the heat of battle, Cornelius escaped. Though Finn had told Conner and Lex to go after him, they refused. There were too many adversaries and it was highly likely Finn would have been overwhelmed.

Chloe and several of the pack wolves were with them. They retrieved the bodies of the two witches who died that night and we left the house as quickly as possible. The ride home was silent, and despite my relief to be safe, I was still tense because I knew that it wasn't over. The night was just the first battle in the coming war.

Finn wanted me to rest after the day I had, but I insisted on talking to the other members of the Council and Chloe and Calder. There were things they needed to know and actions to be taken.

When we arrived back at Conner's house, I was nearly tackled by my friends. Donna lifted me off my feet in a bear hug and Ivie, Ricki, and Shannon crowded around in a massive group embrace. They were talking all at once.

"Girls! Stop talking so fast. You're giving me a headache."

"This kidnapping bullshit has to stop. If it's not the bad guys trying to scoop us up, it's the good ones thinking they're keeping us safe."

Though the day had been hellish, it seemed Donna could still make me laugh.

Ivie pointed to Ricki and Shannon. "No kidnappings for either of you," she stated firmly.

Ricki's smile was wan and her face pale when she answered. "Too late. I was kidnapped by a werewolf."

Shannon just shrugged. "I'll do my best."

Calder appeared behind Ricki. "It's time to go back downstairs, darlin'."

She rolled her eyes but let him support her weight as he guided her toward the door that led to the basement. I could see that the change was upon her, probably tonight or tomorrow morning. It was a bit odd that she seemed to be taking so long for the transition. Most of the bitten would change within twenty-four hours. It had already been two days for Ricki.

Donna finally released me from her tight hug. "Conner said you need to 'debrief' or something equally spy-ish. I'll bring you a cup of tea, okay?"

"That sounds great."

She gestured for Shannon and Ivie to follow her and walked across the foyer toward the kitchen.

Finn wrapped an arm around my waist and walked with me into the study. Though I insisted on sharing the information I discovered today, I wanted to get it done.

✧   ✧   ✧

AN HOUR LATER, I had shared all the information I'd gleaned from my time with the Faction. I began with the fact that Cornelius was a soul eater. Calder and Chloe required an explanation, but the vampire Council members became grim at the mention of the soul eaters. Though the werewolves hadn't had experience with them, Finn and Lex were old enough to know what I was talking about. This knowledge changed a great deal about how we would need to approach future battles.

I also told them that Cornelius was aware of the prophecy of the Five and that he seemed to understand what it meant, more so than we did. The fact that we were in the dark while our enemy was not didn't bode well for the future. I needed to continue my research, though I still felt as though it was futile.

It wasn't until I told them about Cornelius' crazy ideas about what the Faction would accomplish and how he intended to do so that Finn gave any outward sign of his anger. Donna had brought us tea and coffee earlier, and, when I mentioned Cornelius' belief that he and I would birth the next generation of soul eaters, the mug he held in his hand cracked under his grip.

Grimacing, he placed it on the tray. "Sorry."

Conner waved him off, his piercing blue eyes glued to me. "The Slayer specifically said he'd been recruiting for years?" he asked.

I nodded. "Centuries actually."

Conner shook his head and paced in front of the fireplace like a large jungle cat prowling in a cage. "How could the Council be so unaware?" he muttered. I assumed it was mostly to himself because no one answered him.

Still, I had an idea. "I don't think that they were completely in the dark. I think that he has had his fingers in every pie for a long time. He spoke about the recruitment, his plans, as though he had been waiting patiently for years and every contingency was in place. He's not worried in the slightest about the humans, which is frightening in itself. Vampires, witches, and werewolves may possess superior physical attributes, but we are outnumbered and outgunned. The Slayer isn't just talking about establishing a relationship with the humans, but taking complete control. In order to accomplish his goals, Cornelius must have a great number of people to aid him and an excellent plan."

Lex seemed to consider my words and spoke to the room in general. "We need to find out what's happening inside the ranks, what's being planned."

"How are you going to do that?" I asked.

Finn seemed to rouse himself from his brooding and looked up at Conner. "We need to infiltrate."

I frowned, unsure of what he meant. "What?"

Conner seemed to be considering Finn's words and answered absently. "We need someone to join the Faction and report back."

"Like a spy?" I asked.

Finn, Conner, Lex, and Gabriel all nodded. Chloe and Calder were in the room but seemed content to just listen as this was discussed.

"So, who's going to do it?"

Lex shook his head. "I'm not sure, but I have someone in mind."

He and Conner looked at each other and something passed between them. I could understand the need for secrecy. One of their Council members had betrayed them and they couldn't risk revealing important information, even among those they believed they could trust.

A wave of fatigue hit me so hard I swayed. For a moment I wondered if Finn had spiked my tea with herbs again, but, when I looked up at him, he shook his head as though he could read my mind.

"Kerry needs rest," Finn stated. "We can continue this tomor-row."

No one argued, so he pulled me to my feet and lead me from the study. When we reached the base of the staircase, he lifted me into his arms and carried me up.

"I can walk," I murmured, resting my forehead against his neck.

"I know."

I left it at that because I was tired and he wouldn't put me down no matter what I said. Though I would probably never admit aloud, I enjoyed feeling small and pampered.

When we reached the guest room, I reached out and opened the door and Finn carried me inside.

"Shower?" he asked.

"No. Bed." My words were short and weary.

Finn set me on the bench at the end of the bed and disappeared into the closet. While he was gone, I kicked off my shoes and socks and peeled my sweatshirt over my head. I was working on the button and zipper of my jeans when he came back out of the closet with a t-shirt and pajama pants for me.

Finn knelt before me and helped remove my pants. My phone fell out of my pocket and hit the floor with a clunk.

He picked it up, examining it. "I'm so glad you had your phone with you." He looked up at me. "Do you know why they didn't take it?"

I shrugged out of my bra and slid the t-shirt over my head before I answered. "Honestly, I don't think they even considered it. It seems Cornelius' weakness is technology."

Finn helped me into the pants. "Whatever reason that prevented them from turning it off, I'm glad." He helped me into the bed and removed his shirt and pants to join me.

This was one of the things that I loved about being with Finn. He held me close, even in sleep, and didn't shy away from showing me affection, no matter where we were or who we were with.

Going to bed with him, even just to sleep, was my favorite time of day. It never failed to help me forget my troubles.

I laid my cheek against his chest. "There is some good news in all this mess. They couldn't locate me when we were at your house, it's still safe. We can go back home tomorrow."

His arms tightened around me. "Home?"

I smiled. "Yes. Home."

"Are you sure you want to live there?" he asked.

"I love my mother's house and I don't think I'll ever be able to sell it. At the moment, it's no longer safe until the war with the Faction is done. Until then, I would be happy to live in your home. It's beautiful."

"And after?"

"We might have to compromise."

Finn chuckled softly and I enjoyed the vibration against my cheek. "Well, I do love your house, so I'm sure we can work something out."

I couldn't resist the pull of sleep any longer. "Thank you for coming for me," I mumbled.

He kissed my forehead. "I will always come for you," he whispered. "I love you."

"Love you too."

The war may continue but, for tonight, I was safe and I was loved.

Epilogue

Ricki

⌐⌐

I WAS FREEZING and burning up simultaneously. Sweat rolled off my skin as though I were standing inside a sauna, yet I'd never felt so cold.

Shudders wracked my body violently and my teeth chattered so loudly they echoed in my head. When firm hands turned me, I tried to bat them away, but I couldn't escape. The mere touch on my skin was agony.

"Noooo," I moaned.

"Shhh. It's okay. I know it hurts." I was lifted into a semi-reclined position. "Drink this, it'll help."

A bowl was pressed to my lips and I drank the bitter brew, choking a little as it poured down my throat and trickled out of the corners of my mouth.

A gentle hand patted the liquid from my face and chest. My body seized in another bone-rattling shiver.

"You're doing great, darlin'. I know it seems like it will never end, but you're almost done."

My eyes felt swollen and achy but I managed to lift my eyelids and stare up into a pair of gorgeous green eyes. "Is it too late to ask Conner to bite me?" I whimpered.

A rueful smile appeared on Calder's face. "I'm afraid so." He set the bowl on the table beside the bed. "Thank you for choosing me instead."

I hummed in the back of my throat when his fingers stroked over my hair. It was the one place on my body that didn't feel as though it were on fire or submerged in ice. "I'm sure I'll make you pay for it later."

Suddenly, a white hot pain ripped through my body, tearing a scream from my throat. My bones felt as though they were being broken and reset one after another, in rapid succession.

"Don't fight it, Ricki. Just let it take you. I promise it only hurts the first few times, then your body adjusts."

I screamed again, my voice cracking. My wail ended on a high-pitched, pained howl.

With one huge wrenching jolt, the agony ceased. For several long moments, I lay in Calder's arms, panting. Still feeling shaky, I rolled away, putting my hands and feet beneath me, but the bed felt odd. When I looked down, two brown paws rested below me. Turning my head, I looked back, down a lean chestnut colored body, and saw a bushy tail curving over my back.

Well, the next time someone called me a bitch, I guess I couldn't be offended.

The End

Acknowledgements

My deepest thanks to my hubby and father. Without you two, I would have a great deal less time to write stories. And I would be lost without my Lil Bit. She makes me smile every day.

Also, I love you bunches, Donna and Tania. You two do an admirable job of putting up with my crazy, neurotic ass and my avalanche of messages on an almost daily basis. Thank you for keeping me on track, encouraging me, and pushing me to do more and be better.

My Facebook group, C.C.'s Sinners, is a badass group of women. Love you all and thank you for reading and pimping my books. Now, go post a review of this book, dammit!

To my author friends; Tiffany King, Katie Ashley, Tara Sivec, R.K. Lilley, Raine Miller, Leighton Riley, Yara Greathouse, Gina Sorelle, B.L. Marsh, and, last but not least, my future baby mama, Penelope Reid. You all are the best! Thank you for reading my books and sending me books to read when I beg for them.

I also must say that I adore my amazing beta readers; Nikki, Christine, Nerd Herd Nikki, and Amber. Thanks for telling me what I need to hear, good or bad.

Last but not least, I eternally grateful to the readers and bloggers who review and share my books. There are too many of you to name (that would fill up another 200 pages!) but I appreciate each and every one of you.

About C.C.

A native Texan, C.C. grew up either reading or playing the piano. Years later, she's still not grown up and doing the same things. Since the voices in her head never shut up, C.C. decided to share their crazy stories and started writing books.

Now that she has a baby girl at home, C.C.'s non-writing time is usually spent cleaning up poopy diapers or feeding the poop machine. Sometimes she teaches piano, cooks, or spends time bugging her hubby and two beagles.

Contact C.C.

C.C. loves to hear from her readers!

Facebook: www.facebook.com/authorccwood

Twitter: @cc_wood

Website: www.ccwood.net

Titles by C.C. Wood

Novellas:

Girl Next Door Series:

Friends with Benefits

Frenemies

Drive Me Crazy

Girl Next Door-The Complete Series

Kiss Series:

A Kiss for Christmas

Kiss Me

Novels:

Seasons of Sorrow

NSFW Series:

In Love With Lucy

Earning Yancy

Paranormal Romance:

Bitten Series

Bite Me (Bitten, #1)

Once Bitten, Twice Shy (Bitten, #2)

One Little Bite (Bitten, #2.5)

Bewitched, Bothered, and Bitten (Bitten, #3)

Printed in Great Britain
by Amazon